Running for President

A Psychopath is Elected President of the United States

A novel by

Jack Quinn

Published by Micrologic Research
4631 East Hubbell Street
Phoenix, Arizona 85008-3213 USA

I dedicate this book to my daughter
Inge Quinn and to my sister Jean Quinn

Contents

Chapter 1 — Fletcher Street, Chicago

It was nine am in the two-storey house on Fletcher Street on the Near North Side of Chicago. The day was June 13, 1975. Irene Wilder felt a slight twinge of pain in her abdomen. It lasted only about a minute. Could it be a contraction? She sat down to wait to see if it would be repeated. Dr. Adamson had told her that if she felt abdominal pains that occurred at regular intervals, it would mean that labor had begun. She had felt such pains before, but they always went away when she sat down. She looked at her watch. Seven minutes later, she felt the pain again, and again it lasted about a minute. She grabbed the phone on the table beside her bed and dialed Dr. Adamson's number.

The receptionist told her that Dr. Adamson was with another patient, but would be with her in a few minutes. As she waited on hold, Irene felt the third twinge of pain, which again lasted about a minute. Then Dr. Adamson was on the phone. After asking her some questions about the frequency, duration, and intensity of the pains, he confirmed that they were contractions and advised her to go to the hospital.

Her husband Craig was working on a construction site in the Loop, Chicago's downtown, and was unreachable. He was a riveter, working at great heights above the ground erecting the steel frame of a skyscraper under construction. Craig always took the elevated train, which Chicagoans call "The L," to work and left their five-year-old Chevy in the garage. However, Irene had never learned to drive. She called a cab.

At the hospital, no one seemed concerned about the fact that she was in labor, and Dr. Adamson had not yet arrived. She was left to sit in the waiting room despite the occasional contraction. None of the hospital staff paid her any attention. A woman sitting across from her who was obviously also very pregnant sensed Irene's anxiety. "Don't worry, Honey," she assured Irene, "this is my third child, so I can tell you that everything's going to be OK. I was nervous the first time, too." The woman's words did reassure Irene somewhat.

Eventually, Irene was shown to a bed and given a hospital gown to put on. "Now just lie in bed, and don't get up," the nurse told her. She wouldn't have gotten out of bed in any case. She was embarrassed. The gown was open in the back, and if she was sure that if she got up, her backside would be exposed for everyone to see.

Nurses came into her room periodically to check on her, and after what seemed to be an eternity, one of the nurses said, "It's time." Two nurses helped her onto a gurney and one of them wheeled her into the delivery room where Dr Adamson was waiting. "There are complications, and the baby will have to be delivered by Caesarean section," Dr Adamson lied. The truth was that he had a golf game scheduled for that afternoon, and had no intention of missing it by waiting for a normal delivery, which could take hours. His lie was a bad omen on the first day in the life of Irene's son. Later she would ask herself if being delivered by Caesarean section had anything to do with the way Jason turned out.

Irene wished that Craig were with her. He would know how to deal with Dr. Adamson and the hospital personnel, but Craig was unreachable, probably working 20 floors above ground balanced on one steel beam as he guided a second one into place. She would have to face this by herself.

Irene's next memory was of awakening alone back in her hospital room and feeling a pain in her abdomen. She soon realized that there was a white electrical cable by her side on the bed with a button at the end. She pressed the button.

"Ah, I see we're awake," said the chubby nurse who entered the room a few minutes later. It was the same nurse who had wheeled her into the delivery room. "How are we feeling? We must be in pain." Irene nodded to indicate that she was, even though the nurse's baby talk irritated her.

"Dr. Adamson has prescribed an injection for the pain. I'll get it for you. In the meantime, would you like to see your baby?"

"Of course!" It was a baby boy. Irene thought that the red-wrinkled little creature was the most beautiful baby she had ever seen. She almost forgot the pain in her abdomen as she held her son in her arms and then put him to her breast to nurse.

Irene and the baby remained in the hospital three more days while Irene received periodic injections to ease the pain where her abdomen had been sliced open. Craig came to visit her every day after work, and on the third day he took off work to drive Irene and the baby home in the Chevy. They had decided to name the baby Jason after Craig's grandfather who had been a coal miner in England. Craig and Irene were not churchgoers, but they considered themselves Catholics and occasionally attended mass at a nearby church. A few weeks after arriving home from the hospital, Jason was baptized as a Catholic in the Our Lady of Mount Carmel Church on Belmont Avenue.

As Jason grew older, Craig and Irene began wonder if he was a normal child. He babbled baby talk as a normal baby would and took his first steps before his first birthday, but he did not seem to return the affection that Craig and Irene felt for him. "Every time I take the kid in my arms, he turns his head away from me and pushes against my chest like he wanted to get away," Craig complained. Even when Irene was nursing Jason, he would drink his fill from her breast and then push it away and turn his head away from her. Dr. Adamson told them not to worry. "He hasn't started developing yet. Wait 'till he's older. He'll be affectionate. Kids always are."

But, he wasn't. After Jason began walking, he would sit in a corner and play with his box of toys, ignoring his parents. Then at the age of five at his Cousin Lucy's birthday party, he grabbed her Barbie Doll from her hands, threw it on the floor as hard as he could, and jumped on it as the horrified adults in the room looked on. Lucy broke out in tears, and before Craig could stop him, Jason smacked his sobbing cousin in the face. "Crybaby!" he yelled at her.

Craig made apologies to his brother and sister-in-law and promised Lucy that he would bring her a new Barbie Doll tomorrow and a Ken Doll to keep Barbie company. Craig didn't spank Jason. Neither did Irene. In fact, they never spanked Jason. They had heard that the prominent baby doctor Benjamin Spock had written that parents should never spank their children. They hadn't actually read Dr. Spock's book, of course, but they had seen him on television. Craig and Irene never read books. Irene read only recipes, and Craig's reading was limited to the daily copy of *The Chicago Tribune*, which he purchased every morning to read on the L on his way to work.

As Craig put it to Irene that evening at home after they had put Jason to bed, "No matter what we do, Jason just can't learn to play nice with other kids. What are we doing wrong? Are we bad parents, or is there something wrong with Jason? Is it our fault?"

Irene had no answer. She was asking herself the same questions.

Jason became more of a problem when he entered kindergarten. He was constantly getting into fights with other kids and refused to obey the teacher. He seemed to be bright enough, however. He learned his colors and even the letters of the alphabet more quickly than his classmates. Often when the other children were playing during free time, Jason would sit in a corner with a book, leafing through it and pronouncing the names of the animals and objects that he saw in the pictures. Once, when he was paging though a book of animal pictures, his teacher noticed that he was not pointing at the pictures as he said each animal's name. He was pointing at the animals' printed name below the pictures. The teacher realized that Jason had taught himself to read the animals' names. She had never known a kid to learn so quickly before.

In first grade, Jason was suspended from school for three days for fighting. Then, a month later, he was suspended again, this time for yelling an obscenity at a teacher. Jason seemed to learn from the second experience, and he was never suspended again. This was to become a pattern in his life. The first time he was punished for an act of misbehavior, the lesson didn't take hold. On the second occasion, it did.

School was one thing in his life that Jason genuinely liked, and he was determined not to be kept away. He did not like his teachers or classmates, but he did enjoy learning, which he seemed to do with little effort. He could read better than anyone else in his class, and he excelled at arithmetic. Despite his sometimes bad behavior, his teachers and the school principal tolerated him, because he was so bright and eager to learn.

Jason was only ten years old when he first smoked marijuana. Some older kids were passing a joint around in the alley behind his house next to the L tracks. He asked for a puff and inhaled deeply. That set off a spasm of coughing that sent the other kids into peals of laughter. Jason didn't like being made fun of. He took another puff, and this time he held the smoke in his lungs for almost a minute despite an almost overwhelming urge to cough it out. Finally, he released his breath. Afterwards, he felt a sensation of well being that was completely new to him. The world around him seemed brighter. Sounds and sights were more intense, and even the ugly L tracks above his head seen through the wooden ties were transformed into objects of beauty.

Jason wanted to have that experience again, but he had no idea where or how to obtain marihuana. The bigger kids had let him have a few puffs the first time, but now Dan, the biggest kid and the one who knew where to get the stuff, wanted money to supply Jason. "This stuff ain't free, kid. Cough up some dough for the weed and roll your own joints. You ain't smokin' no more a' mine."

Jason was too young to work, and his allowance certainly wasn't enough to allow him to get high. How was he going to pay for weed? He began slipping money out of his mother's purse, just a few dollars at a time, hoping that she wouldn't notice. But she did notice. "I could swear that I had more money in this purse. Now there's just a single $20 bill," she told Craig. "I think Jason's stealing from me."

Irene began locking her purse in a drawer when she wasn't carrying it, and Jason had to find another way of earning money.

"If you can't get money," Dan told him, "bring me things that I can sell—things that are worth money." That was when Jason began shoplifting. At first he stole small items from the shops on Belmont Avenue. Then he began riding the L into the Loop to steal more valuable items, which he would bring to Dan in the alley. Dan always gave him much less for the items than Jason thought they were worth.

Jason never got caught stealing, but he did have some close calls. Once, when smuggling a jade figurine out of Smothers' Bookstore, a clerk spotted him slip the object under his coat and yelled at him. Jason took off running with the clerk close on his heels. Although the clerk repeatedly yelled, "Stop that kid! He's a thief!" as he chased Jason down State Street, none of the people crowding the sidewalk made the slightest effort to intervene. Jason risked his life by running across the street through traffic and quickly left the clerk behind.

Jason was unusually adept at self-analysis for a boy his age. After he had been stealing for about six months, he came to the realization that had been very lucky to have not been caught and arrested so far. He felt no guilt about stealing, but he did not want to be branded a juvenile delinquent and get a police record. He also began to have doubts about the wisdom of smoking marihuana. He liked it too much. Both shoplifting and smoking weed had become habits, and Jason could not tolerate the thought of not being in complete control of himself. He decided that both shoplifting and smoking marihuana had to stop. He gave them up and started avoiding Dan. His decision had nothing to do with morality. It was purely based on logic. Smoking marihuana and stealing to get the money to buy it were not reasonable things to do. This would be the first of many occasions when Jason would do the right thing, not because it was right, but because his logic told him the consequences were unacceptable.

It was two years later that Jason first noticed Sharon Soleri. Sharon was only nine years old and seemed naïve even for a girl that young. She also lived on Fletcher Street with parents who didn't seem to care what she did or where she went. Jason had heard some of the older guys who hung around under the L tracks talk about having sex, and he was anxious to try it himself. He didn't have a strong sexual desire, but his natural curiosity about sex drove him on.

Jason had no skills at dealing specifically with girls, but he was becoming quite skillful at manipulating people in general. He began talking to Sharon and telling her how pretty she was, all the while waiting for an opportunity to get her alone. Finally, that opportunity arrived. It was a Saturday. Jason's dad was working overtime at the construction site in the Loop, and his mother had taken advantage of her husband's absence to go on one of her all-day shopping trips. It was a warm summer day, and Jason was bored sitting alone at home. He left the house with no specific goal in mind, hoping to find some way to entertain himself. He ran into Sharon in the street.

"My mom's gone," he told her. "Come inside and I'll show you where I live."

"I don't think I should," Sharon replied hesitatingly. "Mom said I should never go into other people's houses alone without her or Dad along."

"You aren't alone. I'm with you. Besides, I won't tell if you don't."

Jason took Sharon's hand and led her though the front door. Sharon was reluctant to enter, but she didn't have the self-confidence to refuse.

"Come in here, and I'll show you my bedroom. I've got some neat stuff in here," said Jason. Once they were in the bedroom he added, "I'll tell you what. I'll show you my thing if you show me yours."

Sharon blushed. "No! I don't think that's right."

Jason dropped his pants and underwear. Sharon was completely confused. Her blush deepened. She knew she shouldn't be looking at Jason, but she was unable to look away.

"Now you've seen mine, you've got to show me yours," Jason insisted. Before long they were lying on Jason's bed, and Jason had happily lost his virginity. Sharon had lost hers, too, but her emotion was a sense of shame. It had been a pleasurable experience for Jason but a distressing one for Sharon. This day would be a painful recollection burned into her memory for the rest of her life and would be a secret that she would never share with anyone. She would never marry and never have an emotional attachment to any man for the rest of her life.

Jason had various sexual experiences during his teen years, at first with girls younger than he was. Then he began making use of his gift for manipulating people to seduce girls his age or older. He had no feelings for any of them. He took what he wanted and then forgot them. Then he met Jane.

It was a Saturday in summer when he was 17 years old that Jason spied a woman sitting on a bench alone reading a book. He judged her to be in her late 20s. She was a bit chubby and plain looking, the type of woman that most men would not give a second look. Jason, however, saw her as a challenge. Could he seduce this older woman? Was his personality strong enough to overcome any objections that she might have?

The woman looked at him hesitantly and then looked back at her book. Jason sensed that she felt insecure under his steady gaze. What should he use as a pickup line? He didn't ponder that question more than an instant.

"Mind if I sit down?" he asked. "My legs are getting tired from pedaling this bike."

"Ah….I guess it'd be OK,"

"My name's Jason. What's yours?"

"Jane." She looked back at her book, pointedly trying to ignore this teenager, but Jason wasn't about to be put off so easily.

"What are you reading?" he asked.

"Oh, it's a novel by a Colombian writer named Gabriel García Márquez. Have you ever heard of him?"

Jason hadn't, but he had no compunction about lying. "Yeah, I've heard of him, but I've never read anything he wrote. Is he good?"

"Stupendous!

"Maybe I should read him. What do you like about him? Why do you think he's stupendous?"

"He writes using a style called magical realism. Do you know what that is?"

Jason was getting out of his depth and was anxious to change the subject. "I really like literature, but I'm too young to know much about it. I'll bet you could teach me a lot."

"What makes you think I could teach you?"

"You seem very intelligent. I've always admired intelligent people," Jason lied, "especially intelligent women. Will you teach me about literature and about....what did you call it? Magic realism?"

"Magical realism." Jane didn't know what to make of this young man, a boy really, who suddenly seemed so interested in her. Like many of Jason's victims, Jane was shy and insecure. She timidly tried to end the conversation. "I don't know you. We'll probably never meet again."

"Don't say that, please. Meet me here tomorrow at about this time. I want so much to learn, and I'm sure I could learn a lot from you. I'm really interested in literature, but in school we just read dumb stuff written for idiots. Please don't let me down. I want so badly to learn, but no one cares."

"Well," she relented, "I guess it would be OK. All right, I'll be here again tomorrow."

"What is the title of the book you're reading? I want to read it, too."

She held up the book so that he could see the cover. It was in Spanish. He couldn't understand a word.

"Ah, I can't read Spanish."

"It's available in English translation. It's called *One Hundred Years of Solitude*. Here, I'll write it down for you," she said as she pulled a slip of paper out of her book and began scribbling something on it. "And, the author is named Gabriel García Márquez. I'll write his name down, too."

"OK, see ya tomorrow," said Jason as he swung his leg over his bike and rode off.

That evening Jason stopped by the Lincoln Park branch of the Chicago Public Library and borrowed a copy of the book. He was so engrossed in reading that night in bed that the book finally slipped out of his hand as he fell asleep. Irene noticed his light was still on and went quietly into his room to turn it off and place the book on the nightstand before she went to bed herself.

Jane Jackson had moved to Chicago after graduating from the University of Pittsburgh with a double major in business and Spanish. She had dreamed of teaching Spanish literature at a major university, but that would require a doctorate, and even for people with that degree, jobs were scarce. That was why she had also gotten the business degree. She studied Latin American literature for fun and business to make herself employable.

Pittsburgh, like the rest of Western Pennsylvania, was in an economic slump when Jane graduated from college. The steel mills were going out of business, unable to compete with cheaper imported steel. They had been the backbone of the economy for the entire region. People were leaving Pittsburgh and all of Western Pennsylvania to seek work in other parts of the country. Like many other young people in Pittsburgh, Jane felt she had no future there. Her father advised her to move to Chicago, telling her a person could always find a job in the Windy City, which that was at that time still known as "The Second City."

Jane took her father's advice and moved to Chicago where she luckily had a friend who had also moved there from Pittsburgh and quickly found a job. Jane sent out resumes and managed to land several interviews. Within a month, she was offered a low-level manager's job at a major bank in the Loop. She proved to be a quick learner and within two years was promoted to a mid-level position with a salary large enough to afford a small condominium in a building on Lake Shore drive. Her only social contacts were with people she met at work.

People in Chicago seemed cold compared to those in Pittsburgh. When you walked down a street in Chicago, no one looked you in the eyes. It seemed as if every stranger was viewed as a threat. No man had ever asked her out on a date. Her life consisted of an early-morning workout in the gym followed by an eight- or nine-hour day at the bank with walks in Lincoln Park in the evenings or perhaps a visit to the park's zoo on weekends. Occasionally she went to a movie in the Loop after work before taking the L and a bus home. In the winter, she sometimes went ice skating on a nearby basketball court that was frozen over to serve as a skating rink. She skated alone and never attempted to start a conversation with the other skaters. On warm weekend days in summer she would often rent a bicycle from the American Youth Hostel Association bike shop on Clark Street and ride in Lincoln Park. With the years, she had begun putting on weight and could best be described as plain-looking and chubby. She led a lonely existence and began to feel that life was leaving her behind. Other women her age were getting married and starting families, and she didn't even have a boyfriend.

The next day Jason arrived at the bench in Lincoln Park 15 minutes after the appointed time. He did not want Jane to think he was anxious to see her. However, to his great disappointment Jane was not there waiting for him. Nevertheless, he sat down on the bench and continued to read García Márquez's book. He was unacquainted with literature except for the pabulum he was required to read in school. He was finding this book genuinely interesting. He had never read anything like it before. Suddenly he was aware of someone sitting beside him. It was Jane.

"I hadn't intended to come," she explained. "But then somehow I couldn't help myself. I couldn't bear imagining you sitting here by yourself expecting me to show up."

"I was about to leave"—Jason placed a bookmark in his book and closed it—"but then I got interested in the book that I forgot about time."

"So, you like it?"

"Yeah, I do. I told you that you could teach me things. I never thought of reading a book like this. I didn't know that such books existed. But thanks to you, now I want to finish this one and then read another one just as good."

Jason was only partially lying. Above all, he wanted to get on the good side of Jane. He had not yet had sex with an older woman, but against his expectations, he was also enjoying the book. As to Jane, she was flattered by the respect that this teenager seemed to be showing her.

"Can we go somewhere for coffee?" Jason asked.

"I have to leave now." Jane replied. "I promised I would help a friend move to a new apartment. I have to work tomorrow, but if you want, we can meet here again tomorrow after work. Say, six pm?"

Jason was disappointed at not having made more progress with Jane on their second meeting. However, the next day he was more successful. He not only found Jane waiting for him when he arrived at the park bench, he managed to persuade her to invite him to her apartment under the pretext of wanting to see her book collection.

Once in her apartment, Jason wasted little time. Within five minutes he was sitting next to her on the couch holding her hands, and ten minutes later he was kissing her. She resisted at first. She hardly knew this boy, and he was underage. Why couldn't she stop herself? This was crazy! However, she had gone so long without male attention that her desires overcame her scruples, and soon she was fervently returning his kisses. Not long after, they were in her bed making love. It was a release of years of pent up emotion for Jane. For Jason, it was no more than the thrill of yet another conquest. "The thrill of the hunt," he thought to himself.

Jason had one more year to go before finishing high school. His parents had already decided that he was to go to college, and Jason did not object. Attending class seemed better than getting a job. Both of Jason's parents were first-generation native-born Americans. His father's parents had immigrated from Yorkshire in England where Jason's grandfather had been a coal miner. On Jason's mother's side, his grandparents had immigrated from rural Poland where they had been poor farmers. Neither family had thought to send their children to college. Like most working-class children of immigrant families, Craig and Irene wanted their son to have the opportunities that they had lacked.

In his last year of high school, Jason continued to put the minimum effort into his studies required to get decent grades and continued to visit Jane in her small apartment as often as he could. As much as he wanted to, he couldn't feel any affection for her. His kept seeing her merely for the satisfaction he felt at being able to maintain a sexual relationship with an older woman. He often wondered what it felt like to be in love. It was an emotion that he constantly heard others talk about but that he himself could not feel. He wished that he could be like other people, but he knew he couldn't.

Then one evening shortly after Jason arrived at Jane's apartment and began unbuttoning her blouse with no preliminaries, she told him, 'Jason, I'm pregnant. What should I do?"

Jason didn't know what to answer. This was one complication that he hadn't foreseen and that he didn't need. He had no room in his life for a child. The only emotion he felt at hearing the news was annoyance, which he tried not to reveal. After a long hesitation he asked her, "What are you going to do?"

"I don't know. I'm all alone. I know you don't really love me. We couldn't get married. That would never work."

"Don't worry," Jason assured her. "I'll think of something."

Jason never saw Jane again. When Jane realized that Jason had no interest in her or in the unborn child, she did not attempt to contact him. As strange as this may seem, Jason had never given her his phone number and had never told her where he lived. Jane was also constrained by the knowledge that if Jason reported their relationship to the police, she could be arrested for having sex with a minor. Three weeks later, she had an abortion.

Jason spent a lot of time in his senior year of high school gathering information on universities, discussing them with his parents, and applying for scholarships. Craig and Irene wanted Jason to live at home and commute to one of Chicago's renowned universities. Jason wanted badly to get away from his parents.

Because he was very bright, Jason was provisionally admitted to every university where he applied. However, cost was a factor. As a steel worker, Craig made good money in construction when he was working, but jobs were undependable, and the amount of financial support his parents could give him was limited. One of the replies Jason received looked more promising than the others. It was from Arizona State University (ASU) in Tempe, Arizona, wherever that was. In addition to admitting him, the university promised him a part-time job on campus. With the job came the privilege of paying in-state tuition, which meant a savings of thousands of dollars a year.

Craig and Irene argued against this choice. "I still think you'd be better off living here at home with us and going to a local university," Irene told him. "Your father and I are not rich, but if you lived and ate at home, your expenses would be much lower, and we could afford to pay your tuition."

Jason dug in his heals. "With this job offer, I'll be able to pay part of my own expenses. I won't be such a burden on you and Dad."

"Where is this Tempe place, anyway?" Irene asked. Like many people who were not familiar with Arizona, she pronounced it TEM-pah. Jason was later to learn that locals call the city tem-PEE.

"Ah, I looked it up. It's right next to Phoenix. I've heard a lot of good things about Phoenix. One of my classmates was there on vacation over Christmas break, and he loved the place. It never snows there, he said."

So, it was decided that Jason would attend ASU. He would get a summer job during June and July to save some money for his education and then fly to Phoenix in August.

Chapter 2 — Tempe, Arizona

It was damned hot when Jason stepped out of Terminal Two in Sky Harbor Airport in Phoenix on August 1, 1993. He thought he would suffocate. A nearby electronic sign flashed the temperature, 114 degrees Fahrenheit, 45.6 degrees Celsius! It was humid, too. Jason had always heard that Phoenix had a dry heat, but he was sweating in the humidity as he rolled his suitcase toward the bus stop for the Red Line that would take him to Arizona State University in the nearby suburb of Tempe. Unfortunately, he had arrived in Phoenix on the hottest day of the year at the peak of Arizona's summer monsoon, when not only the heat but also the humidity become insupportable to those not acclimated to the Arizona desert.

The others waiting for the bus seemed to be mainly airport employees. He could see some of the passengers who had been on the plane with him from Chicago lined up to take taxis. One of the people at the bus stop said, "At least it's a dry heat!" The others chuckled. Jason was to learn later that his was a standing joke among Phoenix residents. People from out of state had the impression that Phoenix summers were dry and therefore perfectly comfortable. They had never suffered though the misery of Phoenix's humid monsoon months of July and August.

Jason had to wait 20 minutes for the bus to arrive, and by that time he was thirsty and sweating profusely. The others waiting for the bus didn't seem to mind the heat as much as he did. Perhaps if one lived here long enough, one got used to this inferno. When the bus finally arrived, Jason handed the driver a five-dollar bill. The driver pointed to a sign that said "Exact change only." Jason found a dollar bill in his wallet and attempted to hand it to the driver. "Insert it in the cash box," the driver instructed him. "Do you want a transfer?"

"No thanks." Jason knew that this bus would take him directly to ASU. He carried his suitcases to the back of the bus and took a seat. At least the bus was air conditioned.

When he got off the bus at his stop at the university in Tempe, the heat assaulted him again. In the information packet that the university admissions department had sent him was the name of the dormitory building where he was to live, but he had no idea how to find the building. There was no one on the sidewalk to ask. This wasn't like

Chicago, where the sidewalks were normally crowded with pedestrians. It looked like no one walked in Tempe. However, there were many young people who looked like students riding bicycles, despite the heat. Jason flagged one of them down.

"Say buddy, can you tell me how to get to Hayden Hall."

"Yeah, it's about a block south of here. If you look at that map over there" – pointing to a pillar about 15 feet away – "you can see how to get there."

"OK, thanks."

Jason was really thirsty by the time he reached his dormitory building. A drinking fountain at last, and the building was air-conditioned. With air conditioning everywhere, maybe he could learn to live with this heat after all.

After slaking his thirst, he noticed a young woman sitting behind a desk with a sign in front of her reading "Information." "Hi. My name is Jason Wilder, and I believe I'm supposed to stay in this dorm."

The young woman looked through a sheaf of papers on a clipboard. "Ah, here we go. Wilder, Jason. Here, I'll write down your room number, and here's a key. You'll be sharing a room with another student." Jason would have preferred a small apartment by himself, but a shared dorm room was the best his family could afford.

"If you have any questions, Jason, I'll be right here. Don't hesitate to ask."

She had called him by his first name. Apparently people were more casual here than in Chicago.

When he opened the door to his room, a tall, slender black youth was sprawled out on one of the bunks. He pointed to another bunk, which had a stained mattress. "That's yours."

Jason looked around. The small dorm room wasn't at all what he expected. There was graffiti scrawled on the walls. In addition to the bunks, there were two small writing tables, one of which Jason assumed was his, although both were piled high with dirty clothes. One thing for sure, Jason's new roommate was not a neatness freak. Having grown up in highly-segregated Chicago, Jason was also not comfortable having a black roommate. It wasn't that he was prejudiced. It was just that in Chicago blacks and whites led very separate lives. They worked different types of jobs, and they lived in different sections of the city.

Jason later learned that his new roommate, James or Jimmy Jefferson, was from Johnstown, Pennsylvania. He was a year older than Jason. When he graduated from Johnstown Central High School, Jimmy didn't have the funds to attend university. His parents hadn't completed high school and had low-paying jobs. They were not able to help him very much with college expenses. However, Jimmy worked for a year as assistant physical director in the Johnstown YMCA while his parents allowed him to live at their home on Bedford Street for free. He saved enough during this year to travel to Phoenix and pay his first year's tuition. He could have stayed in Johnstown and completed his first two years of at a junior college operated by the University of Pittsburgh, referred to by the locals as "Junior Pitt," but the highly segregated living conditions in Johnstown felt claustrophobic. He knew enough about the Phoenix area to know that the city's small black community was better integrated than was Johnstown's, although Phoenix also had a few black-only neighborhoods, especially the area directly west of downtown. In need of financial aid, Jimmy was assigned to work 20 hours a week in the university cafeteria.

"You look uncomfortable," Jimmy remarked. "Is it because I'm black?"

Jason decided not to lie. I'm not used to being around black people. I've never lived in the same neighborhood with a black person before, let alone in the same room."

"I'm not used to being this close to white folks, either. In Johnstown, I mixed with white kids at the YMCA or in school, and in the evening, we all went home to our own neighborhoods. Most white people didn't have the courage to enter a black neighborhood after dark. So, this is all new to me, too."

"We'll adapt to it," Jason assured his new roommate. "Can I use one of these desks?"

"Yeah, just push the stuff off that one onto the floor," said Jimmy, gesturing to the desk closest to Jason's bunk. "That one's yours."

Then silence ensued. It was obvious that each of them was shy with the other. Neither of the two young men had even introduced himself to the other, and Jason didn't know how to break the ice. Finally it was Jimmy who spoke, "Like I said, I ain't never lived with no white folks before. Where I come from, blacks and whites live in different parts of town."

"It's that way in Chicago, too. Oh, I'm from Chicago." Jason didn't feel comfortable talking about race and tried to change the subject. "My name's Jason, by the way."

"Well, if we're going to be roommates, we should try to get along," said Jimmy, extending his right hand. "I'm Jimmy."

Jason hesitated a second before taking Jimmy's hand. He had never shaken hands with a black person before. When Jimmy's back was turned, Jason glanced surreptitiously at his own hand to see if any of Jimmy's black color had come off. It hadn't.

"Where's Johnstown?" he asked.

"It's in Southwestern Pennsylvania about 60 miles east of Pittsburgh. Didn't you ever hear of the Johnstown flood?"

Jason hadn't.

Jason quickly settled into university life. He bought an inexpensive bicycle from College Cyclery to get around town, and he landed the promised part-time job at the information desk in the University's Student Union. Because he had to work to supplement the money his parents were able to send him he carried a bit less than a full academic load. He had decided to major in business administration. That seemed to be the field that would offer him the best job prospects after graduation. His roommate Jimmy, on the other hand, majored in elementary education. He wanted to teach in a poor neighborhood in a large city where he felt he could show kids that the way out of poverty was through education.

"I can't understand why you want to do that," Jason said. "Teachers don't get paid very much money. Do you want to end up poor like your parents?"

"I don't care that much about money. I feel that the Lord has called me to help my people."

Jason didn't reply. He had no religious beliefs, and he looked down on people who did, but there was no sense in mentioning that and creating dissention. The two of them would probably have to live together the whole academic year, so it was better to get along.

Jason wasn't happy with all of the courses he was required to take. He could see the utility of the English and math courses, but why was he required to take courses in a foreign language? After two semesters of the language, he wouldn't be able to read, write, or speak it. He decided to take two semesters of Spanish. A lot of people in Arizona seemed to speak Spanish, so maybe it would be of some utility. Besides, Jane, his former girlfriend In Chicago, knew Spanish. It seemed to be a cool language. Also, he had learned to appreciate Latin American literature, but all of the good Latin American writers were translated into English, which made it a waste of time to learn to read them in the original language. But again, if he had to waste his time taking classes in a foreign language, Spanish was probably the least objectionable one.

On the first day of Spanish class, the instructor entered the classroom in the Language and Literature building about five minutes after class was supposed to have started (she had problems arriving anywhere on time) and greeted the class with a big smile and a hearty *¡Buenos días!* Then she pointed to herself and said, *"Me llamo Lupita."* She wrote those words on the chalkboard and then went around to each student in the class saying, *"Me llamo Lupita. ¿Cómo te llamas tú?"* The first student she tried this with sat in her chair and looked befuddled. Lupita then went on to another student who appeared to be Hispanic and repeated the same expression. The answer came back promptly, *"Me llamo Felipe."* Then she went back to the first student and repeated, *"Me llamo Lupita. ¿Cómo te llamas tú?"* The first student had caught on. This time the answer came back hesitatingly but correct, *"Me llamo Georgette."* By the time she had gone around the class, every student had learned how to introduce oneself in Spanish and ask the other person's name. Actually, Jason noted, about one third of the students in class pronounced the words so quickly and with such a good accent that it was obvious that they already spoke Spanish. He didn't know how he was going to compete in this class against so many native speakers.

Jason noticed that Lupita was very intelligent, and intelligence was one of the few qualities that he admired in other human beings. She was also a much better teacher than any of his other instructors. He decided that he wanted to get to know her better. He couldn't spend all of his time with his dumb roommate Jimmy, whose goal in life was to help other people. Besides, he was going to need some extra help if he was going to learn this language. He wasn't enthralled at the idea of learning Spanish, but if he had to do it, he was going to do it to the best of his ability.

He found the opportunity to talk to Lupita outside of class in the second week of the semester when she wrote her office hours on the board and invited any student who had questions to drop by and see her. Jason invented a problem and went to Lupita's office to discuss it with her.

Jason's invented problem was trivial and quickly solved. Then Jason asked Lupita if he could meet her for coffee later in the cafeteria. Lupita, who had just begun her master's program at ASU had not made any friends yet and quickly agreed. "After all," she thought, "even if I am his instructor, we're both students."

That afternoon as they were seated in the cafeteria, Jason drinking a coffee and Lupita sipping a coke, Jason asked her, "Where do you come from? You speak English almost like an American, but with a very slight trace of an accent."

"I'm from Mexico, from Puerto Vallarta. My father was American, and he never learned to speak Spanish well, so we spoke English at home. I grew up speaking both languages, and I'm an American citizen. Actually, I'm a citizen of both countries. I have both an American and a Mexican passport."

"Where is Puerto Vallarta?"

"It's a city on the Pacific coast of Mexico in the tropics. It's a tourist city. My father went to Puerto Vallarta on vacation when it was barely more than a village, and there he met my mother. My father told me that when he saw my mother the first time, he immediately fell in love and knew that she was the woman who would be his wife. My mother worked in a hotel and spoke some English, and she was enchanted by the attention shown her by this gringo. My father proposed marriage to my mother, who said she would accept on one condition. She did not want to live in the United States, so my father would have to move to Mexico. My father flew home to settle his affairs, and when he returned to Puerto Vallarta, he and my mom were married. My dad never left Puerto Vallarta again except for short trips that we took as a family to his home in Seattle to visit my grandparents. What about you? Where are you from?"

Jason ignored the question. He didn't want to talk about himself. "How did he make a living in Mexico?"

"Anybody who is fluent in English can make a reasonable living in Mexico. He got into the timeshare business. Almost all of the Mexican resort hotels sell timeshares. Tourists can buy the right to live so and so many weeks a year in a hotel, and timeshares can be traded. Say you want to spend your vacation in Las Vegas but you own a two-week timeshare in Mexico. You can trade your right to stay in a Mexican hotel for the right to stay two weeks in one in Vegas."

"I suspect that selling timeshares is a rough business."

"My father is a very persuasive salesman. But, tell me about yourself, Jason. Where are you from?"

"I'm from Chicago," Jason replied, "but my story isn't half as interesting as yours. My parents are both American, although my grandparents, my mother's parents, were born in Poland. My mother speaks Polish with them, but she never taught me to speak it. Oh, and my Dad's parents are immigrants, too, from England."

"It's too bad that you didn't learn Polish as a kid. There are a lot of advantages of speaking two languages."

"Yeah, but I can't do anything about that now" Jason felt uncomfortable now that the conversation had turned to his history. He was afraid that if people got to know him too well, he would expose to the world what a shallow person he was. It was time to change the subject. "What caused you to come to Tempe?"

"I graduated from the National Autonomous University of Mexico in Mexico City with a bachelor's degree in Spanish literature. I decided to come to ASU to do my master's degree and perhaps a PhD."

"Why ASU? Why not get your master's degree in Mexico? Wouldn't it be cheaper?"

"Well," Lupita tried to collect her thoughts, "ASU has an excellent graduate program in Spanish. Besides, here I was offered a part-time job teaching your Spanish class. That'll help pay for my studies. Also, I've lived in Mexico all of my life. I wanted to get to know my American half."

"Why did your parents name your Lupita? I've never heard that name before."

"Lupita is a nickname. My real name is Guadalupe, like the Virgin of Guadalupe or Mary, Mother of Jesus, who is said to have appeared to a humble Indian named Juan Diego in Mexico City. The short form of Guadalupe is Lupe, but I've always been called by the diminutive form, Lupita."

"Why is your last name Gonzales? Didn't you say that your father is American?"

"My complete name is María Guadalupe del Carmen Obermeyer Gonzales," said Lupita between sips of her Coke. "Can you see why I prefer Lupita? By custom, we Mexicans take the last name of both our father and our mother, so the short form of my name should be María Obermeyer, but I've always been called Lupita. If I used Lupita Obermeyer, I would feel like a person without an identity, *ni de allá, ni de acá* as we say in Spanish, neither from here nor from there. I feel more Mexican than American, so I prefer Lupita Gonzales. Maybe after I live in the States long enough, that will change."

That was to be the first of many meetings. Jason might have been expected to take advantage of the relationship to get a better grade in Spanish, but he didn't need to. Even when it came to languages, he proved to be a fast learner, and there were plenty of opportunities to learn Spanish in the Phoenix area including an AM Spanish-language radio station, KSUN. He bought a table-top radio and kept it tuned to the KSUN when he was in the dorm room, much to Jimmy's annoyance. As to the Spanish-speaking kids in the class, he quickly learned that although they were fluent speakers, they had never learned to properly write the language. When it came to written tests, Jason consistently got the best grade in the class.

By the time the semester was half over, Lupita and Jason were a couple. They spent the evenings studying together in the student union. By coincidence, one of Lupita's graduate courses was a seminar on the works of Gabriel García Márquez. Lupita was astounded when Jason mentioned magical realism and the invented history of the Buendía Family in the imaginary town of Macondo. She had never before met an American college freshman who knew anything about Latin American literature.

Some of the other students in the Spanish class did not look kindly upon the fact that Lupita and her star student had a relationship, but their dissatisfaction was limited to grumbling. No one took the complaint to the Office of Language and Literature. Lupita seemed unaware of her students' discontent. Jason was aware of it, but he had never cared what others thought of him.

It was during the third week of classes that Jimmy said to him, "Dude, we've been working our asses off. It's time we went a little wild and celebrated."

"What sort of celebration did you have in mind?"

"Let's go to one of the clubs and get smashed. It's the thing all freshman do on weekends."

"But I'm not old enough to drink," Jason objected.

"Don't worry about that, man. I know a place where they don't look to closely at IDs. If you're with me, you'll get in."

"OK, let's go for it. Where should we meet?"

"Friday evening at 8 pm we'll meet here in our room."

Jimmy was as good as his word. When they entered the club, Jimmy said to the bouncer, "He's OK, man. He's with me," as he slipped the guy a five-dollar bill.

The place was jumping. The music was loud, and the club was full of young students. This loud rock music wasn't to Jason's taste—he preferred classical—but the women were luscious, and Jimmy told him they were easy. Jason was sure that he wasn't the only under-age drinker in the place. They went to the bar where Jason ordered a tequila sunrise. "Do you know this world-famous drink originated in Phoenix?" the bartender asked him as he deftly mixed the beverage.

"No idea!" Jason didn't really care.

"Yeah, it was invented by a bartender at the Biltmore Hotel a long time ago. The 1930s I think."

Jason moved away from the bar to avoid this inane small talk. He said to Jimmy, "Look, buddy, I'll catch you later. I want to see if I can make out with one of these chicks."

There was a buxom woman who looked to be about 25 dancing tipsily by herself to one side of the dance floor. Jason liked older women. Drink still in hand, Jason started dancing in front of her. "What's your name?" he shouted above the music.

"Vero! Actually it's Veronica, but everyone calls me Vero."

"Mine's Jason."

"Pleased to meet 'cha, Jason."

The disk jockey was segueing one song after the other. All of the music was very loud and with an ear-numbing bass beat. After the fifth number Jason shouted, "Whadaya say we sit down for awhile? Whadaya drinkin'? I get us each another one."

"I'll have whatever you're drinking."

Jason got two more tequila sunrises from the bar and searched the room with his eyes until he found Vero seated at a table with three other people. In this crowded club, there was no possibility of having a table to themselves.

"Where ya from, Vero?"

"Sasabe."

"Sasabe? I never heard of it."

"It's a little town in Southern Arizona on the Mexican border. More of a village than a town, really. The main industry is catering to illegal border crossers."

Vero had finished her drink quickly. Not to be outdone, Jason emptied his glass again, and went to the bar for two more drinks. After that things got a bit hazy. He remembered going to the bar several times for more drinks and leaving the club with Vero, each unsteadily supporting the other. His next memory was waking up completely nude in a strange bed. A shaft of sunlight coming through the window had stuck his eyes and awakened him. Vero was lying beside him fast asleep and also nude. There was another bed in the room with two sleeping figures upon it, one male and the other female. Had he and Vero had sex? He couldn't remember, but looking at her nude body, he felt desire rising within him. He shook Vero awake, and she responded groggily. She responded languidly to his kiss. Without waiting for any more response from Vero, he slid on top of her and made love to her. He wasn't really sure if she was sober enough to know what was happening.

Then he found his clothes on the floor beside the bed, got dressed, and had the presence of mind to check his wallet. Yes, it was still there, and it had some money in it. He had no idea how much he had spent on drinks the night before, so he couldn't be sure that he hadn't been robbed, but he assumed he hadn't been. He slipped out of the small studio apartment without awaking the three sleeping figures. Vero had fallen back asleep, too. Once outside, he had to orient himself. He didn't know where he was, but there was a main street with heavy traffic just two blocks away. He walked toward it. It was Rural Road, and he saw that he was just south of the Salt River and therefore no more than a half mile from his dorm room.

When he reached the dorm, Jimmy was already awake. "Man! You sure tied one on last night! Who was that chick you left with?"

Jason ignored him. He didn't know the woman he had spent the night with, and at any rate, what business did this idiot have asking him personal questions? Finally he grunted, "Just a woman," and fell down on his bed fully dressed. He vowed never to have so much to drink again. Jason couldn't stand not being 100 percent in control of himself.

The semester passed much more quickly that Jason had expected, and soon it was time for the yearend vacation. Jason flew home to Chicago during the Christmas break. His father Craig was waiting when Jason got off the plane at O'Hare Airport and gave Jason a big hug, but he released him when he felt his son stiffen in his arms. "The kid hasn't changed," Craig thought to himself. He had hoped that being on his own would make Jason more human.

"Let's go home," Craig said aloud. "Your mother's been cooking all day. I think she'll have a good meal for us."

"Yeah, I've really been missing Mom's home cooking," Jason, lied. Inwardly he cringed at the thought of eating greasy meat with vegetables boiled to a mush and served with a cheesy sauce and some gross, fat-laden, unidentifiable type of chocolate pudding served as desert.

The two weeks that he spent with his family dragged on slowly in Jason's mind. His parents, in contrast, were delighted to have him home and felt that the time was passing far too quickly. Even though Jason was uncommunicative, he was their son, and they loved him. They just wished that he weren't so distant all of the time.

As often as he could, Jason took the L to the Loop or borrowed his father's old Chevy and drove north toward Wisconsin, just to get out of the house. He found that the cold Chicago wind bothered him much more that it used to. He had become accustomed to the warmer Phoenix weather. In Chicago, he shivered even in his winter coat anytime he was outside.

Finally, the Chicago vacation was over, and his father drove him to O'Hare Airport for his flight back to Phoenix. Irene didn't go along, claiming that she didn't feel well. In truth, she was glad to be rid of Jason and didn't want to go through the pretense of a loving mother saying good-bye to a loving son.

"Things ain't goin' so good, Jason," his father began as they were driving out the Kennedy Expressway toward the airport. Work's been slow, and I haven't been makin' as much money as I used to. I'm afraid I'm not gonna' be able to send you as much money as I have been."

Jason thought in silence. How was he going to complete his studies? The money he was making working during the school year staffing the Student Union information desk wasn't enough to pay tuition and meet his other expenses. He'd have to figure something else out.

Then his father added, "Your Mom and I have enough saved up to help you through the next semester. After that, you're going to have to figure out a way to make it on your own."

Jason saw an advantage to the situation. Once his parents stopped helping him financially, he would no longer be obligated to visit them. He knew that they would be as glad to see the last of him as he was to get away from them. He was unable to maintain the pretense of being a loving son. He despised his parents. What a pair of uneducated dumbbells!

Lupita was not waiting for him at Sky Harbor Airport when he landed in Phoenix. Public transportation in the Phoenix area was very primitive compared to Chicago, and Jason assumed she hadn't been able to persuade anyone to give her a lift to the airport. If nobody cared enough about him to pick him up, he would have to take the bus to ASU in Tempe. He didn't bother calling Lupita to tell her he was back. She knew which flight he was arriving on, and if she couldn't be bothered to take the bus to the airport to greet him, why should he bother calling her?

"I'm so happy that you're back," Lupita told him the next day when they met in the cafeteria of the Student Union. "I missed you so much."

"I'm glad to be back, too," Jason replied. This was true. In the few months he had been living in Tempe, he had learned to appreciate the warm weather and the more casual culture of the Phoenix area. He hoped to never see Chicago again. "And I also really missed you," Jason added. This was not true. Jason viewed his relationship with Lupita as a convenience, but he felt no affection for her. He knew he was incapable of falling in love, but if he were going to be in a relationship, it might as well be with Lupita. She would serve as well as anyone else. Jason didn't know what type of career he wanted, but he envisioned great things for himself. He believed that a great man needed a wife to support him, and he thought Lupita might be that wife.

School was ending for the summer when Jason suggested to Lupita that they live together. Lupita wasn't sure that was a good idea. "Besides," she added, "we don't have enough money to rent an apartment." That was true. Lupita had been offered the opportunity to teach Spanish classes during ASU's two summer session, but that job wouldn't bring in enough money to support them both, and Jason no longer had a job at all. His boss had informed him that due to the decreased enrollment in the summer, he had to cut back on staff. Jason also remembered what his father had told him. He could expect little financial help from home. He had to find a better job. He needed a full-time vacation job that could turn into a part time job when school resumed at the end of the summer. The job definately had to pay more than he had been earning at the university.

"My parents can't ever know that I'm living with a man without being married," Lupita fretted. "They're very conservative Catholics."

"Well, my parents are Catholics, too," Jason countered. "We can't spend our lives worrying about what our parents think. It's time we made our own lives. I love you, and I want to live with you."

Jason began searching the advertisements in the *Arizona Republic* and the *Phoenix Gazette*, which were both owned by the same publisher and generally carried the same classified advertisements. The *Republic* came out in the morning seven days a week, and the *Gazette* appeared in the afternoon Monday through Saturday. Not many of the ads in either paper appealed to Jason. He needed a job with flexible hours. A used car lot called Friendly Motors on East Van Buren Street ran an ad almost daily looking for car salesmen "Must be good with people, sales experience preferred but not necessary. Flexible hours. Call Texas Bob for an interview." Jason had ignored the ad for several weeks, but not being able to find anything better, he finally called the number in the ad and set up an appointment.

Jason had seen Texas Bob on TV commercials. What a smooth talker! He made the used cars he sold seem like unbelievable bargains. "Friends, we jist got a notice from th' bank sayin' we have to sell some of them thar cars you see behind me, so we're discountin' 'em to move 'em on out. Look at this one, a 1960 Edsel. Friends, they jist don' make cars like this no more. Come in and check out this here car, and if you like it, we'll make you a deal that will knock your socks off. It will fit your pocketbook with easy weekly payments. We're so anxious to find a good owner for this car, friends, that if we think you'll give it a good home, we'll almost give it to you. We carry our own contracts. Bad credit, no credit, slow credit, low credit, it don' matter, folks. We can finance yew. Have somethin' to trade? If you can drive it in, tow it in, push it in, or ride it in, we'll take hit in trade. We'll take almost anything in trade except for yer mother-in-law, but if you insist, bring 'er in and we'll take a look at 'er and see what we can dew." Texas Bob finished every commercial with the same line, "Friendly Motors. Where you come in walkin' and go out drivin'."

It was a long bike ride to the car lot on streets with heavy traffic, but Jason was at the car lot 15 minutes before the scheduled interview. The lot was on seedy East Van Buren Street, which was famous in the Phoenix area for the prostitutes who walked its sidewalks, cheap motels, drug dealers, dangerous bars, used car lots, and frequent violence.

When he sat down in the small portable office at one corner of the small car lot, it turned out that Texas Bob was not at all what Jason had expected. For one thing, the hokey accent of the TV commercials was gone. Texas Bob had the tones of a Midwesterner, perhaps from Minnesota, Jason guessed. Except for his dress, he had the manners of a sharp businessman. He was wearing cowboy boots and faded jeans held up by a wide leather belt with an enormous brass buckle in the form of a star. His vertically striped blue shirt was covered by a leather vest, and around his neck hung a bolo tie with a clear plastic slide inside of which was entombed the body of an oversized scorpion. His enormous cowboy hat hung on a wooden peg behind his desk. To the left of his desk, a confederate battle flag adorned the wall, and to the right was a no-smoking sign, looking out of place.

Texas Bob saw Jason's glance linger on the no-smoking sign. "I used to smoke," he explained, "but since I quit years ago, I can't stand the smell of cigarette smoke. If I breathe it, it sets off a coughing spell. I'd really like smoking to be banned altogether someday, but I would never say that to my customers. Almost all of them smoke." Then suddenly, "What makes you think you can sell cars?"

"I learn things faster than other people do," Jason explained. "I think I can learn to do anything if I set my mind to it."

Texas Bob's real name was Robert Samuelson, but no one called him anything but Texas Bob. He was largely self-taught, so he appreciated other people who were quick learners. Business school did not prepare its students to sell used cars, but he sensed that Jason had the street smarts needed to learn. Then he looked out the window and noticed that a couple had entered the car lot. He pushed a form toward Jason. "Fill out this application and leave it on my desk. Drop back again tomorrow, and we'll discuss terms. In the meantime, I have work to do."

"Does that mean you're offering me the job?" Jason asked.

"Yeah, I don't know much about you, but I'll give you a chance. At any rate, I'm not taking much of a risk. You'll only get paid if you sell, and if you can't sell, I won't have much invested in you. Now let me go outside and see if I can sell these yokels a car."

Texas Bob's business model took into account a big turnover in sales personnel. Most of them stayed only a few months. If Jason didn't work out, it wouldn't be a big loss. However, Texas Bob had a feeling that Jason might stick around longer than the typical used car salesman.

As Jason filled out the job application, he could hear Texas Bob outside. He had changed not only his accent but his entire personality. "Howdy, folks! I see ye'r lookin' at that thar Ford. You sure do have an eye for quality, you sure do. That thar car is pbob'ly the best bargain we got on the lot. We took it in trade from a preacher man who hardly never drove it."

Chapter 3 — From Selling to Managing

Jason was back at the car lot when it opened at eight the following morning. "Let's get started, Kid," Texas Bob said. "I want you to follow me around for a few days to learn how to sell a car. After that, you're on your own. As I told you yesterday, your only pay is your commission on what you sell. Simply put, you're an independent contractor in business for yourself. You're not technically my employee, but nevertheless, you'll do as I say."

The first four days, Jason was not allowed to talk to customers other than to say hello and shake hands when Texas Bob or one of the other salesmen introduced him to a potential customer. Of course, that meant that Jason made no sales and earned no money.

Between customers, Texas Bob explained the business to Jason. "I buy these used cars on the wholesale market or I take them as trade-ins. Some of them have serious problems. I contract with a mechanic to bring them up to saleable condition, meaning that if there are any defects, the mechanic makes sure that they aren't problems that our average customer is going to notice before signing a contract to buy. The car's not going to burn oil and a fender is not going to fall off when the customer drives it off the lot, although those things may happen a few weeks later. If we can't fix up a car good enough to sell without too much work, we sell it to a wholesaler, and somebody else gets stuck with it.

"Our customers are all low-income people who couldn't buy a car at all if it weren't for businesses like ours. We'll do almost anything to make a sale, even sell a car at a loss if necessary, because selling cars is not our main business. We make the big bucks from financing them ourselves at a high interest rate. Our customers in general have little or no experience with borrowing money. We get them to trust us, and they are grateful to us for making it possible for them to get a car loan. We set up easy payment terms, weekly if necessary. Most of the loan payments go toward interest and into our pockets. Very little goes toward principal. By the time a customer pays off the loan, he has paid for the car several times over. We also have an arrangement with an insurance company to insure the car. The insurance premium is included in the car payment, and we get a rebate from the insurance company."

Jason asked, "But don't some people realize that they're being fleeced and stop paying their loans?"

"Don't use the word 'fleece!' These people couldn't finance a car if it weren't for us. We seldom have problems with payments. When a customer buys a car, we tell him, usually it's a man, how much he's going to pay each month or each week. We don't talk about interest rates or payoff dates, and our customers wouldn't understand if we did. All they know is that for so-and-so many dollars a week, they have a car to drive. Have you ever tried getting around Phoenix without a car? The public transportation here is deplorable. The buses don't run at all on Sunday. We make it possible for people to get to work."

Jason had been getting around without a car, and he conceded that it was very difficult, even impossible at times. With his bike, he was limited to traveling to areas within a few miles of the university. He moved on to his next question, "Don't people sometimes stop paying their loans even if you are doing them a big favor? What do you do then?"

"Yeah, that happens. In that case we have the car repossessed, and we sell it again. The buyer is unfortunately out all the money he has made in payments. In addition, we sell the loan to a collection agency at a discount, and the collection agency hounds the customer to try to get the loan paid off plus interest plus collection fees. Almost anyone who defaults on a loan is going to be very, very sorry. It'll cost them a bundle. If anybody comes in and complains, we say that it's out of our hands. We'd like to help, but the collection agency refuses to listen to us. In general, we make more money from deadbeats than we do from people who pay their loans. We repossess the car and get to sell it twice and finance it twice. The original car buyer ends up with no car and is still required to pay the loan, which keeps accumulating interest and late-payment fees. However, most people pay their loans, and as I said, we make it possible for people to buy and finance a car who wouldn't be able to afford one. We're performing a public service."

"Don't the authorities cause problems?" Jason wanted to know.

"We're in Arizona. Arizona is not exactly a consumer-friendly state. Naw, we don't get hassled. I make political contributions to the right people, just to make sure it stays that way. The sheriff is a good buddy of mine."

When Jason explained his job to Lupita, she was aghast. "How can you take money from these poor people who can't afford to pay? Don't you have a conscience?"

Jason thought about the question. The truth was that he didn't have a conscience, he had to admit to himself. In fact, all of his life he had be puzzled over exactly what a conscience was and how it could cause people to act against their own best interest. However, he said to Lupita, "I'm doing this for us. Once I sell a few cars, we'll able to rent an apartment and live together, and I'll also be able to pay next semester's tuition." And then he added, parroting what Texas Bob had told him, "Besides, it's an honest business. We sell cars to people who otherwise couldn't own one."

Jason went to the car lot every day, seven days a week during the summer university vacation. Texas Bob let him take one of the cars home at night so that he had a way to get back and forth that was more reliable than his bicycle. Within a few weeks, Jason had become adept at selling cars, and more importantly, of convincing customers that financing with Friendly Motors was a real bargain, a deal too good to pass up. When he received his first paycheck with his percentage of the sales, "the take" Texas Bob called it, and of the payments on the financing contracts that he had sold, it was more money than he had expected. He decided it was time for him and Lupita to go apartment hunting.

There were apartments near the university that catered almost exclusively to students, but they were noisy. Jason couldn't stand the loud music that the other students played at night nor the noise of the weekend parties that seemed to start Friday evening and continue until the wee hours of Monday morning. Many students were in no shape to show up for Monday morning classes.

Jason took a day off work so they could check out apartments. Lupita wanted to rent an apartment in one of the large complexes, but Jason overruled her stating that those places were too expensive. He wanted them to rent an apartment in a smaller, family-owned building. Following up several ads in the *Arizona Republic*, he finally decided on renting a unit in a triplex on East Taylor Street, a small residential street in a declining neighborhood a short commute from Friendly Motors. The family that owned the building lived in the front unit. Lupita and Jason rented the rear unit, farthest from the street but with a rear entrance from the alley, which allowed them to come and go without being noticed. The apartment was not only near Jason's work; it was within a reasonable distance of the university. When school started again in August, Jason would borrow one of the cars from the Friendly Motors lot to drive the two of them to the university in the morning then drive himself to work from the university in the afternoon. In the evening, he would drive back to the university to pick up Lupita and drive them both home. Because Lupita was a graduate student, and many of her fellow graduate students were also teaching assistants, some of the classes she took were seminars held in the evening when the job of teaching undergraduate students was over for the day. Jason would take classes in the morning and work in the afternoon three days during the week plus an eight-hour shift on Saturdays and Sundays.

When the time came for Jason to cut back his hours at the Friendly Motors lot to part time and recommence his studies, Texas Bob took him aside. "Look, Jason, you've got a real gift for selling. If you get your business degree, what are you going to do with it? Get a job as a nameless low-level manager in some humongous corporation and hope you can work your way up the ladder? Most of those professors at ASU have no idea what it means to be an entrepreneur. Most of them have never held a real job. This car lot is what business is really about. This is where money is made, and the whole point of business is to earn an income. You're a natural. You're the best salesman I've ever had."

Jason half agreed with Tex, but he wasn't yet convinced that giving up his studies would be a good idea. So, he returned to school, taking classes in the morning as planned so that he could work at the car lot in the afternoon. It was not easy. The intense heat made working in the open lot in the afternoons exhausting. The humidity of Arizona's summer monsoon added to the misery of working outdoors. The office offered some respite, but the evaporative cooler that had kept the office at a comfortable temperature in the early summer now just blew hot, muggy air.

One day Jason had an idea. Many of the car lot's customers where Hispanic, mostly Mexicans who came to Phoenix a few months each year to earn money to send to their families. Many of them were perpetual migrants. They would work in Phoenix at manual labor until they had saved some money, and then they would return home to their families in Mexico until the money was spent. Then it would be time to go back to Phoenix to earn some more.

Crossing the border from Mexico was easy in those days. The border fence was full of holes in cities such as Nogales, and the few people that the Border Patrol caught crossing illegally in the morning were sent back to Mexico before noon only to be back in Arizona again a few hours later. Sometimes the Border Patrol deported the same person two or three times in the same day.

On weekends, long lines of people could be seen crossing the border on the hill above the twin cities of Nogales, one in Mexico and the other in the USA, to go shopping on the Arizona side and perhaps treat themselves to a Big Mac at McDonald's. Almost all of them would be back in Nogales, Sonora on the Mexican side before nightfall. The lax border enforcement gave Mexicans access to cheaper products in Arizona, and it made the businesses on the Arizona side of the border profitable.

For those illegal border crossers who wanted to do more than just spend a day in Nogales, it was easy to get to Phoenix. Anyone with luggage who visited McDonald's was bound to be approached by someone asking if the person needed a ride. The trip from Nogales to Phoenix could cost as little as $30 in an unlicensed taxi, and the smugglers jammed as many people as they could into each car. There was always the danger that the car would be stopped by the Border Patrol and anyone without permission to be in the USA would be transported back to the border, but again, the person would probably be back in Arizona within an hour and on the way to Phoenix once again shortly thereafter. The system worked well for everyone. Mexican laborers got to earn some dollars and then return to their families in Mexico, Arizona residents got the benefit of their cheap labor, and the Border Patrol got to pretend that it was doing something to combat illegal immigration.

Jason's idea was that the car lot should do more to attract Mexican car buyers, even if they were not in the country legally. Not only did these Mexican laborers require a car for transportation, they could also take the car with them back to Mexico and sell it for much more than they had paid for it in Phoenix. There was a flourishing business in those days of Mexicans and Mexican-Americans who routinely purchased used cars in the USA and resold them for a handsome profit back home. Texas Bob had already tapped part of this market. If the customer had no fixed address in the Phoenix area, Friendly Motors demanded payment in cash. To those traffickers in used cars who had a history of buying at Friendly Motors and a Phoenix address, Texas Bob was more than happy to extend credit at a high interest rate. However, this business was still a small portion of Friendly Motors' sales, and Jason wanted to expand it.

In those days, despite the high number of illegal border crossings there was little true illegal immigration. People didn't come from Mexico to Arizona to stay. They came to work for a period of time and then return to Mexico to live from their earnings. There was a constant back and forth with almost as many people returning to Mexico as were entering the US illegally to work. It wasn't until years later as an unintended consequence of increased border security that Arizona's undocumented population began to balloon. People who made it from Mexico into Arizona began staying, because if they returned to Mexico for a period of easy living, it would be too difficult to return to Arizona.

How to attract more of these buyers, who spoke little or no English? Even though he was only in his second year of Spanish at ASU, he already spoke the language well enough to communicate basic ideas. Because he was the only person at Friendly Motors who spoke any Spanish at all, he dealt with the Mexican customers. He decided that the best way to attract more of them was by having the car dealership do a radio commercial in Spanish. Together with Lupita, he came up with enough text in Spanish for a 30-second spot. Lupita even reluctantly managed to translate the car lot's motto, "Friendly Motors, where you come in walking and go out driving." In Spanish it read, "Friendly Motors, *donde entras caminando y sales manejando.*" In fact, it sounded better in Spanish than in English, because it rhymed.

There were few Spanish-language radio stations in Phoenix at that time other than KSUN. The others that had been started had mostly gone bankrupt or had abandoned the Spanish format in the hopes of avoiding bankruptcy. Even KCAC, another Spanish station that Jason had once listened to, had changed its format to progressive rock in English. However, Jason knew from talking to Lupita that many Mexicans listened to country music, which reminded them of the *norteña* music of northern Mexico. He persuaded Texas Bob to run the commercial for a week on KHAT, a daytime-only radio country music station where I was working my way through ASU as a disk jockey, to see if a commercial on that station could produce any results. That was the first time that I met Jason, although I had no idea at the time that he was destined for great things.

But who was to do the commercial? Texas Bob did all of the Friendly Motors radio commercials himself, but he couldn't do one in Spanish. That left either a professional announcer or Jason, whose Spanish was still rudimentary and heavily accented. If Texas Bob couldn't do the commercial himself, he at least wanted someone from the car lot to do it. Jason didn't have to be fluent in Spanish. All he had to do was read it into a tape recorder with the best pronunciation he was capable of. He rehearsed every evening with Lupita coaching him and correcting his pronunciation. Thanks to her prodding, he finally was able to read the 30-second commercial aloud into the microphone, although still with a very noticeable American accent.

The commercial was a success! The first day it ran, three potential new customers showed up who had heard the commercial on KHAT, and two of them bought cars. Financing was a problem that Texas Bob had not thought through. Most of his Mexican customers up to that point had been legal US residents or, in the case of people who trafficked used cars across the border, people with whom he had established a relationship over time. It was one thing to sell a car to a permanent US resident, who could usually be tracked down if the purchaser failed to keep up the payments, but these men were not legal residents. If one of them took the car across the border into Mexico, the chances of recovering it were next to zero. Even if Friendly Motors retained the title, Texas Bob knew that the car could be sold on the Mexican black market without one. Mexico was then (and largely still is) a country where the normal rules of legal procedure didn't operate.

Texas Bob finally came up with a solution with the advice of his attorney. He would allow anyone to buy a car who could come up with two cosigners who were US citizens or legal residents of the United States. If the car purchaser skipped the country, the collection agency could still go after the cosigners. Many of the Mexicans who were undocumented in the US had relatives or immediate family members who were legal residents or even citizens. Sometimes in the same nuclear family, some members would be in the country illegally and others, having been born on the US side of the border, were US citizens. A boy who was born in Arizona and therefore a United States citizen could live with an older sister who had been born in Mexico and was in the United States illegally.

Texas Bob had his lawyer draw up a new loan contract designed to be used specifically with buyers who were in the United States illegally. The contract was written in legalese obscure enough that even most native English speakers would not be able to understand it. He purposely didn't have it translated into Spanish. In the end, the requirement to have cosigners would prove to be an unnecessary precaution. Most of the undocumented car buyers turned out to be very responsible about paying their loans, much more responsible than many of the American citizens that the car lot dealt with.

Jason was soon overwhelmed with the influx of new car buyers, so Texas Bob hired a bilingual Mexican-American salesman, and as business picked up even more, a second one. Although Jason was still working part-time, he was put in charge of the two new salesmen and received a percentage of their commissions as well as commissions on his own sales. Jason was moving up the income ladder. Thanks to his inventiveness and gift of gab, he was now a manager as well as a salesman. Texas Bob was grateful to Jason for the increased business and gave him one of the better used cars as a bonus. He began to ask himself if he should take Jason in as a business partner. He didn't need a partner to run Friendly Motors, but Texas Bob had ambitions of expanding into the new car market. Jason appeared to have the brains to make them both rich.

Jason also wanted to be rich. He remembered Texas Bob's earlier advice. Graduating from business school would land him a job as a faceless bureaucrat in some large company with sufficient income to support himself and Lupita or another woman in a comfortable manner, but he would never be rich. He couldn't see himself working in a bureaucracy taking orders from clueless higher management for the rest of his life.

Jason dropped out of ASU and started working at Friendly Motors full time. He had decided that Texas Bob was right: If he wanted to be rich, a degree in business administration was not going to get him there. Although he resented taking orders from Texas Bob, he managed to hide the resentment from his employer. Ultimately, he wasn't going to get rich working for Texas Bob either, but for now Texas Bob and Friendly Motors would serve as stepping stones to something better. What that something better was, Jason didn't yet know.

Jason suggested to Texas Bob that it was time to expand the size of the car lot. The property next door was occupied by a boarded-up motel that had once rented rooms by the hour and sold pornography at the front desk but which had been unable to compete with the large number of other dilapidated motels along Van Buren Street that rented double rooms in the slow summer season for as little as $5 for an entire day. The motel next door had gone bankrupt and had been repossessed by a bank that was willing to sell the property at a low price just to get it off its books. That section of Van Buren Street was not an area where many honest businesses wanted to locate. It was taken over at night by prostitutes, drunks, and drug addicts. A few blocks farther up the street was the Arizona State Mental Hospital, many of whose inmates were criminally insane. This was the mental hospital from which the infamous trunk murderess Winnie Ruth Judd had escaped six times. Van Buren was also the birthplace of the Miranda rights (You have a right to remain silent....) after a man named Ernesto Miranda murdered a woman who was walking along the street. No other section of Phoenix had such a lurid history as did Van Buren Street.

Even though the Van Buren area was decaying, away from this infamous street business was booming. Phoenix was growing rapidly, and a high percentage of new residents were people with no more than a high school education, if that, who had had been attracted to the Phoenix area's ample low-wage jobs. These were just the sort of people who were routinely turned down for car loans by honest lenders but who could buy a car from Friendly Motors, the car seller of last resort. The area's Hispanic population continued to grow as more people moved to Phoenix from Mexico and Central America, legally or illegally. Most of these new immigrants took jobs in such low-paying industries as gardening, restaurants, hotels, and car washes. The construction industry, which had once supplied good-paying union jobs, began hiring these immigrants at a fraction of the wages that it had formerly paid. Texas Bob viewed all of these new residents as potential customers.

Jason's radio commercials in Spanish had proved successful enough that he began placing classified ads in the Spanish-language weekly newspaper *Prensa Hispana* in addition to the English-language adds that Texas Bob was already running in the *Arizona Republic*. The ads brought in more business, and soon Friendly Motors was serving the Hispanic working-class community almost exclusively.

Jason became so wrapped up in the business of the used car dealership that he had little time for Lupita. They saw each other only in the mornings over breakfast and at night before they went to bed. At times, Jason arrived home so late that Lupita was already asleep. He would shake her awake and make love to her in order to rid himself of the stress of the day. He didn't ask himself if Lupita enjoyed this lovemaking. Lupita didn't like having her sleep interrupted this way, but she had grown up in a culture were a woman does her wifely duty and satisfies her man. If a Mexican woman didn't do that, her husband would find his satisfaction elsewhere.

As to Lupita, she was very busy with her dual role as a graduate student and a Spanish teacher. She did miss having Jason around, but she didn't have time to sit and pine for him.

Chapter 4 — Fame and Fortune

During the next two years, business increased greatly. It was now 1998, and Texas Bob had become a rich man. Jason's salary and commissions had increased to the point that he felt comfortably well off, but he wasn't satisfied. It was through his hard work and innovation that Friendly Motors had become such a profitable business. He deserved to be rich. Texas Bob did not! Texas Bob was a leech who had was prospering because of Jason's drudgery.

However, Jason was careful to hide his resentment. He still needed Texas Bob. Without him, he would be out in the street looking for a job instead of earning a good living in the used car lot. Outwardly, Jason did his best to appear grateful, and he even flattered Texas Bob by frequently remarking that it was thanks to him that Jason and Lupita now had a more comfortable life. He and Lupita were no longer renting. They had bought a small house in Scottsdale, and both of them were now driving new cars, not the jalopies that they used to borrow from the Friendly Motors used car lot.

Lupita was in the last year of her PhD program at Arizona State University and was hoping to land a professorship after she received her doctorate. She would have preferred to apply for positions throughout the country and even abroad, but Jason was doing so well at Friendly Motors that moving to another state was out of the question. In Metropolitan Phoenix there were only three choices, Arizona State University itself in Tempe, the Thunderbird School of Global Management in the Glendale, almost an hour's drive away, and Grand Canyon College in Phoenix. The latter was a Protestant-oriented religious college, and as a Catholic, Lupita didn't feel comfortable with the idea of teaching there. She applied at both ASU and "T-bird". She patiently waited for replies.

Texas Bob and Jason were sitting in the office alone during a lull in the normally busy day. Texas Bob cleared his throat as if he were preparing to say something important. "You know, Jason," he began, "I think of you almost as a son."

Jason smiled inwardly. So far, things were going according to plan.

Texas Bob continued, "It's largely thanks to you that I now have a comfortable income. I'd like to pay you back by helping you make a little money, too."

More money? Jason had to exercise his self control to hide his excitement. "I haven't done anything," he replied with feigned modesty. "It's you who have built this business. If I know anything about the car business, it's because of what I've learned from the great marketing genius, Texas Bob. You're a great teacher."

There was a silence during which Jason impatiently waited to learn what Texas Bob was going to propose. For Christ's sake, why was the idiot stalling? Texas Bob seemed to be gathering his thoughts.

"I've been offered a chance to buy a Ford dealership up on Camelback Road. I would be selling new cars at a good profit, and the used cars I would sell would be reconditioned and come with a guarantee. They wouldn't be the crap that we sell here. If I buy the dealership, it will be a completely different type of business from what I'm used to."

"And, how do I fit into this deal?" Jason asked.

"I'm still mulling it over. My first thought was to run the new car business myself and leave you in charge of Friendly Motors. But I don't think that would work. I'm too associated with the low-end used car business. I've done so many TV and radio commercials over the years that people in the higher income brackets, those who can afford a new Ford, associate me with selling junk, and they're not wrong. I need someone to front the new business, and you're the logical choice. Except for your commercials in Spanish, the public in general doesn't know you and doesn't associate you with Friendly Motors."

"I'm flattered," Jason lied, "but I don't think I'm capable of taking over a new business by myself and running it."

"You won't be alone," Texas Bob explained. "You will be the manager of the lot and its public face. I will be a silent partner. You'll run the business, and I'll supply the money, but I will always be there behind the scenes to guide you. I'll take you in as a partner. Because it's my money that's at risk, I'll own 80 percent of the business, and you'll own 20 percent. You'll also get a salary as manager and a bonus at the end of each year based on the business's performance in addition to your 20-percent cut of the profits."

Jason was pleased at this step upward. However, he still viewed his relationship with Texas Bob as temporary. He had no intention of spending the rest of his working life as the junior partner to some airhead like him or to anyone else. Someway, he would find a method of being his own boss and amassing his own fortune instead of making someone else rich.

Meanwhile, Lupita was becoming increasingly dissatisfied with her marriage. She admired Jason's intelligence, but he seemed to put it to use only for the purpose of promoting himself and taking advantage of other people. She couldn't have a meaningful conversation with him. When he was home all he did was complain about his situation at work. He had to kiss up to Texas Bob, and he had to be nice to the salesmen, who were all dumb as rocks. The car buyers were even dumber. If they ended up paying three or four times what a car was worth, it was their own fault for being born imbeciles.

Lupita, on the other hand, was immersed in a world of good literature, philosophy, classical music, and she was even beginning to take an interest in liberal politics. She wished she could discuss these topics with her husband, but Jason had no interest in abstract discussions. He had even lost the interest in literature that he had as a kid. Literature had no practical value. As to politics, his only interest was in keeping Republicans in power in local and state government, because they were more tolerant of the shady business dealings of companies such as Friendly Motors.

Jason and Lupita had no children. Lupita had been using birth control since before she and Jason had married. At first, it was because she wanted to finish her graduate studies before having children. Later, she came to realize that Jason would make a terrible father. She didn't want to bring children into a family where the father would be distant, unemotional, and uncaring. At any rate, Jason was only moderately interested in sex, and he was a lousy lover. When making love, he just wanted to get the job over with and satisfy his own desires. He didn't seem to care whether Lupita got pleasure from the act or not.

She began to ask herself if she might not be better off without Jason. She no longer had the strong Catholic beliefs that she had been brought up with, but the years of Catholic indoctrination in her youth had shaped her character nonetheless. She still believed that marriage was "to death do us part." Intellectually, she no longer believed that it was a wife's duty to submit to her husband's will, but some of the old conditioning remained, and she couldn't shake off that conditioning merely by willing it away.

She certainly had no interest in Jason's car business. Jason had a brain. Why hadn't he stayed in the university, gotten his degree, and gone on to graduate school? He had the intelligence to excel in college. She was sure that Jason could have gone far in business with the right education, perhaps become an economist, although she wasn't certain exactly what an economist did. That thought led her to acknowledge to herself that she was painfully ignorant of business. She was never going to become self sufficient by relying on her PhD in Spanish literature. A little business knowledge would be a good thing.

What if she and Jason did split up? Despite her framed diplomas hanging on the wall in the house she and Jason shared, she was hardly in a position to support herself if she were to start a new life on her own.

Texas Bob decided to call the new auto dealership Wilder Motors to hide the fact that the dealership was owned by the same shady character who ran Friendly Motors. He also decided that neither he nor Jason was qualified to run the business, at least not yet. Both of them had something to learn about selling cars to a more sophisticated clientele. Therefore, as part of the deal to buy the new car dealership, he arranged for the manager, Elliot Camacho, to stay on for a year as a salaried advisor. Elliot would teach Jason the business. After the year was up, the three of them, he, Jason, and Elliot, would discuss whether Elliot's contract should be extended.

It didn't take Texas Bob long to realize that he was out of his depth in this new business, where attracting customers required at least giving the appearance of honesty. His old selling habits were too deeply ingrained. At Friendly Motors, he could get away with almost any type of fraud, which he preferred to call "smart business practices," but he couldn't get away with those tricks in this new enterprise. Nevertheless, he deluded himself into believing that he could adapt to the new business. He couldn't. His fraudster habits were too entrenched. No matter how he tried to unlearn his old way of doing business, as soon as he met a prospective customer, his mind started searching for ways to get the maximum amount of money out of the person while giving as little as possible in return, legalities be damned.

Texas Bob finally conceded that he could never adapt to a more honest method of doing business when Wilder Motors took in a 1985 Ford as a trade-in on the purchase of a new car. Texas Bob wanted to clean up the old junker and put it up for sale on the used car lot at a substantial markup. Elliot nixed the idea. "That car's got problems," he explained. "If someone buys it, the person will be back within days complaining. Word will get around that we sold a lemon, and it will hurt our reputation. We'll sell the car to a wholesaler."

"But if we wholesale the car, we'll get less for it than you gave the customer for the trade-in," Texas Bob complained.

"That's true," said Elliot, "but we still made a pretty penny on the deal. Believe me, every penny above the trade-in value that we gave the customer, we more than got back by padding the price we charged for the new car. It's OK to take advantage of a car buyer, but you can't let the customer know that you're doing it. The customer should drive away thinking that he or she has taken advantage of you."

After several similar incidents, Texas Bob reluctantly admitted that he was out of his depth. He gradually participated less and less in the management of Wilder Motors and spent more time running his used-car lot on Van Buren Street, where he felt more at home and was a master at prying every last cent out of a car sale. Without really planning to do so, he left the running of Wilder Motors entirely in the hands of Jason and Elliot.

Elliot was a good teacher, and Jason was a quick learner. "You can divide the customers into two groups: male and female. If a woman comes in by herself, no matter what she says, she's primarily interested in style. If you can show her a car that she falls in love with, she'll buy it. Often, she'll be willing to pay the sticker price, and you won't even have to bargain. I usually try to give these ladies a bit of a price break. I'd feel guilty taking too much advantage of them."

"What if she brings a man with her? Jason asked

"Ahh," Elliot replied, "in that case you're dealing with someone who thinks he knows more about the car business that you do. You treat the guy like a god. It's to your advantage to let the guy think that you admire his knowledge. Complement him on how smart he is. Tell him what a pleasure it is to deal with someone who knows the ropes, all the while subtly steering him to the car that you want him to buy at the price you want him to pay.

"Let's start with the sticker price on the windshield. As everyone knows, it's padded. Almost no one is dumb enough to pay it. Anyone who comes in is going to try to negotiate a lower price. Every salesperson on the lot knows what the minimum price is that the car can be sold for, but with a male customer, a good salesman plays dumb and pretends to be on the customer's side and eager to help the customer pull one over on the arrogant management. Once the customer and the client negotiate a price, the salesman asks the client to wait a few minutes, because the deal has to be OK'ed by the sales manager. He's never sold a car at a loss before, so he has to somehow smart-talk the sales manager into approving the deal. That's even partially true. We'll never permit a sale without reviewing the tentative agreement that the salesperson has obtained to see if we can get a few more hundred bucks out of the customer. In reality, that salesperson is turning the deal over another branch of the sales department, whose job it is to try to sell the customer some expensive additional features."

"I suppose that as long as the lot can make a couple of hundred bucks on the sale, the deal will be approved," Jason interjected.

"Ultimately it would be, but first, the so-called sales manager, who in reality is a closer, tries to get more money out of the customer. While the salesperson is apparently trying to persuade the manager to accept the deal, the two are actually discussing how to get the customer to pay a bit more. Both the sales person and the closer receive a paid a commission based on the profit made on the sale, so they are both motivated to increase that profit as much as possible while allowing the customer to believe that he's getting a great deal. Perhaps the salesperson will return to the client with the story, 'I'm sorry, my manager says we'd be losing too much money on the deal. The lowest he is willing to go is....' then he'll name a price a few hundred dollars higher. He'll pretend to be mad at the sales manager and tell the customer he thinks he's being taken advantage of."

Jason asked, "And, if the customer refuses to pay that price?"

"The salesman will show the customer the factory invoice and plead that the car lot has to make some profit on the sale or it will go out of business. Of course, the manufacturer's invoice isn't really what we pay for the car. There are factory incentives, rebates, etc. that we get from the manufacturer that lower that price but which are not shown on the invoice. The sales manager then names a new price, and says that he'll quit if the sales manager doesn't accept it. This price will still be higher than what the customer and the salesperson originally agreed to."

"And if the customer insists on buying the car at the agreed-on price?" Jason asked.

"If the customer is persistent, there are a number of other tactics that we use," Elliot continued. "The salesperson can tell the customer that he'll go over the sales manager's head to the general manager, who is not available at the moment, but if the salesperson can just have the customer's phone number, he promises to call the potential customer the next day if the manager agrees to the lower price. The salesperson does call the next day and tells the customer, 'You've won! The manager agreed to your price.' Or, if it seems too risky to let the customer leave the lot, the salesperson will go back into the manager's office with the appearance of persuading the manager to accept the customer's price.

"In either case, the next stop is for the salesperson to turn the customer over to a clerk to complete the paperwork. However, this person is not really a clerk. Like the so-called sales manager, she is also a closer with an extensive sales background, and she receives a commission on any extras she can add to the sales contract. Emma Thompson is our prize closer, one of the best in the business. It's her job to get add on extras to pad the price without letting the customer know he's being scammed. She can't work all of the time, of course, so our second closer is Paul Sanders. If both Emma and Paul are absent, I take over. Paul is not quite as good as Emma, but he's coming along."

"How does the closer get the price up?" Jason wanted to know.

"The most important thing she does is to keep the customer talking so he doesn't notice that fee after fee is being added to the invoice. For example, the starting price will be the price that the salesperson offered the day before, not the lower price that the manager supposedly agreed to. Sometimes the customer feels so victorious at having pulled one over on the car dealership that he doesn't notice that he's paying the higher price. If the customer does notice, Emma or Paul will apologize profusely for the mistake, 'correct' the price, and complement the customer on being sharp enough to spot it. By now the customer is feeling that he's much smarter than Emma, who after all is only a dumb clerk, and he will be putty in her hands."

"How can she boost the price of the car beyond what the customer has already agreed to without having the customer just get up and walk out?"

Elliot explained, "First, the customer is usually feeling so good about the car that he is about to own that his sales resistance is low. Also, every car buyer knows there are going to be some add-ons. There is a license fee and state sales tax to be added to the price. That money goes to the State of Arizona, of course. Then there is the document preparation fee. That is preprinted on the invoice, and we tell the customer it is required and non-negotiable, which is actually true. The fee is pure profit."

"What do you do if the customer refuses to pay the document preparation fee and threatens to walk out?" Jason asked.

"Under Arizona State law, we can't lower the document preparation fee for one customer without lowering it for all of them. It is true that we are not obliged to charge a document preparation fee at all, but if we do charge one, Arizona law requires that we charge the same fee to everyone. If we were to eliminate or reduce the 'doc fee', for one customer, all prior customers could demand the same rebate. We could have a class action lawsuit on our hands. If the 'doc fee' threatens to keep a sale from happening, we offer some offset such as a few free oil changes to make the customer happy.

"There are also other fees. Every sale includes a preparation fee, which in theory compensates us for preparing the vehicle for sale. That is pure profit. The manufacturer pays us to remove stickers and protective coverings from the car, wash it, and prepare it for sale, so when we charge the customer for doing that, we're getting paid twice.

"Oh, and then there is a charge for undercoating and rust protection. We tell the customer that this treatment is optional, but we highly recommend that buying it to protect the underside of the shiny new car. We don't actually do anything. The car comes from the factory with all of the underside protective coating required. But if we can get away with charging for it, we do. In Phoenix even the undercoating that the manufacturer puts on is overkill. We don't have ice and snow or salt put on the streets to melt them in Phoenix as they do in cities back east.

"We also arrange financing with companies with which we have an agreement. We often make more money on the kickback from the finance company than we do from selling the car. The kickback can amount to several thousand dollars on a big loan. The customer thinks that since the loan comes from a well-known bank, he is getting the best interest rate possible, but the bank charges enough in interest to pay us a fee for sending them the business. Oh, I almost forgot. We also add a two-percent loan origination fee to the car's selling price. That adds hundreds of dollars to our profit, and all we do is make a call to a credit agency to check the customer's credit score. Of course, some customers are smart enough to shop around for their own financing, but most aren't, and those who don't are the ones we like the best."

"I see something on the sticker of each car called a destination charge. What's that."

"That's a legitimate charge," Elliot explained. The manufacturer charges us for delivering the car to us, and we pass that charge onto the buyer. It's a strange situation. The manufacturer charges the same delivery fee to every car dealer in the country for delivering a specific model, no matter how much it actually costs them to ship the car to us. There is no way for us to get out of paying it to the auto manufacturer, which means that there is no way for the customer to get out of reimbursing us for it. No matter which dealership the customer goes to in order to buy a specific model, the destination charge or delivery charge or whatever the dealer chooses to call it is going to be the same."

Jason was beginning to realize that this dealership was just as crooked as Friendly Motors, but new car dealers fleeced the customer in a more sophisticated and less obvious manner. "There are high-class crooks and low-class crooks," Jason thought to himself. "Texas Bob is a low-class crook. I want to be a high-class crook, and I can learn a lot about becoming one from Elliot."

"We also get something called a holdback from the dealer on every car, Elliot added. We have to finance our inventory, and the holdback typically covers two-months of financing, say $250 a month. In that case the holdback will be around $500. If we sell the car a month after we receive it, we make $250 on the holdback. Of course, if the car sits on the lot for months without being sold, we pay interest every month to finance it. We can't afford to pay cash to buy cars from the manufacturer. We have to take out loans to finance our inventory, and we have to pay insurance on every car we have in stock. What if someone steals one of the cars, or worse yet, what if an unusually strong monsoon storm damages every car on the lot? If our stock weren't insured, such a disastrous event could send the dealership into bankruptcy.

"I don't want to overwhelm you," Elliot continued, "but there are a few more tricks. We install a cheap burglar alarm on all of our cars, and at closing, we attempt to add on an $800 charge for it. If the customer objects, we mention that it's a lot of work to uninstall a burglar alarm and that we'll let the customer have it for our cost of $400 to save the work of uninstalling it. We will etch the vehicle identification number into the glass for $150. We offer pin striping to make the car look sexier. It costs us almost nothing, and we charge a good price for applying a few strips of cheap plastic. Did I mention that we arrange financing and get a kick-back from the finance company for sending the business its way?"

"Yes, you covered that."

Well, in addition to collecting kickbacks from the finance companies, we also offer credit life and credit disability insurance, which pay off the loan if the customer dies or becomes unable to work. We get a kickback from the insurance company on those. Oh, and I forgot to mention fabric protection, which consists of spraying on some Scotchgard, and paint sealant, which costs us almost nothing to apply, but we charge a good price for both options. It the customer agrees to a few of these options, we can easily add another $1,000 to the price of a car. Cars are clear-coated these days at any rate, so paint sealant doesn't really server a purpose, but we don't tell the customer that.

"We add all of these charges to the amount the customer finances, so it doesn't affect the down payment. By this point in the negotiations, the customer is only interested in two things: What's the down payment and how much does he have to pay a month? We don't emphasize the second figure unless the customer makes a point of asking. Of course, most customers trade in an older vehicle, which more than covers the down payment even though we give the customer much less for the trade-in than it's worth. All of the fees we charge are folded into the loan."

Jason's head was spinning. "There seems to be a lot to learn," he told Elliot. "This is quite different than the way we sell at Friendly Motors. I think the best thing for me to do is spend my time with you during the hours that you're here and spend the rest of my day learning the operation of the other departments, following a sales representative around, spending time with our closer, a few days in the repair department, etc. I need to learn both the new and used car business, because you sell even used cars much differently than we do."

"Yeah," Elliot replied. "One thing that you'll find different here is that our used cars are in better condition. When we sell one, it comes with a three-month guarantee against defects. Even if a tire blows out, we replace it for free. We may use a few tricks to overcharge the customer, but it's to our advantage that the customer drive away happy and stay happy. We want the buyer to think well of us and recommend us to his friends, and the worst thing that could happen is for us to get a reputation for selling lemons. We also hope that in two or three years, when the used car customer is ready to move up to a newer model, he or she comes back to us to buy it.

We make good money on used car sales. When a buyer trades in a used car, it often rattles. We replace a few rubber gaskets, etc, and no more rattle. We clean the car up and repair any defects. Then we sell the used car at a good mark-up, but we also make sure that it's in tip-top shape. If it isn't, we sell it to a wholesaler, and it ends up at a used car lot like Friendly Motors. Our used car department brings in about a quarter of our profits, so it's very important that they have a good reputation."

Jason had always been a fast learner. He soon knew everyone who worked at the car lot by name. He quickly learned the techniques of selling to a higher income and more sophisticated buyer than he was used to dealing with at Friendly Motors. He knew that he had to modify the way he spoke to potential car buyers, but at the core, the selling game was the same. Jason was a gifted actor who easily slipped into and out of different roles, and he quickly learned to slip into the role of the helpful new car salesman. His gift of gab served him well, and he quickly gained the respect of the sales staff at Wilder Motors.

Learning the ins and outs of the service department was more challenging. Unlike the greasy part-time mechanic who worked for

Friendly Motors and always had a saliva-soaked unfiltered cigarette dangling out of the corner of his mouth, the mechanics here wore clean uniforms and kept their work areas neat. Smoking in the work area or anywhere in view of a customer was strictly forbidden. As they worked, the mechanics were plainly visible to the customers through a large plate glass window in the waiting room. The mechanics, however, had no direct contact with the customers. All communication between the mechanics and the customers were routed through a service advisor. At Friendly Motors, employing a mechanic was a necessary expense to bring used old cars up to a standard that enabled them to be sold. At Wilder Motors, the repair department was a lucrative profit center.

When a customer arrived with a repair problem or for routine maintenance, he or she was greeted by the neatly dressed, slim service advisor wearing a white shirt and conservative tie and carrying a clipboard. The service advisor would take down the customer's information and information about the car including the mileage and write down the customer's name and phone number, which could be used later as leads by the sales department to try to convince the customer to trade in the old buggy on a newer model.

The sales advisor also noted the reason for the visit and gave the customer an estimate of the repair or service costs and then directed the customer to the waiting area, where there was a television playing, stacks of magazines, free coffee, and even free snacks. Clean restrooms were located immediately adjacent to the waiting area. The customer was assured that if there was any work to be done that was not included in the estimate, the service advisor would discuss it with the customer before that work was started. It all looked very professional, and as mentioned, the customer could watch the car apparently being professionally serviced through the large window in the waiting room. What the customers thought they were observing and what the mechanics were actually doing were not always the same thing, however.

The customers were led to believe that the service advisors were professional mechanics who through their skill had worked their way up to a management position. They were nothing of the sort; they were salespeople who often had no idea which end of a wrench to hold but who had memorized the buzzwords of auto repair and had been trained to project a knowledgeable image. They were paid on commission and encouraged to "up-sell" or talk the customer into service work that was not needed. For example, the service assistant might say, "You're due for an oil change in another 1,000 miles. Would you like us to take care of now so you won't have to come back in?" Most customers, who hate sitting in a waiting room, no matter how attractive it is, would be grateful for the suggestion and agree. If the car was in for an oil change, the service assistant would bring the car's air filter into the waiting room to show the customer and ask, "Should we change this while we're at it?" In most cases the air filter would be very slightly soiled and in the worst case might need some dust blown off it, but few customers knew enough about the inner workings of a car to say no. In fact, a simple oil change offered a plethora of opportunities to sell a number of products at inflated prices such as windshield wiper blades, filters of different varieties, radiator flushes, and an upper intake cleaning."

"What is an upper intake cleaning?" Jason asked. "That's a new one on me."

"We make it sound complicated, but all we really do is spray some solvent into the intake airstream with the engine idling. It cleans out carbon deposits, although most cars don't have that much carbon buildup. We charge $89 for it, and it only takes a few minutes, although if the customer is watching through the window in the waiting room, we do a song and dance to make it look more complicated. Our mechanics not only have to be highly skilled at car repair, they have to be actors who can put on a show for the customer.

"We also recommend that customers upgrade to a high-mileage or synthetic grade of oil. Unless we think the customer is sharp enough to spot it, we charge for the more expensive oil but put in the same basic oil grade that the customer would have gotten anyway. When we change the oil, we're supposed to change the oil filter—it's included in the price—but we often don't."

"But, the customer is watching! What if the customer catches you not changing the oil filter?" Jason wanted to know.

"In that case," Elliot responded, "we apologize profusely, change the filter, and give the customer a certificate for a free oil change.

"Recommended service inspections are another big money maker. Basically, the service inspections consist of checking the belts, brakes, etc. and changing the oil and perhaps the brake fluid. For a half hour's work, we bill several hundred dollars. We almost always find some extra work that needs to be done at an extra charge. At the minimum, we sell the customer some new belts whether they're needed or not. If we think the customer is especially gullible, we throw in a brake job, a tune-up, or on a high-mileage car, even a complete transmission overhaul.

"If the customer leaves the car, he or she is almost sure to receive a call during the day saying perhaps, 'We noticed that your front end is out of alignment. Would you like to get that taken care of while the car is here?' Most of the time the front end is in perfect alignment, but most drivers have no way of knowing that. The only work the mechanic actually does if the customer isn't present is to rub a few areas under the front of the car with a rag soaked in cleaning fluid, so that if the customer actually looks under the car, it would appear that some real work had been done. If the customer is in the waiting room and watching through the window, the mechanic actually has to go through the motions of doing an alignment. We have no compunction about cheating the customer, but we are very careful not to give the customer any reason to suspect that we are doing so."

The service department profited from the fact that customers trusted its employees, Jason learned. No one trusted the auto salespeople, but the public thought the service department was on their side. They weren't! Customers had no idea that the car dealership made more money from inflating charges in its service and parts business than from selling new cars.

After a year of working in every department in the car dealership, Jason felt competent to run it without help. In fact, he thought he could run it more profitably than Elliot could, and he didn't want Elliot looking over his shoulder as he made changes. Elliot had no compunction about inflating the prices that the dealership charged customers, but Jason didn't want to stop there. He wanted to take over complete control and ownership of the business and route some of the money that the customers were overcharged into his own pocket. He didn't yet know exactly how he was going to do that, but he felt that it would be easier if he had full management responsibilities. Somehow, he had to get rid of Elliot.

Elliot owed his job to Texas Bob's decision to keep him on, so the first step of getting rid of Elliot had to be getting Texas Bob's approval. Jason knew that Texas Bob had a weakness for Henniger Beer, brewed in Frankfurt, Germany and almost impossible to find in Phoenix, but he managed to find a liquor store that sold it. He purchased a cold six-pack of the brew and drove to Friendly Motors to have a chat with Texas Bob, whom he found in his office on the car lot. He put the six-pack on Texas Bob's desk, pried the caps off two bottles with the bottle opener of his Swiss Army knife, and took a seat next to Texas Bob's scarred wooden desk.

"Ah, great beer! If you brought me this, you must want something. Well, a few more swigs of this delicious beer and you can have anything you want," Texas Bob joked.

"No, I don't want anything," Jason replied. "I just thought maybe we should talk over business."

"Speaking of business, how are things going at Wilder Motors?"

"Better than we expected. Have you gone over the sales figures for last month?"

"Yeah, I did. It looks like taking over that car lot was a great idea." Then Texas Bob added, "Keeping Elliot on was the right decision."

"Now we're getting to the point," Jason thought to himself. Out loud he said, "Elliot is one of the subjects I wanted to talk to you about. He's been a great teacher, but I think he's taught me enough that I'm ready to run the lot by myself. There's no sense in two of us collecting a manager's salary. I think we should let his contract expire and give him enough advance notice that he can find another job. I'm sure almost any car dealership in town would be glad to hire him."

"I'm not sure that I agree with you, but it's your decision to make, Jason. You're running the place. Should you tell him that we're not going to renew his contract or should I do it?"

"As you say, I'm running the place. I'll take the responsibility. I think we should give him a golden parachute, a nice little parting bonus. He'll be working for one of our competitors soon, so it's best to part friends. We don't want him out there bad-mouthing us."

When Jason broke the news to Elliot that his contract would not be renewed, he made sure to add that the severance bonus was his idea. "I want us to part friends," Jason told him. "You never know when one of us may be able to do the other a good turn in the future. Job turnover is high in this business. If it had been up to me, we would have kept you on with a raise, but Texas Bob feels that we should cut management expenses. I'll give you a stellar recommendation, because you've been an excellent teacher. I'm sure you'll soon land a better job than this one. You are very talented, and we were extremely fortunate that you agreed to stay on for a year as manager after we bought the dealership."

Elliot left thinking that Jason was his friend. He never did learn that it was Jason who wanted to get rid of him and who figuratively pushed him out the door. If he is reading this book, perhaps he knows it now.

Texas Bob was increasingly distracted by problems at Friendly Motors and made the mistake of not keeping an eye on Jason. His suspicions were not awakened when Jason fired old Mrs. Whiting, who had been the accountant at the new car lot for years and hired a young, inexperienced graduate from ASU to replace her. Jason now had someone working in accounting who owed his job and his loyalty to him and who seemed naïf enough to be manipulated.

"Mrs. Whiting is getting on in years and is not as sharp as she once was," he told Texas Bob. "She had begun to make mistakes. We'll save money by hiring this new kid at a lower salary. Being the accountant for one car dealership is not a full-time job at any rate now that it's all done on computers. The new kid could also take over the books at Friendly Motors and save you the expensive fee you're paying to your accounting firm. If he gets overwhelmed, I can jump in to help him a bit."

Texas Bob admitted that he needed to cut expenses. His legal fees were mounting. He had been too brazen about cheating his customers and had made the mistake of angering a customer who took his complaint to the state attorney general. He also made a political miscalculation. He had always made generous campaign contributions to candidates who were likely to be elected to state and county law enforcement positions. There was not much he could do to influence law enforcement in the City of Phoenix, whose police chief and city manager were not elected, but because the city generally left fraud cases to the county and state, he felt he had nothing to fear from the city police.

Texas Bob's political instincts failed him; he backed the wrong candidate for state attorney general. In 1998, he made a generous contribution to the Republican candidate, who went on to lose the election. The following year the new Democratic attorney general took notice of the numerous complaints against Friendly Motors and began an investigation. The straw that broke the camel's back was a complaint by a Hispanic immigrant named Carlos Vásquez who claimed that he had traded in a used car and made a $1,000 down payment to buy a used pickup truck. Mr. Vásquez spoke only Spanish and had not understood the contract he signed, which was in English. He did not receive the pickup truck even though Friendly Motors had kept his trade-in and down payment. Friendly Motors alleged that Mr. Vásquez had indeed received the pickup truck but had not made payments on his loan. In reality, Texas Bob had sold the truck to another customer. Because Mr. Vásquez was in the country illegally, Texas Bob thought that he wouldn't dare complain to the authorities. He was wrong.

The new attorney general, a former federal prosecutor, had been looking for a case that would get her publicity and enhance her political career, and in Friendly Motors she found one. She decided to make an example of Texas Bob. She held a press conference in which she announced: "My office is charging Friendly Motors with a number of fraud offenses including false advertising, padding registration and license fees for a profit, stating that cars were in good condition when they weren't, collecting and retaining down payments on cars that the car dealership subsequently refused to sell, and failing to honor warranties.

"Friendly Motors and its owner, Robert Samuelson, better known as Texas Bob, have been defrauding the citizens of Arizona for decades. I will do everything in my power to shut down this illicit business and put Mr. Samuelson behind bars."

However, the attorney general's job was not that simple. The case dragged on for a year during which time Texas Bob spent a huge sum on legal fees. Nevertheless, she did prevail in the end. The court fined Texas Bob $130,000 and sentenced him to six months in jail. Friendly Motors was shut down, and Texas Bob was prohibited from owning any stake in a car retailer in Arizona for the rest of his life. The attorney general got quite a bit of favorable publicity from the case, and she used it to point out that Texas Bob had been a generous contributor to the campaigns of her predecessor. When Texas Bob was sent to jail, his only asset was his stake in Wilder Motors, which he was now obligated to sell, and he had even borrowed against that.

It had been Jason who had attracted most of Friendly Motors' customers with his ads in Spanish, but luckily for him, the investigation stopped with Texas Bob. The attorney general's office decided not to prosecute any of the used car dealership's present or former employees, considering them, too, to be victims of Texas Bob's machinations.

Jason breathed a sigh of relief. He was not only delighted to not have been caught up in the fraud case, he was equally delighted when he realized that this was the opportunity that he had been waiting for to take over the dealership. Texas Bob was not only serving a jail sentence, but being barred from the car business meant that he would have to sell his controlling interest in Wilder Motors. Sitting in jail and still faced with a mounting stack of legal bills, Texas Bob was in no position to bargain.

Taking control of Wilder Motors was a complicated affair. A local bank held a lien against the automobile dealership for the loan that Texas Bob had taken out when he originally bought the business, and as mentioned, he had borrowed additional money against it to pay his legal expenses. The bank was not happy to learn that Texas Bob was in jail. It wanted the loan paid off immediately. Texas Bob's lawyers also took out liens against Wilder Motors to recover their fees. The business was in danger of going belly up and being shut down or sold at auction if something were not done quickly. Jason hired a team of lawyers and an accounting firm and charged them with straightening out the mess.

Finally, the various lawyers and the bank that held Texas Bob's loan came to an agreement. The car lot had increased in value, so the bank was willing to give Jason a loan big enough to buy Texas Bob's share, and pay off Texas Bob's loans, and cover the liens against the business. There was even a modest sum left over for Texas Bob, who was therefore not dead broke when he was released from jail at the end of his sentence and disappeared. Years later, he was to reappear as the owner of a car lot in Las Vegas Nevada, where law enforcement against fraudsters was even laxer than in Arizona. You can't keep a bad man down.

Now that Jason was the sole owner of Wilder Motors, it was essential to increase the car lot's business in order to meet expenses including the higher monthly loan payment to the bank. He decided to risk all on an advertising blitz to attract more customers. The campaign would be expensive and if it didn't pay off, he could go bankrupt and lose the car lot to the bank. However, Jason thrived on risk, which was to him like heroin to a junky. Instead of feeling depressed by his shaky financial situation, he was exhilarated at the challenge that he had to face.

Jason fired the car dealership's old advertising agency and hired a new one with more modern ideas. He and the agency worked together to design a completely overhauled radio, TV, and print campaign. Jason, who trusted no one but himself, insisted on doing the radio and TV spots personally against the advice of the advertising agency, which wanted to hire a professional announcer for the job. Jason also insisted that his photograph feature prominently in the print advertisements. What the advertising agency didn't understand was that Jason not only wanted to promote Wilder Motors, he wanted to promote himself. He had plans, and in order to carry out those plans, he needed to become known as a pillar of the community.

Deciding on the target market was important. Jason was willing to sell to anyone, of course, even to people who couldn't possibly pay off their loans, but together with the advertising agent and a consultant he hired, it was decided that the best target audience for the commercials consisted of working-class white men and women. These were the very same people who consistently voted Republican and thereby kept the crooks in power who ran the State of Arizona and Maricopa County and made it possible for cheats like Jason to stay in business. Jason couldn't understand why so many people would vote against their own interest, but he was happy that they did.

The advertising agency convinced Jason not to disguise his distinct Chicago accent in the commercials. Phoenix-area residents came from all over the country, and there was therefore no distinct Phoenix accent. A Chicago accent would do as well as any other.

The advertising agency decided to give the ad campaign a western slant, because a large portion of the target market consisted of country music fans. Lawyers in Phoenix were known to dress in western boots and bolo ties to go to the office. Jason was to dress in western clothes not only for the TV commercials but also at the car lot and at any other public appearances. His new uniform was a western hat and boots, a leather vest, a bolo tie, and a long-sleeved colorful shirt. Dressed this way, he felt a bit like Texas Bob, but the advertising agency assured him that he had to have an image. Jason's image would be that of the sophisticated Phoenix immigrant who had taken to western customs. In other parts of the country, a man with a Chicago accent who dressed in fake cowboy clothes might have made a bizarre impression, but in Phoenix, such a man fit right into the working-class culture.

He filmed his first TV commercial at the car lot inside the dealership's showroom where several cars had been parked especially for the occasion. He walked from car to car, briefly describing how special each car was and the low monthly payment that each car could be bought for. Then looking straight into the camera with a smile on his face he said the words that were to become Wilder Motors' motto, "Visit Wilder Motors for the drive of your life. All roads lead to Wilder Motors on East Camelback" and then added, *Hablamos español.*"

The advertising agency was very pleased with the commercial, but Jason wasn't, although he reluctantly gave his approval to let it run. Except for the fact that he was dressed in a western getup, nothing differentiated it from all of the other car lot commercials on TV. Wearing western clothes was hardly unique in Phoenix. He needed some sort of gimmick to make his commercials stand out from those of his competitors. Nevertheless, the commercials did cause a modest increase in visits to the dealership and a small increase in Wilder Motors' sales of both new and used cars.

It was about three weeks after the commercials began running on TV that he was first recognized by a stranger. He walked into a Denny's restaurant for lunch, and as soon as the hostess saw him, her eyes went wide. "You're that guy on TV, Jason Wilder, aren't you?" she gushed. Jason admitted that he was.

"Here, let me seat you in a good booth. Oh, and can I have your autograph? It's for my five-year-old little girl. She's seen you on TV so much that she repeats your slogan along with you at the end of each commercial. 'Visit Wilder Motors for the drive of your life. All roads lead to Wilder Motors on East Camelback.' She can even say the Spanish part that comes after that, even though she doesn't know what it means. I don't either. She'll be thrilled to know that I met you in person."

"I'll be glad to give you my autograph."—Jason was flattered—"and the next time I come in, I'll bring a special present for your little girl." The present that Jason had in mind was a stuffed toy donkey. He had had 500 of them made for a special promotion he was about to launch.

All during lunch, he noticed the waitresses congregating near the door of the kitchen in their spare moments, casting glances his way, giggling, and chattering with each other in a low voice. Apparently, Jason was causing a bit of a sensation.

Jason's advertising agency entreated him not to go ahead with his plans for a new series of TV commercials. They told him the new commercials would be much too hokey for his target market and would drive customers away. Jason ignored their advice. About two weeks later, the first of the new series of TV commercial appeared. It showed Jason standing next to a donkey, holding it by the reins. Jason spoke first, "Howdy, folks! I'm Jason Wilder of Wilder motors, and this is my pal Moses."

Next came a tight shot of the donkey, whose lips moved in time with a gruff voice that said, "Howdy, folks!"

The camera then panned to Jason, who recited the first line of the commercial and then switched to the donkey, which appeared to recite the second line. The donkey's lips were moving, and the words seemed to be coming out of its mouth. The donkey promised that if any parents "brought their kids to visit Wilder Motors and stopped by to say hi to me," the kids would each receive a free toy.

The camera switched back and forth between the two for most of the duration of the 60-second spot until Jason said "Visit Wilder Motors for the drive of your life," and the donkey added, "All roads lead to Wilder Motors on East Camelback." Finally they appeared onscreen side by side one last time and seemed to recite in chorus, "Hablamos español."

The next day, the commercial was the subject of conversation at many water coolers throughout the Phoenix area. Those who hadn't seen it made a point of watching the local newscast the following evening to catch it. Many kids saw it, too, and they begged their parents to take them to Wilder Motors to see Moses the talking donkey and get a free toy. The toy was a fluffy stuffed toy donkey, just like the one that Jason had dropped off at Denny's for the daughter of the woman who worked at the reception stand.

The commercial proved to be popular and brought in lots of families with kids, and most parents took the time to look at the cars on sale. Some of them ended up buying one. Jason had to explain to the kids why Moses didn't talk to them the way he talked on TV. "Moses is a big ham. He'll only talk when he's in front of TV cameras. However, you can talk to him, and he'll understand every word you say."

One person who was not happy with the commercials was 63-year-old Maricopa County Sheriff Paul Balboni, who had the reputation of being more interested in animal rights than in the welfare of crime victims. He went before the TV cameras and said he was going to arrest Jason Wilder for cruelty to animals. He didn't know what Jason did to get the donkey to move its lips as if it were talking, but Jason was certainly inflicting some kind of torture on the poor beast.

A local fundamentalist preacher called a press conference and accused Jason of committing blasphemy. "Moses is one of the holiest men in the Bible, and anyone who has the temerity to name an ass after him is condemned to Hell for all eternity." The preacher demanded that Jason "be arrested and locked up for the rest of his life in Florence prison for heresy."

Both the sheriff's and the preacher's remarks served to make Jason better known and more popular. More people poured into the car lot than Jason's sales staff could handle. Sales personnel were actually running from customer to customer. One of the customers showed interest in a used car, and when the salesman couldn't find the key to open it, the Jason ordered him to give the car to the customer without charge if the customer would return with a locksmith and drive the car away. The sales people were so busy that no one had time to search for a lost key, and that story, too, appeared in the press and served to make Jason more popular.

A weekly alternative newspaper did an investigation into the donkey incident and, unlike the sheriff, actually went to Wilder Motors to interview Jason and examine the donkey. It was obvious that the donkey's voice came from an announcer off camera, but how did Jason get the donkey to move its lips as if it were talking. At first, Jason was coy. Like a good magician, he didn't want to give away his trick. However, the young female reporter had dealt with men like Jason before. She leaned over Jason's desk, revealing more cleavage than was seemly, and asked, "You'll tell little old me, won't you?"

Jason opened his desk drawer and pulled out a jar of peanut butter. "This is the secret."

The reporter was puzzled. "How could a jar of peanut butter make a donkey move its lips as if it were talking?"

"We feed it to Moses, and some of it sticks to his gums," Jason explained. "He moves his lips to get it off his gums so he can swallow it."

When the weekly paper came out the next Thursday, the sheriff was made a laughingstock. TV and radio cited the incident as the closing, humorous story in their newscasts. No one could be accused of animal cruelty for feeding peanut butter to a donkey. When one of the TV stations interviewed Jason about the story, he said, "Perhaps Moses isn't the only talking ass in Maricopa County." The TV station bleeped out the word ass—Phoenix was full of religious fundamentalists who would object to the word—but everyone who saw the newscast knew what was bleeped out and at whom it was directed. The whole incident and the sheriff himself were the subjects of much hilarity during the following weeks.

Jason had made an enemy of the sheriff, but he was smart enough to know that he had gone too far. Sheriff Balboni was a powerful political figure in Maricopa County, and Jason needed to have him on his side. Jason held a press conference to publicly apologize to the sheriff. "I am truly sorry that my remarks were misinterpreted as being directed at Sheriff Balboni. I realize now that I have unintentionally given offence, and I greatly regret it. Paul Balboni is an outstanding law-enforcement officer, and we residents of Maricopa County are very fortunate to have him as our sheriff. I offer him my sincerest apology."

The sheriff, who himself had a continuing battle with the people he called "the liberal press," forgave Jason, and the two would later become political allies. However, that is getting ahead of the story.

We've been neglecting Lupita. She was becoming more and more disenchanted with her marriage to Jason. Jason only came home to sleep, and he seemed to have no interest in talking to her. She had hoped to obtain a professorship at a university teaching Spanish literature, but none of the universities or colleges in the Phoenix area had an opening. She could have found a job in another state, but that would have meant leaving Jason. She was beginning to regret that she had not made that choice. When she and Jason had married, she had been convinced that he sincerely loved her, but now she had serious doubts. Jason seemed very distant, almost as if he had no emotions whatsoever.

To avoid being economically dependent on Jason, Lupita took a job as a secretary in the local offices of the European semiconductor company Olivari Technology. There she thought her graduate degree gave her a chance to move into a management or marketing position, even though she had no business or marketing experience. She began taking business courses in the evening at Arizona State University.

She felt very lonely. Another woman would have taken a lover or divorced her husband and married someone more suitable, but Lupita's strict Catholic upbringing in Mexico kept her from doing either, although at times she wished that her religion didn't have such a hold on her. Jason had no religious beliefs. Why should she? Jason didn't seem to have any beliefs at all. Why should she?

Out of desperation, she decided that she and Jason should go to a marriage counselor. When she broached the subject with Jason, his response was, "No way! I'm not going to let some shrink poke around in my head!"

Jason knew from long experience that he was not like other people, and he was not about to interact with someone who might expose his true inner nature. It was not fear that made him resist analysis. Fear was an emotion that Jason seldom felt. It was logic. He had nothing to gain from psychoanalysis, and logic told him that it was not a good idea. He knew that he was a psychopath, a condition for which there was no treatment. He imagined that Lupita suspected that also, but if she had her suspicions confirmed and their relationship changed, she might blab the news all over the place. Jason had delusions about becoming a famous person, and he didn't want questions about his mental stability to become public knowledge.

"I've been thinking about this for a long time," Lupita explained. "I've come to the conclusion that our marriage is over unless we do something to save it. This is our last chance. If you refuse to go to marriage counseling with me, I see no way to save our marriage."

"What do you mean? Don't we have a great marriage?" Jason asked. "I'm happy with our marriage, and I thought you were, too."

"No wonder you think I'm happy," Lupita replied. "You take no notice of me. Except for when you want sex, I might as well be a painting on the wall. If I were a dog, you'd give me more attention than you do now. Even when we make love, I might as well be one of those inflatable sex toys as far as you're concerned. All you care about is getting off. You have no consideration for what I might be feeling. Either you agree to go to counseling, or I'm leaving."

Jason reluctantly agreed. "OK," he said, "you make the appointment, and I'll be there."

Lupita made the appointment, but when she called Jason to tell him about it, his secretary answered the phone. "He's not available," the secretary told her.

"Tell him that it's his wife who's calling."

"I'm sorry. He's in a meeting, and I can't disturb him. As soon as he gets out, I'll tell him that you called. Do you want to leave a message for him?"

Lupita gave the secretary the details of the appointment. Had it gotten to the point where the only way she could communicate with her husband was through his secretary?

That night, Jason didn't come home. He spent the night in a hotel with Alice O'Hara, the same secretary to whom Lupita had given the message and with whom he had been having a clandestine affair for months.

Lupita showed up at the counselor's office the next day hoping that Jason had received her message and would also appear, but he didn't. Lupita spent the next 50 minutes explaining her situation to the counselor, and answering the counselor's questions. At the end of the session, the counselor gave her opinion of the situation. "I can't tell for sure without examining him, but from the way you describe Jason, I suspect that he has what we call antisocial personality disorder. Laymen know it as psychopathology."

"But don't psychopaths go around killing people until they're locked up in a mental institution?" Lupita asked.

"That's a popular misconception," the counselor explained, "and in some cases it's accurate. However, most psychopaths are not violent. Psychopaths have no conscience and are unable to feel such normal human emotions as love, empathy, and sympathy, but they are good actors and can fake them, at least for a time. Many of them don't even feel fear and therefore take enormous risks. If they retreat from a dangerous situation, it's not out of fear but because they calculate that the situation is not in their best interests. They are very good at manipulating people to get their way. They are not easy to spot, because they are so skilled at mimicking emotions and appear very friendly and outgoing when you first meet them. At some point, they turn on everybody, however. One characteristic of psychopaths is that they cannot form long-term friendships or relationships of any type. They can't keep up the act long enough. Few of them are murders. It's not that they have anything against killing people. What holds them back is the threat of punishment."

"I don't think that's Jason," Lupita responded. "I'm sure he used to love me. He used to be so nice to me and treat me with great tenderness. I'll try to get Jason in here so you can help us and see that Jason is not the type of person you described."

Inwardly, the counselor thought she had pegged Jason exactly, but she didn't say that to Lupita. "I hope you can get him to come in with you for counseling. I have no way of knowing for sure what causes him to act as you say he does without spending some time with him. However, I'm worried about you. You strike me as being the perfect victim. I don't think you're capable of standing up for your own rights where Jason is concerned."

Lupita never was able to get Jason to go with her to the counselor. "I know I promised I'd go, but I've changed my mind. I'm not going, and that's that!" Jason shouted as he stormed out of the house one day later.

Lupita cowed under Jason's angry outburst. She felt as if he had struck her, although even in his angriest moments, he had never done her physical harm. She thought about the counselor's words. Yes, she realized now, Jason was very good at manipulating her. She also realized that she would never be able to stand up to Jason, even though she still believed that Jason had once genuinely loved her. She had two choices. She could live the life of a masochist, or she could leave.

The next evening, while Jason was still at the car lot, she called her parents in Puerto Vallarta, Mexico, explained what was going on in her life, and asked their advice.

"I had no idea you were so miserable," her mother said. "You need to get away from that *pendejo*. Come and stay with us. We still have your room ready, and you can stay as long as you want."

When Lupita got off the phone with her mother, she picked it up again and called America West Airlines. Yes, there were several flights from Phoenix to Puerto Vallarta tomorrow. Yes, there were seats available on each of the flights. Lupita gave her credit card number and purchased a one-way ticket on the early afternoon flight.

"Are you sure you want to fly one way?" the agent asked her. "Americans are limited to how much time they can spend in Mexico as tourists."

"I'm a Mexican. I was born in Puerto Vallarta."

After booking her flight, Lupita had time to think over how she would handle Jason. She didn't dare tell him that she was going to leave him the next day while he was at work. It would be best if she could avoid talking to him altogether. She had grown to fear Jason's angry outbursts, despite the fact that he had never hit her. She didn't want to provoke an outburst now on her last day at home. By the time Jason came home around 9 o'clock, she had come up with a story. She was not used to lying, and she felt guilty doing it, but she would try to pull it off.

"Hi, Honey," Jason said cheerily as he came in the front door. "Are we over that silly little disagreement we had? Is it safe for me to come home again?"

"I've had bad news, Jason. My father is gravely ill. I'm flying to Puerto Vallarta tomorrow. Mom says it might be the last chance I have to see him alive."

"I'm sorry to hear that," Jason lied. "I've always liked your father. What's wrong with him?"

"Mom says he might have had a heart attack."

"Might have had? Doesn't anyone know?"

"You know how the public health system is in Mexico," Lupita answered. "It's not the best."

"This is going to be damned inconvenient," Jason said. "I have an important social event next Thursday, and I need you to go with me."

"Does that mean that you don't want me to go home?" Lupita asked.

"Naw, I guess it's all right. Just be back no later than Wednesday. Don't forget that I need you on Thursday."

"I'll be back on time," Lupita fibbed.

Jason was normally very good at reading people, and if he had been attentive, he would have noticed that there was something strange about the way that Lupita was acting, despite her assertion that her father was sick. Lupita was not accustomed to lying and hadn't done it well. However, Jason's mind was elsewhere, and he was paying little attention to his wife. He seldom did pay her much attention.

Lupita called her work in the morning and informed her boss that she was quitting for personal reasons.

"But you've become indispensible here," her boss countered. "Is there something we've done that's made you want to quit?"

"No," Lupita answered, "it's a personal matter, and I'm afraid I can't discuss it. I just wanted you to know that I'm going."

"But, what should we do with your paycheck? You have some pay coming. Should we mail it to your house?"

Lupita hadn't considered that she might have money coming. She had some savings, but she was not wealthy. Every extra dollar would come in handy. "Can you mail the check to my parents' house in Mexico?"

Her boss agreed to do that. Lupita gave him the address and bid him good-bye.

When Lupita didn't return the following Wednesday as promised, Jason dialed her parents' number in Mexico. Lupita's father answered. He refused to let Jason speak with Lupita. "She's pretty shaken up. I think you should give her some time to recover."

"Recover? Recover from what? I thought you were the one who needed to recover. She promised me she'd be home today."

"Jason, maybe you don't realize it, but Lupita is quite traumatized. I don't think she's going back to Phoenix very soon. She needs to gather her thoughts and decide what to do."

"This whole thing was a ruse, wasn't it?" Jason shouted into the phone. "Lupita said you were gravely ill. There is nothing wrong with you whatsoever, is there? "That bitch just lied to me just so I would let her leave!"

Jason slammed the phone down angrily. "Damned bitch! Maybe I should have knocked her around a bit." But no, that wouldn't have been a very good idea. It would have landed him in jail on domestic violence charges.

Jason got a beer out of the refrigerator and sat drinking it until he calmed down. Then he picked up the phone and dialed his secretary. "Alicia? This is Jason. Are you busy?"

"No."

"Can I come over? I need someone to talk to."

"Of course! I'll be waiting for you, Sweetie."

As Jason lay next to Alicia after the two had made love, his mind was elsewhere. He had to get Lupita back. Arizona is a community property state. That meant that any wealth that Jason had acquired during the marriage was half Lupita's, and she would be entitled to claim it in case of a divorce. Somehow, he had to persuade Lupita that he still loved her, although he didn't. He had to come up with a plan.

Chapter 5— Politically Outspoken

It was late spring in 2002. Jason and Lupita were seated at the breakfast table in their home in Paradise Valley, a bedroom community for the more affluent members of the Phoenix business community. It had been two years since Jason had persuaded Lupita to return. When her parents refused to let him talk to her on the phone, he flew to Puerto Vallarta to bring her back. When he rang the bell at her parents' house, it was Lupita herself who answered. She was shocked to see Jason. She had had no idea that he was coming.

Although it seemed melodramatic, Jason had planned what he would do. He fell to his knees before Lupita and swore that he loved her. He said he had been miserable ever since she left and now realized that he could not live without her. Jason felt pleased with himself thinking back on that day. It was one of his better pieces of acting. He was so convincing that Lupita agreed on the spot to go back to Phoenix with him. Keeping up the pretence of loving her in the two years that followed had not been as easy, but somehow Jason managed it. He couldn't afford to have Lupita leave him. A divorce settlement would ruin him financially.

"What are you smiling about," Lupita asked across the breakfast table.

"Oh," Jason replied, "I was thinking back to the day I went to Puerto Vallarta and how glad I am that you agreed to come back to me, and I was thinking of how much I love you."

"I know that you love me, *Corazón*. I am also so happy that I came back. Our life together has been so much better these past two years." Then she thought to herself, "Well, our sex life could be better, but no marriage is perfect."

Financially, things had gone very well for Jason the past two years, also. Nationally, car sales dropped after the terrorist attacks on the Twin Towers in New York City on September 11, 2001, and some of Jason's competitors had gone out of business. Thanks to Jason's sharp sense of marketing, he had grabbed a larger share of what was left, and his sales had increased. He now had three dealerships in the Greater Phoenix area thanks to his being able to buy two bankrupt dealerships at fire-sale prices. All were mortgaged up to the hilt, of course, but Jason was not the type of person to lie awake at night worrying about how to pay off his debts. His financial situation was shaky, but Jason delighted in taking risks and felt that he was smart enough to always come out on top. He was certainly smarter than those dumb-assed bankers.

"I've been talking to Martin Glover, the big cheese in the Arizona Republican Party. He wants me to run for the state legislature. I'm thinking of taking him up on it."

"I'm shocked!" Lupita really was astounded. "I had no idea you were interested in becoming a politician. You've always said you despise them. At any rate, aren't you a Democrat just like me?"

"If I enter politics, it will be good for us financially, Honey. I don't want to be just a car dealer the rest of my life. I've got bigger ambitions. As to partisanship, the Republicans run things in this part of the state. If you want to represent Paradise Valley in the State Legislature, you've got to be a Republican. The Arizona Democrats are a bunch of losers. They're always talking about the poor people, Hispanics, the uneducated, and other losers like that."

Lupita sighed inwardly. She bit her tongue, but she was hurt at Jason's remark. He had lumped Hispanics, the uneducated, and losers together in one sentence. She wandered if he thought that she was a loser. He probably did. He couldn't consider her to be uneducated. She had much more schooling that he had. But then, who knew what Jason thought? His opinions didn't always reflect the facts.

Lupita had been happier when she and Jason were first starting out and were both poor students. Now that they were well to do, Lupita's life had become routine. With the money that Jason earned, there was no economic reason for her to work. She could only earn a fraction of what Jason brought in. Nevertheless, she didn't want to be dependent on Jason, and she didn't want to hang around the house all day. She needed something to challenge her mind. She recalled the day that she had gone back to Olivari Technology and asked if she could get her old job back. The receptionist in the personnel office had asked her to take a seat. "I see you've worked here before," the receptionist had remarked as she glanced through Lupita's résumé. "Just make yourself comfortable and let me make some phone calls."

Jason interrupted her daydream. "Why the sigh, Honey? Don't you want to be the wife of an important man?"

Lupita didn't realize that she had sighed out loud. She hoped that she hadn't been thinking out loud, as well. "I don't care about such things, *Corazón*. But if it's important to you, I'll go along with it."

In her heart, Lupita didn't feel that way, however. She was Hispanic and a trained educator. Even though she was not working in the field she trained for, her educator's mind made her very sympathetic toward the poor. Her mother's family in Mexico was dirt poor. In her mind, the Republican Party in Arizona was led by rich people whose pretended interest in ordinary people disappeared quickly after each election.

Jason suppressed a feeling of irritation as he poured himself a second cup of coffee. Ever since he had brought Lupita back from Puerto Vallarta, she had been calling him *Corazón* or *mi Corazón*, a Spanish term of endearment that meant my heart. There was a rising antipathy toward Hispanics among influential Republicans in Arizona, and his wife's brown skin and occasional use of Spanish did nothing to help him fit in with the Republican crowd. In hindsight, he felt he would have been much better off marrying a blond with lily-white skin. But, it was too late to do anything about that now. The last thing he needed was a messy divorce. Given his growing prominence in the Phoenix area, it would be the subject of conversation among all of the gossip mongers who had begun to dominate local talk radio.

Despite her PhD, Lupita didn't seem to have good sense. She even volunteered twice a week at a food bank to feed the losers who couldn't get a job. In this world, you had to look out for yourself. Worrying about people who were not smart enough to fend for themselves was a waste of time. How did he end up with such a dumb-assed wife?

"I've got to go, Sweetie," he said. He kissed her on the cheek and parted with the words, "I love you."

It was time for Lupita to leave, too. She went to her car and drove to her office at Olivari Technology. She was no longer a secretary. When she reapplied for a job after returning from Mexico, she was offered a position in international sales. While getting her PhD, she had not only taken classes in Spanish literature, she had been required to take classes in Portuguese and French. France, with its high-tech industry, was an important customer for Olivari Technologies, and most educated French people do not communicate well in English. Perhaps she had a natural gift for sales, or perhaps Jason Wilder's reputation as a businessman helped her, but more likely it was her sharp mind plus the fact that she spoke four languages that had enabled her to quickly rise to the post of manager of European sales. The business classes she had taken in night school at the university had doubtlessly helped, too. She was not making as much money as Jason, but she now had a comfortable income of her own, and she made a point of saving a substantial portion of each paycheck. As she became more skilled in the ways of business, she began investing her savings in secure stocks.

An hour after leaving Lupita, Jason was sitting in the Caf' Casino French restaurant on Camelback Road looking over the table at Martin Glover. The two had coffee and croissants in front of them.

"Look!" said Martin. "You're an important man in the Phoenix business community. I know you will have the support of the people who matter if you decide to run for the State Legislature. You also have name recognition among the voters. Ordinary people will vote for you."

Jason was disappointed. "Being in the State Legislature isn't exactly an important position. I was hoping for more."

"No, being a legislator is no big thing." It's just a first step. You have to start at the bottom and work your way up. I see you as our governor in a few years if you play along with us."

Jason wasn't convinced. "If I'm so well known in the business community, why don't I run for governor now?"

Martin couldn't help showing his impatience. This guy had an exaggerated sense of his own worth. "The business community supports you and so do we party leaders, but Rome wasn't built in a day. You have to prove yourself at the bottom of the ladder before you move up. How well do you operate under fire? Will you support our policies even when the going gets tough? As soon as you run for office, you're going to be criticized, because there are a lot of people who don't like how we run things in this state." By "we" Martin meant the Phoenix Forty, an informal group of 40 families who ran local and state politics from behind the scenes.

"How long do I have to settle for being a legislator?" Jason wanted to know.

"Let's say you serve two terms in the House of Representatives. That's four years total. Then you run for the Arizona State Senate from your district. Let's say you serve two terms in the Senate. That's four more years. If you have a good record during those eight years in the legislature, it will be time to think about running for governor."

Martin Glover had an uneasy feeling as he left the restaurant. He didn't trust Jason. If he and his group backed Jason, he wasn't sure that Jason would remain loyal to them. His only hope was that Jason was smart enough to understand that it was in his best interest to support the existing Republican power structure. After all, Jason was one of them. He was part of the business elite. It was time that he showed some loyalty to the rest of them. If Jason played his cards right, he and Lupita might be invited to join the Phoenix Forty someday. But, no. Lupita was a Mexican. She wouldn't fit in. Why didn't Jason dump her and marry a younger, white trophy wife with money as John McCain had done when he entered politics?

When Jason got to his office, he sat down alone to think about what Martin had said. If he was going to run for governor someday, there was no way he was going to spend eight years dinking around in the Legislature first. "No! I'm not going to let that dumb-assed Martin Glover dude tell me what to do!" he said out loud.

If he was going to get on the primary election ballot, there wasn't much time left. The primary was only months away, and there must be a deadline for turning in petition signatures. If he would just do what the Republican Party wanted him to do, he would get loads of help from Party volunteers and would be a shoo-in to get on the ballot. No! He wasn't going to do that! He was not going to be beholden to these people. On the other hand, if he played along with Martin Glover and his gang for now, he could stall for time as he picked up some political education. But, no! He couldn't play second fiddle in this game!

If he was going to be in charge of his own political campaign, he didn't have much time to get organized. He had to announce his true plans as soon possible, or he would never get everything done on time. To hell with Glover and his whole stuck-up crowd! Going it alone would mean hard work, but Jason had never shied away from putting in the necessary effort to get what he wanted.

Early the next morning Jason let the press know that he would be making an important announcement on the grounds of the State Capitol

Building that afternoon at 2 pm and promised that it would be worthwile for each news organization to send a reporter. He hurriedly had a podium and public address system set up on the Capitol's lawn. Martin Glover made sure that the right people in the press were informed. He was still under the delusion that he was in charge and that Jason was about to announce his candidacy for the Arizona State Legislature.

About 15 reporters showed up, but they were the important ones, a reporter from the *Arizona Republic*, one from each of the wire services, and the four most important Phoenix TV stations had camera crews on scene. Two of the radio stations had also sent reporters. There were also a few local political commentators in the audience. Jason stepped to the podium and got right to the point.

"Ladies and gentlemen of the press, I hereby announce that I intend to run as a Republican candidate for governor of the State of Arizona."—Martin Glover's ears couldn't believe what they were hearing.—"I would rather devote myself to my business, but things are not going well in our state and as a concerned citizen, I think it is my duty to do something about it. I am appalled by how our state is being overrun by illegal immigrants. The president refuses to adequately protect our border with Mexico with the result that criminal gangs composed of wetbacks operate freely throughout the state. Our border communities are under siege. I intend to build out the fence on our southern border with Mexico that the Federal Government promised but has never delivered and send Arizona National Guard troops to the border to seal it completely. I'll have every truck that comes across the border searched right down to the last tomato and head of lettuce so that not one wetback and not one ounce of drugs makes it through.

"We also need to cut taxes to attract industry and out-of-state investment. I intend to reduce the taxes on business, cap Arizona's top-bracket personal income tax rates, and cap property taxes. I promise to make Arizona the state with the lowest taxes in the nation. We need to do this to create jobs for our citizens.

"I find it disgusting that state agencies operate in Spanish as well as English. This is America, folks, and everyone should speak American. When we go to vote, we are confronted with a ballot printed in two languages. That is unpatriotic. You're supposed to be able to speak American in order to vote in this country, and if you can't, you should stay home. When I get into office, it will be American only! Real red meat American English! None of that pansy British-speak!

"Another thing I find unacceptable is that only 11 percent of the land in Arizona is in private hands. The federal government claims most of the rest. That land belongs to us, the citizens of Arizona, and it's high time the federal government gave it back to us. When I am governor, I will introduce a bill in our state legislature declaring that federal government's title to all of the land it claims in Arizona to be null and void. I will return that land to the people, who are its rightful owners.

"We all know that the lefties in government want to take away our right to bear arms. As long as George Bush remains in the White House, we have some protection, but there are plenty of people in various government agencies who want to take away Americans' right to defend themselves, and if some leftie Democrat gets elected president next time, the first thing he'll do is try to take away our guns. When I am elected governor, I will give every American citizen over 14 years of age living in Arizona the right to carry a gun everywhere in the state including in schools. I'll make sure that no left-wing politician in Washington interferes with our gun rights. No business and no government building should be allowed to violate our Second Amendment rights by prohibiting people carrying firearms from entering any building they want to. I'll make sure that they don't. And gun owners will not have to pass background checks either. There's such a thing as gun rights in this country, and I intend to make sure that they are respected in our state. If those liberal states back east want to do something different and violate our sacred Constitution, that's their problem. Everyone living in Arizona has a right to carry a gun. No exceptions!

"Finally, there's the problem of the Washington Beltway liberals imposing laws on us that take away our rights. I intend to prohibit any law enforcement official in Arizona from enforcing federal laws or regulations that trample on our rights. It's time we stood up for our own rights and stopped kowtowing to the lefties in organizations like the Environmental Protection Agency, who have come up with the fiction of global warming. Our planet is not warming, folks. It's cooling off. The lefties invented the fiction of global warming so that they would have an excuse to take over more control of our lives."

Pandemonium broke out among the reporters. Martin Glover had summoned them here to cover the announcement of someone who was going to run for the state legislature, not governor! As local politics in Arizona go, this was a sensation, and the press was going to make as much of it as it could.

There were many questions during the next half hour, and Jason handled them all well as the TV cameras rolled. One reporter asked, "But, didn't you used to do radio and TV commercials in Spanish?"

"Yes, I did," Jason admitted, "but I was wrong to do so. I was younger then, and I made a mistake. We have to protect America from those who would undermine our culture by coming here and refusing to learn our language. All of those people come here and have lots of children, and the children grow up speaking Spanish. Even their kids refuse to speak American. This is the first time that people with their pants up have been overrun by people with their pants down." Jason had heard that remark somewhere before and decided to appropriate it for himself.

The same reporter persisted, "But isn't your wife Mexican?"

"My wife is an American. She was an American citizen at birth. She could be president some day. It's true that she was born in Mexico, but her father was an American. She is just as much a native United States citizen as George Romney, who was also born in Mexico, or our own great senator John McCain, who was born in Panama. She could run for the office of president of the United States someday, just as both of those men did."

Another reporter asked, "How are you going to overrule the federal government and take over federal lands?"

"Don't you worry," Jason replied, "when I'm elected governor, I'll just do it. I'll send the national guard out to reclaim what is justly ours if the federal government refuses to let us have it peacefully. Some of us may have to take up arms to protect ourselves from the government."

The press conference went on for hours. The TV camera operators sent runners back to their TV studios with rolls of video tape from which editors could extract sound bites for the afternoon news and kept recording. No one knew what outrageous remark Jason would make next as he answered the reporters' questions.

Finally Jason said, "That's all folks. Thank you for coming."

The TV crews started packing up. They had much more than they bargained for, and as the word spread, the viewership of the evening news was bound to take a big leap. In the meantime, they had some great video coverage from which the studio editors could extract juicy sound bites.

Martin Glover was not at all happy with Jason's announcement. He was supposed to run for the state legislature, not for governor! Who the hell did that bastard think he was, anyway? Well, he'd show him. The Phoenix Forty had handpicked Alice Dickerson as the next Arizona governor, and it would put all of its resources behind her. That lousy, low-class car salesman would soon learn what it meant to buck the Republican machine.

Another person who was not happy was Lupita. Jason had not asked her to stand with him as he made his announcement, and now she understood why. He couldn't have gotten away with the things he said had his brown-skinned wife been standing by his side. Jason's attack on Mexicans was an attack on her. She was so agitated that she couldn't remain still. She strode back and forth in their living room while she waited for Jason to come home. Uncharacteristically for a woman who was usually passive, she was seething with anger.

When Jason arrived home a few hours later, she let him have it. "I saw your announcement on the news. How could you say those things, you bastard? You insulted and belittled your own wife in front of millions of people."

Jason, who had barely made it beyond the front door, stopped dead in his tracks. He had never heard Lupita use such language. He stuttered in trying to reply. Finally he managed to get a few words out, "It was Hobson's choice. If I want to get elected in Arizona in today's climate, I have to take an anti-immigrant stance. There is no alternative."

"Is running for governor so important to you that you will publicly insult your wife, your mother-in-law, and my people?" Lupita wanted to know.

"Ah, Honey, I didn't insult you. I love you."

"You damned well did insult me! You insulted my roots; you insulted where I came from; you insulted my identity, who I am."

"You know I didn't mean you, Honey. You're one of the good Mexicans."

"Good Mexican? That is the last straw!" Lupita turned red in the face and held her breath as if she were on the verge of losing control and exploding. Then, she turned on her heal, marched into their bedroom, and slammed and locked the door.

Jason tapped timidly. "Let me in, Honey, please."

There was no answer. Jason could hear drawers opening and then slamming shut. He had no idea that Lupita could get so angry. Then, the door burst open in his face and Lupita pushed by him and strode to the front door of the house. She was carrying a suitcase.

"Honey, let's talk about it," Jason pleaded.

Lupita paused in the door. "I can't talk about it now. I don't know if I ever can. I'll be in touch with you when I decide what to do."

Jason heard her car start in the garage and then back out into the street with a screeching of tires. Another screeching of tires, and he heard the car round the corner at the end of the street. Then it was very quiet.

Now Jason was angry, too. "That bitch! That hussy! That whore! I'll show her that she can't get away with this!" he shouted out loud. But then he remembered again that everything he owned was also legally Lupita's property. He got a beer out of the fridge, grabbed the cordless phone off the kitchen counter, and sat down in his favorite chair in the living room. After taking a sip of beer, he dialed his lawyer at his home phone number. What the lawyer told him did not make in happy. "Your wife can take you to the cleaners if she gets a good attorney. All things being equal, I'd rather be on her side than yours."

"Let her stew in her own juices!" Jason shouted to himself after hanging up. "She'll come crawling back."

Lupita drove around for awhile aimlessly and aggressively, taking her anger out on the car. Then her better sense prevailed. She had to calm down, or she would have an accident. She pulled into a shopping center parking lot and sat in the car trying to get her emotions under control. Finally she drove to a nearby motel and checked in. She had to get some shuteye to be ready for work in the morning. It was after midnight when she finally fell asleep, and she awoke groggily six hours later to the sound of the alarm of the clock radio on the night table beside her bed.

She showered, dressed in some of the clothes she had brought with her in the suitcase, put on her makeup, and headed for work. On the way she stopped in a restaurant for breakfast. As she sipped her second cup of coffee, she thought back to what the psychologist had told her when she had sought marriage counseling. Yes, the councilor had been right. Jason was a psychopath. He could put on a good act as a loving husband for a time, but inside he cared for no one but himself. This time, she would not let him sweet-talk her into going back.

Arriving at her office, Lupita gave her secretary instructions to not put through any calls from her husband. She told no one at work about the problem that she was having in her private life, although her secretary easily divined that all was not well in the Wilder household.

Jason didn't give Lupita much thought in the following days. He had a business and a political campaign to run. Because he had defied Martin Glover's instructions, he could expect no help from the Arizona Republican Party, at least not until he beat that slut Alice Dickerson in the primary. What the hell made them think that a woman could be governor, anyway?

His first step was to get on the primary ballot. That meant setting up a campaign committee and registering it with the Arizona Secretary of State. Then he would be allowed to circulate nominating petitions. Because he would get no help from the Republican Party, he couldn't rely on volunteers to circulate the petitions. He would have to hire professional petition circulators and get the petitions turned in by June 1. That didn't leave much time. It also meant a very large expense.

Help came from an unexpected quarter. Jason received a phone call from Maricopa County Sheriff Paul Balboni. "Jason, we had our differences in the past, but I remember that you apologized and even made a contribution to my campaign. Now I think that I can help you."

Jason was so surprised that didn't know what to say. "That's great!" he managed to stammer. "What do you propose?"

"I've got a big list of people who worked in my last campaign and a list of donors, some of them quite wealthy. I'm willing to turn those lists over to you."

"But, what do you get out of it?" Jason wanted to know. Jason knew enough about Paul Balboni to understand that he was a lot like

Jason. Neither of them did anything unless they could obtain some advantage from it.

"I don't get along with the Republican establishment any better than you do. If that Dickerson broad is elected governor, or worse yet, if a Democrat gets elected, I'm going to have lots of problems. I have a feeling that you and I can work together."

"I'd be happy to work with you Paul and for any support you could give me."

"Ok, Jason, but don't cross me. I have ways of making the lives of my enemies very unpleasant."

"Don't worry," said Jason, "if you help me get elected, I will be eternally grateful. I'll owe you big time."

A few hours later, a sheriff's deputy dropped off a packet of information from Paul, and Jason noticed that a large proportion of Paul Balboni's political supporters either lived in Sun City or Sun City West, both retirement communities outside of Phoenix. Eighty percent of the residents of those communities had no more than a high school education and nine percent hadn't even finished high school. The population also consisted of 98 percent whites of European descent with a median age of 75. This was exactly the demographic that Jason could appeal to. These people voted, and having little exposure to ethnic minorities, they were highly susceptible to Jason's message of a state under siege from people not like them. They were also a group with little trust in the Federal Government, and they always voted for the most conservative Republicans.

Jason called several people on the list. He didn't have to talk to too many of them before he found a core of people who were willing, even anxious, to help him in his campaign by telephoning others to ask for support, five-dollar donations, and to request them to circulate nominating petitions.

The reason for the five-dollar donations was that Arizona had an organization called Clean Elections, which funded the campaigns of candidates for state office provided they met certain conditions. The candidates must collect a minimum number signatures and five-dollar donations to qualify for Clean Elections funding. The advantage of Clean Elections funding was that once qualified, a candidate could spend full time campaigning without having to devote time and resources to additional fund raising. Jason decided to go with Clean Elections funding, although he had no intention of running a clean election. Jason appointed Paul Balboni as his campaign manager.

Chapter 6 — Political Shenanigans

Thanks in large part to the aid of Sheriff Paul Balboni's political machine, Jason did receive enough petition signatures to get on the Republican primary ballot, and he had raised enough five-dollar donations to qualify for Clean Elections funding. Jason had a feeling that many of the people who donated five bucks had their contributions reimbursed from Sherriff Balboni's immense campaign war chest, but he preferred not to know if that was true so as to be able to plead ignorance in case of any future ethics investigation. Now that he was on the primary ballot, his next task was to beat Alice Dickerson in the primary election, which would be held on September 7. Most voters sent in their ballots by mail much earlier than that. However, Jason had a trick up his sleeve to get enough of an advantage on Election Day voting to make up for any deficit in early balloting. The trick had been suggested to him by Paul Balboni.

The Arizona's Republican primary voters tended to be exactly the sort of people that Jason had designed his campaign to appeal to white, older, and less educated. For some reason, most of the younger and better-educated voters didn't bother with the primaries, which might explain why the people who were elected to office in Arizona were frequently the type of people who would have been locked up in a nut house in earlier times.

It was difficult enough to get most voters to turn out for the general election. The people who did participate in the Republican primary tended to form their opinions of the basis of emotional appeal instead of facts, logic, and reason. Promise to build a wall on the Mexican border, and you could get elected in Arizona, even though the state government had almost zero say on immigration matters, which had been proven time and time again when Arizona's racist immigration laws had been overturned by the federal courts. Most people who got elected to office in Arizona did so by railing against the federal government.

Sheriff Balboni had demonstrated that he could be reelected repeatedly by standing in front of the TV cameras and making macho, chest-thumping comments about how tough he was while mountains of un-served arrest warrants piled up in his office and allegations of sex crimes against juveniles went uninvestigated. The 2000 census showed that 18 percent of Arizona's population hadn't even finished high school, and another 50 percent had finished high school but not earned a degree of any sort. Arizona was below the national average in the percentage of its population that had earned either a bachelor's or graduate degree. Its public school system was ranked third in the nation. Third from the bottom that is.

Jason looked at those figures and smiled. He was an expert in just the type of demagoguery needed to appeal to this electorate.

Alice Dickerson, mistakenly in Jason's opinion, had published a 200-page white paper that laid out a logical plan for the future of Arizona including care of public lands, an improved education system, and a committee to attract high-paying companies to the state with an emphasis on the technology industry. Almost nobody read the white paper except reporters, editors, and analysts in the press who were required to. She was trying to appeal to more educated, logical people, of whom there were few among Arizona's Republican voters. Alice's traditional Republican political campaign might appeal to the business bigwigs who made up the self-styled party leadership, but the average working-class or retired Republican could only understand simpler, more emotional language. They found Alice's plans incomprehensible.

Jason's tactic was to make frequent accusations about the unsuitability of his opponent to hold office with little regard for the truth. His voters would be people who wouldn't bother to check facts or even care about them. He portrayed her as an egghead who was out of touch with "ordinary folks." His gut feeling told him that mud-slinging would prove to be an effective weapon in this primary. He said she was a woman with many female friends, and let people draw whatever conclusion from that remark that they wanted to.

Jason ignored the advice of his political advisors, whom he considered to be a bunch of nincompoops, and designed his own three-pronged primary campaign. He would use Paul Balboni's campaign workers to conduct a traditional door-to-door campaign among Republican voters. If a campaign worker sensed that the voter was likely to cast a ballot for Jason, the campaign worker would help the voter fill out a request for a mail-in ballot. If the voter seemed more likely to vote for Alice Dickerson, the campaign worker would thank the voter and move on to the next address on the list, after leaving some literature accusing Alice Dickerson of being a tool of out-of-state, leftwing liberals.

The second prong was to create as much free press publicity as possible, which was not difficult. All he had to do to get on the news almost every night was to make at least one shocking statement at a campaign rally or press interview every day. The more outrageous the statements were, the more likely they were to get press coverage. He accused his opponent of hiring illegal immigrants to landscape her lawn and to clean her house. He claimed that her campaign was financed by anti-gun activists from liberal eastern states. The fact that none of this was true didn't bother him in the least, because he knew that most voters didn't care about the truth either. He belittled the fact that Alice Dickerson spoke French and Spanish. "Real Americans speak American!' he never tired of saying. "Do you really want a governor who can speak French?"

The third prong of his campaign was something that had been suggested by Sheriff Balboni and which Jason didn't reveal to anyone except to the out-of-work actress from California whom Sheriff Balboni had recommended as the perfect person to carry out the plan. The sheriff promised that they could count on her discretion as long as she was well paid. People might suspect that Jason was behind the scheme, but no one would be able to prove it. Just to be sure, Jason was careful to have no direct contact with the actress and to make sure she was paid in cash by a person who could not be traced to him.

Jason began holding political rallies in north Phoenix, Glendale, Sun City, north Scottsdale, Yuma, and especially in small communities with a high percentage of retirees such as Sun Lakes, Goodyear, Peoria, Mesa, and Sun Tan Valley. These communities might have small populations, but their residents tended to vote in large numbers, and they overwhelmingly supported the most conservative Republicans. He avoided places with a more liberal reputation such as Tempe, Tucson, and Central Phoenix. He held his first rally in Sun City West where the auditorium was filled with enthusiastic gray-headed men and women. His speech was repeatedly interrupted by wild applause, whistles, and shouts of "Go, Jason!"

"I know what you're suffering," Jason began. "You hire landscape companies to take care of your lawns, and the workers who come out are scruffy brown-skinned men who can't even speak American. We all know they're illegals, but what can we do? The landscape companies pick them up off the street as long as they'll work cheap. Then, the next day when you are at the doctor's office or on the golf course, the same men come back, break into your house, and take your TV and jewelry. Instead of respecting the elderly as they should, these people prey on you. They need to be sent back to Mexico, and I plan to send them there!

"When I am governor, I promise you that senior citizens will be treated with respect. I will secure Arizona's border with Mexico, something our federal government refuses to do, and I will stop these Beaners from coming into our country.

"When we elected George Bush to the presidency, we thought we were electing a conservative, but he has turned out to be really soft on immigration. He wants to turn these illegals into American citizens, even though most of them don't know a word of American. If Alice Dickerson gets to be governor, she'll work with Bush, and the next thing you know these people will be living next door to you with the same rights that you have. You'll have to sleep with your gun beside your bed at night, and you'll be afraid to leave your house in the daytime for fear that it will be cleaned out while you're gone. You won't be safe; your children won't be safe; and your grandchildren won't be safe.

"If George Bush refuses to secure our southern border, I promise you that I will. This is America, and it should be for Americans. It's time someone stood up for white people and sent all of these lazy Mexicans back home. I know the other side is going to call me a racist, but I'm not. I'm a loyal American who wants to protect our country from thieves, gangsters, rapists, and drug smugglers from south of our open border. I know that there are many Hispanics who live in this country legally, but they are just as bad. Half of them are on welfare, and they're all in favor of open borders so that their friends and relatives can come here and live off the American taxpayer. And, Alice Dickerson wants to be one of them. She speaks Spanish as well as French, for Christ's sake. Do we really want someone on the Ninth Floor of the State Capitol Building who will spend her time watching Mexican soap operas in the company of a bunch of brown-skinned people who haven't had a bath in a week?"

The crowd whooped and hollered in approval. The Phoenix TV stations all had camera crews covering the event. They edited Jason's most radical statements down to sound bites, which were featured on the evening news and on all the local newscasts the following day. Channel Six Speedy News' coverage was typical. After transmitting excerpts from Jason's speech, it included a few remarks from people in the audience. One elderly male Swiss immigrant speaking with a Germanic-sounding accent said, "Jason tells the truth. He says the things we all think, but most people are afraid to say. He's the only politician I've met who speaks for me. I support Jason Wilder."

A local self-appointed Hispanic leader named Julia Sepúlveda was invited to respond live. The idea was to give balanced coverage. "Mr. Wilder is a racist," she began. "That Gringo should be sent back to England or wherever the hell he came from. We were here in Arizona before all you white *gabachos* arrived, and as far as I'm concerned, all of you can leave now and take Jason Wilder with you." She finished by raising a clenched fist above her head, thereby convincing more people that Jason was right.

While Jason was holding his rally in Sun City West, Alice Dickerson was holding her political rally in the upscale bedroom community of Paradise Valley among Jason's neighbors: traditional, moneyed Republicans. In measured tones, she laid out her plans for tax reform, balancing the state budget, and improving K-through-12 education in front of a listless audience and three drowsy reporters. Her rally did make the TV news, but the next day almost no one who had attended the rally remembered what she had said. The gossip around the water cooler in the plentiful call centers across the state was about Jason Wilder and how he had the courage to stand in front of the TV cameras and say what everyone knew was true but which career politicians like Alice Dickerson were too chicken to acknowledge.

A day later, the TV newscasts carried more-reasonable responses to Jason's invective. US Republican senator Hampton Brown stood in front of the cameras at a press conference that he had called and read a statement in a wooden voice, "Everyone who comes to our country legally, works for a living, pays taxes, and accepts American values is welcome. Hate mongers like Jason Wilder, whose aim seems to be to divide us and sow hate among us, are not welcome in the Republican Party. The Arizona Republican party is open to all people of all races and religions."

"Nonsense!" was Jason's reply the next day. "It's time we cleared out the slackers and returned this state to real Americans. It's time for sclerotic political hacks like Senator Brown to get out of the way. They not only don't want to be part of the solution, they are a big part of the problem."

Sheriff Balboni would later remind Jason to watch his language. "Not many of your supporters know what words like sclerotic mean. If you use highfalutin language, they'll think you're talking down to them and you'll lose their support. Stick to simple words and short sentences."

Alice Dickerson herself called a press conference to criticize Jason for his intemperate remarks. "My opponent has chosen to run on a racist agenda. All Americans, whether brown, black, or white, are guaranteed the same rights under our laws. If Jason Wilder becomes governor, our state will be in turmoil from which it will be difficult to recover. There is no place for ethnic hate in the State of Arizona. I call on all of Arizona's residents to repudiate Mr. Wilder's chauvinistic remarks."

Few potential voters paid attention to these statements. At least she and Jason were now even on vocabulary. Most Arizona Republican voters didn't know what the word chauvinistic meant either.

If Ms. Dickerson's remarks had any effect at all, it was to arouse Jason's supporters even more and to contribute to their belief that he was right. What did that woman mean by going on TV and bad-mouthing white people, and who gave that Sepúlveda broad the right to say anything? This was a free country, and people like her should not be allowed to criticize it.

Other events cemented Jason's support even more. A pro-immigration demonstration was held in downtown Phoenix the following afternoon. There were only a few dozen protestors, but the close-in shots of the TV cameras gave the impression that there were hundreds. The demonstrators were brown skinned and waved Mexican flags. They marched down Washington Street, tying up traffic, beating on drums, and shouting slogans in Spanish, "¡Jason! ¡Escucha! ¡Estamos a la lucha!" Few Republican voters could understand what that meant, but it sounded very threatening.

Then one of Jason's supporters, who had slipped in among the marchers, threw a large stone that smashed a storefront window. Suddenly, the police officers, who had been standing by, charged the marchers with nightsticks raised and began beating anyone who came within reach.

Analysts later noted that all of the marchers had been peaceful with one exception until the police charged them. The police had rioted. However, when video of the event appeared on the TV news, most white viewers blamed the riot on the Hispanics. The Hispanics, in turn, blamed the police. It was astounding how two groups of people could watch the same video and interpret it so differently. Jason's demagoguery was opening up a racial divide among people who had previously lived together in peace. Few people could calm down enough to think rationally about the situation, however. More and more people began to think that Jason was right. What they believed they saw in the videos on the nightly TV newscasts confirmed it.

Jason was quick to seize his advantage. He went in front of the TV cameras to attack his opponent. "Ms. Dickerson would open our borders to people who want to destroy our American way of life. Look at what those marchers were yelling, 'We're going to fight.' Call Ms. Dickerson's campaign committee and tell them that we don't want open borders for violent criminals in Arizona. Elect her to office, and every city in Arizona will have nightly riots like the one those immigrant hoodlums conducted in Phoenix last night. Elect me, and I will restore law and order."

The next day, there were two opposing demonstrations in front of the State Capitol Building. Again, there were only a few dozen people in each group, but the TV cameras zoomed in so that anyone watching on TV got the impression that there were hundreds. One group was composed principally of Hispanics who were carrying signs in Spanish and English with slogans with the words "Down with Jason!" and "We are human beings, too." They were carrying American flags in a show of patriotism but they made the mistake of chanting in unison the same slogan that the press microphones had picked up during the previous demonstration: "¡Jason! ¡Escucha! ¡Estamos a la lucha!" To anyone who understood Spanish, the words were inoffensive, but to anyone who didn't understand Spanish, the chant sounded like a threat.

The group opposing the Hispanics was composed of about 15 middle-aged and older white people who were shouting insults in an uncoordinated manner. Over half of them were scruffy-looking males dressed in leather and sporting substantial beer bellies. One voice could be heard above the others yelling, "Get those wetbacks out of here!" and "America for Americans!" One of the leather-clad demonstrators carried a sign reading "White Power" and another carried a sign with a large red swastika painted on it.

About four dozen police officers stationed themselves between the two groups to keep them apart. The police officers outnumbered the demonstrators, and the police thought they had everything under control. They were used to opposing groups yelling at each other, and these small loud demonstrations seldom turned violent. The Phoenix police chief later admitted that his department was unprepared for what happened.

Three of the leather-clad men in the anti-immigrant group suddenly formed a tight wedge and charged through the police line, taking the officers by surprise. These three mean-looking dudes managed to throw some punches at four elderly Hispanics. The police tried to pull the leather-clad hooligans off their victims and managed to handcuff two of them. The third evaded the police and kicked one of the Hispanic men in the groin before knocking him to the ground with the butt of a pistol that he yanked out of his boot. The police reacted to the presence of a gun with a hail of bullets that struck the leather-clad man in seven places, leaving him writhing and dying on the ground.

Suddenly more police officers appeared as if from nowhere. They surrounded both groups of demonstrators and began handcuffing them with the exception of a young Hispanic who started running from the scene. A police officer drew his service revolver, fired six shots, and fatally wounded the fleeing man in the back.

The event was breaking news all over the world. In Germany, the news reported that the American South was in the midst of a racial war. (German news outlets seldom get their geography right.) French TV reported that a civil war had broken out between "Anglo-Saxons" and Latinos. (The French stereotype almost all Americans as Anglo-Saxons.) In China and Russia state television reported that the racist American government was no longer content to suppress minorities, the government was now massacring them. All of the newscasts included video of the Phoenix police officer shooting the fleeing Hispanic youth in the back.

Never mind that only a few dozen people had been involved in the demonstrations and that the Hispanics in the demonstration had not lifted a finger to harm anyone. Jason called a press conference and implored the governor to activate the Arizona National Guard "to protect Americans from the invasion of these foreign terrorists." Other voices took up the demand. The governor managed to resist for less than a day. By the next afternoon, groups of men in military uniform and carrying rifles began to be stationed on street corners throughout the central Phoenix area and in major shopping centers all over the state. The governor also declared a state of emergency and banned all demonstrations. Legal scholars questioned his right to do so, but no one paid any attention to them. People were frightened and began to look suspiciously at their neighbors, especially if the neighbors had a different skin color.

The president went on television the next afternoon in a live broadcast from the Oval Office. He revealed that the Hispanic who had been shot in the back was "a 16-year-old American citizen who had been born in Phoenix. I have instructed the FBI to investigate the incident. I don't have the power to initiate a murder investigation," he added. "That power rests in the hands of the attorney general of the State of Arizona. However, I am instructing the justice department to carry out a civil rights investigation. In the meantime, I urge the citizens of Arizona and especially the residents of Phoenix to remain calm and await the results of the investigations."

But, they didn't.

Jason was too wrapped up in events to give any thought to Lupita, but Lupita hadn't forgotten him. How could she? He was on virtually every newscast. "I'm married to a monster!" she thought.

Over lunch in the office cafeteria the next day, Lupita made it a point to sit with the oft-divorced Laura Cunningham. "Laura," she began, "can you recommend a good divorce lawyer?"

"Oh sure!" Laura replied. "I've used Lincoln Horowitz on my last three divorces. He's a real peach to get along with, and his rates are reasonable. He also managed to bleed dry every one of those sons-of-bitches I was married to. I've got a nice little nest egg, thanks to him."

"I'll give him a call. Do you have his number on you?"

Laura pulled a small address book out of her purse and began jotting on a paper napkin. "Don't tell me you're going to divorce the famous Jason Wilder? You're going to get a fortune out of him in any divorce settlement."

"I am going to divorce him, but I don't care about his money. I just want to get rid of the bastard." Lupita's use of the profanity was uncharacteristic and showed the extent of her anger.

The divorce didn't go as smoothly as Lupita had hoped. At their first appointment, Lincoln Horowitz explained to her that "Jason would have to agree for the divorce to proceed. Unless you can prove abuse, alcoholism, or adultery, you two will have to be legally separated for at least a year before you can obtain a divorce over Jason's objections."

"I'm pretty sure that Jason has committed adultery," was Lupita's response. "I'm pretty sure he's screwing his secretary."

"Can you prove that, or can you get the secretary to testify in court?" Lincoln asked.

"No, I have no proof. I have no idea if his secretary hates him enough to testify against him or not. I suspect that she wouldn't want to be dragged into a court case."

"In that case," Lincoln replied, "let me file the papers and see what we hear back from Jason's lawyer. Maybe Jason will agree. After all, he's running for office and may not want his dirty laundry washed in public."

Three weeks passed before Lincoln called Lupita at work. "Jason is refusing to agree to a no-fault divorce," Lincoln told her. "His lawyer hinted that the problem is the property settlement. Jason doesn't want to split the marriage's community property with you. At least, that's my impression."

"But, what if we threaten to make public that his wife wants to divorce him. Won't he back off out of fear of negative publicity during his political campaign?"

"Not according to his lawyer. His lawyer says that Jason would welcome the publicity. He's running for office as the badass who is going to set this state straight. The lawyer says that Jason's having his Mexican wife mad at him would enhance his stature among chauvinistic angry white Republicans."

"Then, what can I do?" Lupita asked.

"You have three choices, as far as I can see. You can accuse him of adultery and we can subpoena his former secretary to testify. Another possibility would be for you to file for a legal separation and wait a year. You abandoned him; he didn't abandon you, or we could do it without the legal separation. As a last resort, we can negotiate a property settlement that he will accept. That would probably mean giving him more than he deserves."

Lupita thought if over then replied, "Let's go with the last option. I don't want any of his filthy money. I don't want it said that I profited one cent from that scumbag. What I have in the bank is mine, and everything else is his. He is responsible for his own debts, and I'm responsible for mine. Oh, and I want him to pay my legal costs for the divorce." As it would later turn out, by separating her finances from Jason's, Lupita made a very wise decision.

It was another week until Lupita heard from Lincoln again. "He's agreed to your terms. He's signed the papers. I need you to come into the office and sign some papers, too. Then we'll schedule a court date."

Jason felt relieved when Lupita accepted his conditions for the divorce. He had worked hard to build up the business, and he was paying the mortgage on the house. Everything he had was due to his own hard work, and there was no way he was going to share it with someone who had no claim to it. Other than that he gave the divorce little thought. He had a car dealership to run and a political campaign to carry on. He was grateful that Sheriff Paul Balboni had agreed to be his campaign manager. That took a big load off his mind. Paul had one of his deputies arrange Jason's speaking engagements and for volunteers to go door to door with campaign literature, collect donations, etc. Jason was happy when he drove around town to see more and more yard signs popping up with his name and campaign slogan on them. "Jason Wilder for governor. Keep Arizona strong and free." Jason didn't know that not all of the cash donations made it into his campaign kitty.

Appearing at campaign rallies was no longer easy. There were always large groups of demonstrators outside anywhere he tried to hold a meeting, and Paul Balboni had to provide off-duty sheriff's deputies to keep the demonstrators from crashing his events.

The community was divided. The more some people called Jason a racist and demonstrated against him, the more his core supporters rallied behind him. His campaign rallies became noisy events with opposing large groups of people shouting at each other, waving signs, and occasionally throwing rocks and bottles. The off-duty sheriff's deputies were no longer able to maintain order. The Phoenix Police assigned a large number of officers to each of Jason's appearances, and the governor reinforced them with a contingent from the Arizona National Guard.

The police officer who had shot the teenage boy in the back was "suspended from patrol duties and assigned to a desk job" according to the police chief "while the department conducts an investigation." There were large demonstrations demanding that the officer be charged with first-degree murder and counter demonstrations calling the officer a hero. Most of the demonstrations and counter demonstrations took place at Jason's rallies.

Jason also had problems within his own campaign organization. Paul Balboni kept asking Jason for more money to keep the campaign going. "I'm not even taking a salary," was Paul's story. "I'm doing this because I believe in you. But, this campaign has expenses. You can't run a political campaign without investing in it." Paul didn't mention that most of the campaign work was being done by his deputies whose salary was paid by Maricopa County. He also neglected to mention that most of the money Jason gave him was deposited directly into his own bank account.

"What about the Clean Elections people? Aren't they giving us money?" Jason asked.

"Sure they are, but it costs more to run a campaign than they give us, and in order to comply with Clean Elections, we are not allowed to ask for donations. You have to put in some more of your own money, or this campaign is sunk. If you get elected governor, you'll have plenty of opportunities to get that money back and a lot more to boot."

"But, if I give money to the campaign, isn't that a donation? Isn't that cheating on the pledge I made to get Clean Elections money?"

"Jason, if you give your own money to your own campaign, I think that's only fair. Besides, who's gonna' know? If we ask for donations, Clean Elections will find out, and we'll end up in court, and you'll probably be disqualified as a candidate. No one's gonna' know if you write me a check. Make it out in my name so that it doesn't show up in the campaign financial records."

Jason felt uneasy, but what was he to do? After all, as Paul said, he was working for free. Not only that, Paul had some of his deputies in civilian clothes distributing campaign literature and putting up campaign signs. If that ever came out, he was in trouble in any case. "In for a penny, in for a pound," as his English granddad used to say.

Jason was obliged to take out a second mortgage on the house to keep the campaign going. His car dealership was already mortgaged up to the hilt. If this run for the governorship paid off, it would be worth it. There were almost unlimited opportunities for a governor to make a little "side money." If it didn't pay off, Jason was sunk.

Despite Jason's relentless campaigning, the polls that Paul Balboni commissioned in his name showed that he and Alice Dickerson were running neck and neck within the margin of error right up to the week of the election. Alice had seemed to be running a lackluster campaign up until the police officer had shot the teenager to death. Since then Alice had become very vocal in denouncing police violence and implying that Jason was at fault. It was as if she had had a personality makeover. She stopped being the timid campaigner and became very aggressive in her verbal attacks on Jason. "That guy wants to be our governor, but why would we elect a jerk like that to be dog catcher? That guy's racism is what triggered the police violence and brought our state to the brink of civil war." Alice now always referred to Jason as "that guy," and the polls showed that her campaign was catching on with voters who had previously declared themselves undecided. Jason still had the lead among white voters, especially older males, but Alice had the Hispanic vote almost all to herself. One thing that Jason counted in his favor was that Hispanics tended to turn out in smaller numbers to vote. He bet that a lot of the Latinos who were demonstrating against him were not even citizens. In fact, most of them were probably illegals.

As Election Day approached, it was time to put the plan into action that Paul had hatched and Jason had financed. They sprung the trap the afternoon before the election as Alice was giving an outdoor campaign speech to a large crowd on the grounds of the Arizona State Capitol building. A few weeks ago, she had had trouble attracting an audience at all, but now large numbers of people attended her rallies. What had started as a desultory primary campaign was being called "a pivotal moment in Arizona politics." The TV crews of all of the Phoenix stations and several TV stations from Tucson and Flagstaff were present. Alice was sure that she would get a boost from her final appearance on the evening news before tomorrow's balloting. She did get a prominent spot on the news, but it wasn't the favorable coverage that she had envisioned.

Alice was just about to wrap up her speech and take questions when a woman with short blond hair wearing a green miniskirt and a very low-cut halter top pushed her way through the spectators to the podium, grabbed the cordless mike out of its holder, and shouted, "Don't elect this woman. She and I have been lovers for 15 years, and now that she's running for governor, she's abandoned me. I could tell you a lot of dirt about her. She's not the saintly Christian that she..."

Just at that moment, a security guard grabbed the microphone out of the woman's hand, and another tried to grab the woman herself, but she slipped under his arm, ran across the capitol grounds, and jumped into a car that had been waiting on 17th Avenue with the front door on the passenger's side standing open. She slammed the door, and the car roared off.

Alice stood at the podium in a state of shock. She didn't know how to react. Then tears started rolling down her cheeks. "I don't know that woman," she blubbered into the microphone. "What she said isn't true. I'm happily married. I've never done anything like what she accused me of. I've never seen her before." Someone put his arm around her shoulders and led her off crying.

The incident was a sensation of the evening news. Channel Six Speedy News devoted half of its newscast to it. First, it showed a long video segment beginning with the woman's approach to the podium and ending with her jumping into the front passenger's seat of a car, which then sped off. The newscast focused on that incident and completely ignored Alice's speech.

Then there was a short discussion of the event featuring Alice's campaign manager and Jason Wilder. The campaign manager asserted, "It was a put-up job" and accused the Wilder campaign of being behind it. Jason claimed no knowledge of the event other than what he had seen in the video clip. "I feel very sorry for my opponent. It was the worst possible time for this to happen. I don't know if the woman's accusations are true or not, but I want to express my deep sympathy for

Alice in any case. I hope the press will start an investigation to get to the bottom of this." Then he coyly added, "I do not want Alice's sexual orientation to be an issue in this election. Her private life should not enter into her run for governor."

"Are you implying that the woman's allegations are true?" the interviewer asked.

Jason replied, "I know absolutely nothing about Alice's private life. I'm just saying that whether they are true or not, they should not influence the outcome of this election."

The press did start an investigation, but it was too late, of course; the election was the next day. Many of the people who had intended to vote for Alice Dickerson suddenly had strong doubts about her, but they couldn't bring themselves to vote for Jason either, so they just stayed home. Jason's voters, on the other hand, turned out in large numbers to vote against "that lesbo."

When the votes were counted the night of the election, Jason had won with 51.8 percent of the vote. Alice Dickerson had been leading in the mail-in balloting, but Election Day balloting had turned the vote in Jason's favor. Jason was now the Republican nominee for governor.

The press had little success in uncovering who was behind the incident at the State Capitol that had torpedoed Alice Dickerson's campaign. Most suspected Jason, but there was no proof. The press did manage to find that the car had driven to Deer Valley Airport north of the city where the mystery woman had boarded a private plane. The plane had filed a flight plan to fly to Lindbergh Field in San Diego. They located the plane's owner in San Diego, but he wasn't much help. "She paid me in advance for the flight in cash. She said that she was fleeing an abusive husband and she didn't want him to be able to find her. I don't really know her whole name. She called herself Clara. No, she wasn't wearing a miniskirt. She was dressed in a conservative business suit." She had apparently changed clothes on the way to the airport.

No one at Lindbergh Field remembered having seen the woman. The press inquiry ended in an investigative cul-de-sac. It wasn't until many years later when the truth would come out, when the actress stepped forward and confessed. By then Jason was in a place where her accusations did him no harm.

The primary election had been a squeaker, but Jason won the nomination, and that was all that mattered. Alice had been leading in early mail-in balloting, but among the people who voted in person on election day, Jason won enough of a majority to defeat her. Now the first half of the job was done. Jason was the official Republican nominee for governor of Arizona. Next, he would have to win the governorship itself in the general election.

Once Lupita had come to an agreement with Jason, the remainder of the divorce proceedings went smoothly. Legal proceedings were certainly much more complicated in Mexico. She met Lincoln outside the courtroom, and they entered together. There were already about 20 people waiting inside. Soon, a young woman entered and took her place at a desk to the side of the judge's bench. She busied herself with a stack of papers that she had brought with her. Each time the door at the back of the courtroom opened, Lupita turned to see if it was Jason. After a few minutes, the woman seated beside the judge's bench looked up from her papers and said, "All rise!" The judge entered wearing a black robe and took her chair behind the bench. "Be seated," the judge said. Then she called the first case.

Lupita was fascinated as she watched and listened. The proceedings went quickly. It seemed to take about 10 minutes to get divorced in Phoenix. Then her case was called, and she walked to the front of the courtroom with Lincoln, who motioned her to take the witness stand, which was not a stand at all but rather a seat behind a low railing with a microphone mounted in front of her. Lupita noted that Jason still wasn't there. The clerk approached, asked her to raise her right hand, and asked her if she swore "to tell the truth, the whole truth, and nothing but the truth." She did.

Then Lincoln asked her a few brief questions, the last of which was "Are you pregnant?" Lupita blushed but managed to stammer "no." That was it. The judge said, "You may step down." Lupita returned to her seat among the spectators while Lincoln handed some papers to the judge who signed them and then passed them on to the clerk. The clerk made some notations before making duplicates at a copying machine conveniently located next to her desk. She handed the copies to Lincoln and kept the originals.

Lincoln returned to Lupita, handed her some papers and said, "Let's go. Those are your copies of the divorce decree. Keep them in a safe place. You may need them. You are now a free woman."

"You mean that's all there is to it?" Lupita asked. She couldn't believe that a few minutes ago she was married, and now she wasn't. After all of the preliminary work and negotiations, the divorce itself seemed anticlimactic. Lupita felt a bit depressed. She almost wished she could undo the process. Almost.

"That's all. You are free woman. If you want, you can walk down the hall, find another judge, and marry someone else."

"Fat chance!" Lupita responded. "I hope I'm smart enough not to make that mistake again soon. But, I still don't understand why Jason wasn't there."

"He didn't have to be. In Arizona, when a divorcing couple has signed an agreement in advance of the hearing, only one of the parties has to show up to testify, actually to answer a few simple questions under oath as you did. Then, if the papers appear to be in order, the judge almost always accepts what the couple has agreed to.

Jason paid no attention to the divorce. He was just happy to have gotten rid of Lupita so cheaply. He would be far too occupied with politicking in the following weeks to be concerned with her. The general election would be held on November 5. Winning the Republican primary in a conservative state was one thing. Winning the general election where Democrats and Independents would be casting votes would be more difficult. Although Arizona is a Republican-leaning state, it has a history of electing the occasional Democratic governor when the Republican candidate is especially weak.

Jason was fortunate in his enemies. In the Democratic primary race for governor, Barbara Lahti had defeated Federico (Fast Freddy) Martinez by a narrow margin. Freddy Martinez was unsatisfied with the result and took the matter to court. The Arizona Supreme Court refused to accept the case claiming it had no jurisdiction to overturn the will of the voters, so the election results were allowed to stand. However, Fast Freddy was stubborn and unwilling to accept the court's decision. He filed papers with the Arizona Secretary of State's office to run for governor as an independent candidate. Jason couldn't believe his luck. Fast Freddy's decision and the resulting intraparty bickering almost certainly meant that the Democratic vote would be split, and he would win the governorship with a plurality of votes. There was no run-off election in the Arizona governor's race. Even if the candidate with the largest number of votes failed to win a majority, that candidate was declared the governor elect.

Jason wouldn't be the first car dealer to win the Arizona governorship with a mere plurality. Evan Mecham, who had passed away a year earlier, had been elected to the governorship in a three-way race against two Democrats in 1986. Evan Mecham had not only been a perennial candidate, the Harold Stassen of Arizona, he had owned an automobile dealership. It was quite a shock when Mecham finally won an election.

Jason hoped that the similarities would end there and that he wouldn't be impeached as Mecham had been just over a year after taking office. Jason made a mental note not to repeat Mecham's mistake of having a terrible relationship with the legislature while claiming he was only answerable to the Constitution, which he believed had been handed down by God. Mecham had also named several accused criminals to important posts including an accused murderer as superintendent of the Arizona Department of Liquor Licenses and Control. Jason made a mental note not to appoint anyone to public office who was under indictment for murder or had recently been released from prison.

Jason was the only one of the candidates who had absolutely no political experience. Fast Freddy Martinez had been born in Nogales, Sonora, just across the Mexican border in 1949. When he was five years old, his father had moved the family to the US side of the border to Nogales, Arizona, and several years later his father and mother became naturalized US citizens, which meant that their son Federico was also naturalized.

In later life, Freddy was elected to a four-year term as mayor of Nogales, Arizona in 2003. Since then he had been running his business as a fruit and vegetable wholesaler, importing produce from Mexico and selling it to grocery chains in the US. Now he wanted to do something to serve the state that had been so kind to him and his poor immigrant parents. If he had managed to be elected Arizona governor, he would not have been the first immigrant from Mexico to serve in that post.

Mexican-born Raúl Castro, no relation to the man of the same name in Cuba, was elected governor of Arizona in 1974.

Barbara Lahti was a rarity. She was a native-born Arizonan in a state to which almost everyone had moved from somewhere else. She had been born in Phoenix in 1953 and as an adult had served three terms as a representative in the State Legislature followed by two terms in the State Senate. In her second term in the Senate she was elected president of that body. Like Jason, she had statewide name recognition, whereas Freddy Martinez was better known in the less-populated southern third of the state. However, most people felt that either of them would make an excellent governor. It was a shame that they were running against each other. A poll taken weeks before the election showed that almost two thirds of Arizonans thought that Jason was completely unqualified for the post. However, he had a minority of hardcore supporters who could be counted upon to show up on election day and vote for him. With the Democratic vote split, many Democrats were disheartened, and Jason figured that some of them would stay home and not cast a ballot.

Jason was so sure of victory, that he decided to have a little fun. He brought Moses the talking burro back before the TV cameras who proclaimed, "I'm voting for Jason Wilder. I sure don't want one of those other donkeys to be governor. You should vote for him, too, so we don't end up with the wrong ass sitting in the governor's chair."

The TV stations had not become any more willing to allow the word "ass" in the commercial than they had been years ago to allow it in a news report when Jason said it. Jason showed them that the word was used in the Bible to refer to donkeys to no avail. Finally, they compromised. The word was partially bleeped out so that the "a" sound was heard at the beginning of the word and the rest was left to the viewer's imagination. That made the commercial even funnier. What Jason had done as a joke turned out to be a stroke of genius. Even those who had been vehemently opposed to him had to admit that he had a sense of humor. He was human after all.

Jason won only 38.6 percent of the vote in the November 5th election, but it was enough to get him elected governor with a plurality. Barbara Lahti came in second with 34.9 percent of the vote, and Fast Freddy Martinez garnered 26.5 percent. Sixty-one point four percent of the electorate had voted against Jason, but still he was elected governor. Jason was sworn into office on January 6, 2003.

Jason was well aware that most Arizonans disliked him, and everyone in the State Legislature knew that, too. The establishment politicians wouldn't make it easy for Jason to govern the State of Arizona.

The first thing he wanted to do was to get a new budget through the legislature. His predecessor had already come up with a budget, but Jason decided to start over again from scratch and get rid of some items that he regarded as handouts. He wanted to reduce taxes on business, and he wanted to cut the income tax on the upper income brackets. He also felt that his predecessor's budget was far too generous in the money allotted to schools, community colleges, and universities. He thought that the budget also allotted too much money to the Arizona Health Care Cost Containment System (AHCCS), which was Arizona's version of Medicaid or government-subsidized health care for lower income residents. Why should business owners, the people who actually created wealth, pay the doctor bills for those loafers?

Jason had some fence mending to do with the State Legislature if he wanted to get his ideas passed into law. Both chambers were dominated by Republicans, which was a plus. However, he had defied the Republican establishment by running for governor against the party bosses' wishes. Merely getting elected did not earn him any respect with his fellow party members. Jason had far more enemies than he had friends. The senators and representatives in the legislature were not about to cozy up to him.

As to the Democratic minority in the legislature, Jason could expect no help whatsoever from that quarter. More than half of the Democrats in the legislature had Spanish surnames, the very group that Jason had disparaged in his political campaign. Many of them held university degrees. The Republicans in the legislature, on the other hand, tended to be of European descent and lesser educated. Jason thought he could convince the Republican legislators to see things his way. If an appeal to their party loyalty wouldn't work, there were other, less-subtle methods of persuasion.

Two days after his inauguration, Jason telephoned William Kandinsky, the president of the Republican majority in the State Senate. "Bill, now that I'm governor, I think it would be a good idea for us to get together informally to see if there's any way we could cooperate."

Senator Kandinsky was wary. "I'll tell you right off the bat that I'm no fan of yours, Jason. In fact, I'll do everything in my power to make sure that your term in office is as short as possible."

Jason responded, "I'm sorry you feel that way, Bill. Look, we'll just have an informal talk off the record. We'll do it at my house so no one will be the wiser. How about this evening, say at seven? After all, we're both Republicans."

"No way!" was Bill's terse response. "I want nothing to do with you. As to your being a Republican, you still have to prove that to me."

"In that case, I could go public. I could say that I tried to negotiate with you and you refused."

"That would just backfire," Bill responded. "The public doesn't like you either, and refusing to meet with you would be a feather in my cap. Don't forget that most people voted against you, and they still don't like you."

"Perhaps. However, the public is fickle. Can you be sure that they would put the blame on me and not on you? You could be committing political suicide."

"I don't think so."

"Look!" Jason implored, "We'll meet privately at my house. No one will know you were there. I promise to keep it secret if you don't want anyone to know. I'll dismiss my security detail for the night so that you can enter the house unobserved. What have you got to lose?"

Kandinsky was skeptical. "I could lose my reputation if it gets out that I met with you in private at your house, but OK, I'll trust you this once. I'm probably making a mistake, but I guess it can't hurt to talk off the record. Seven did you say?"

"Yes, I'll see you then."

It was well known around the Capitol Building that William Kandinsky had a weakness for strong drink and pretty women. Although he made it a point to appear frequently in public with his wife and children, it was also whispered that he wasn't always faithful to his spouse. Jason was aware of Bill Kandinsky's weaknesses. He had once showed up at the Senate dead drunk, but his colleagues had managed to hustle him out of the building and somehow kept the affair from becoming public. They couldn't stop the gossip about the drunken senate leader among the political insiders, however.

When Bill Kandinsky arrived at Jason's house, Jason invited him to sit in an overstuffed chair in the living room. On the coffee table before the chair stood a bottle of Speyburn Arranta single-malt Scotch whisky, a bottle of cold water, ice cubes, and two glasses. "May I pour you a drink?" Jason asked.

"Just a small one. I'm driving, you know."

Jason poured a generous drink into Bill's glass and a smaller amount into his own. "That's far too much," Bill objected. "I'll just take a few sips." Bill took a rather large sip of the amber liquid and let out a satisfied sigh. "That's really good stuff."

"I'm hoping we can work together for the good of the State of Arizona," Jason began.

"I don't want to be rude to a man when I'm in his house drinking his whisky, but I can't see you and me working together," was Bill's response. "I don't like the way you got yourself elected, and I think the sooner we get ourselves a new governor, the better off the state will be. I'm sorry to be so blunt, but that's the way I see things."

Jason topped off Bill's glass, which was already nearly empty. Bill took a big swig and then set his glass down.

"Alcohol seems to act as a diuretic by me," Bill said. "Do you mind if I use your bathroom?"

"Down the hall and to the right."

Jason judged that Bill had already consumed enough alcohol to not notice a slight change in the taste of his whisky. He pulled a small envelope of white powder from his pocket, dumped it into Bill's drink, and stirred it. Then he dropped in another ice cube and topped off the drink with more whisky.

When Bill returned and had taken his seat and another large swallow of whisky he said, "I really don't see this discussion going anywhere. I think it was a mistake for me to come. I think I'll be on my way."

"I'm sorry if that's the way you feel," Jason responded. "Let's just finish our drinks, and then I hope we can part friends, although I'm sorry that this meeting couldn't have been more productive."

Bill took an extra large swig of whisky that half emptied the glass. "Jason, you and I are never going to be friends."

The whisky seemed to taste even better than it had when he started drinking. Bill didn't notice that Jason had barely touched his drink. After Bill emptied his glass, he tried to get up to leave, but it felt too comfortable in Jason's chair. Jason didn't seem to be such a bad guy after all. Bill had a sense of well being that he hadn't felt in years.

Then the doorbell rang, and Jason went to answer it. Bill heard a female voice say, "Uncle Jason! May I come in for a short visit?"

"Of course you may, my dear."

"Bill tried to get up out of his chair to great the newcomer, but he felt unsteady and allowed himself to fall back into his seat. "Glad to mee chuu," he managed to murmur. Maybe he didn't need to leave right away after all. This woman was a pretty hot-looking dish. He pushed his empty glass forward so that Jason could refill it.

The next thing Bill was aware of was waking up in a strange bed. He was completely undressed, and he had a terrible headache. He had no idea where he was. Then he remembered drinking with Jason the night before, He must have drunk too much. Perhaps he was still at Jason's house. He found his clothes on a chair next to the bed, dressed himself, opened the bedroom door, and walked out into the hall.

"Are we awake?" Jason asked cheerily. "Man! You really tied one on last night!"

"How did I end up in that bed? Did you undress me?"

"No, you undressed yourself. Either that or she did. Don't you remember? You got pretty rowdy last night. Man! You were really drunk! I had no idea that you'd had that much to drink. I thought the best thing was to invite you to stay. Are you sure your don't you remember? I couldn't let you drive home in that state, so I invited you to stay, and you accepted. Are you sure you don't remember?"

"What about that young woman? The one who called you uncle."

"Man! Your really don't remember, do you? You made a big impression on her. She went into your room to bid you good-night. I was a bit drunk myself and went to bed. I don't know what you two did after that. She's not really my niece, so whatever happened in your bedroom is no business of mine."

"I, I, I don't remember any of this. Nothing," Bill managed to stammer. "Are you sure that's what happened?" Inwardly the thought that he had made a conquest pleased him, but he wished he could remember it. What good did it do to get laid if you could remember nothing about it? That is, if he had gotten laid. He wasn't sure of anything.

"Look, Buddy, I've got some bacon and eggs cooking. Let me get you some breakfast, and after you've eaten, I'll see you to your car. Do you think you're in shape to drive? Do you want to shower up here?"

"I don't feel well. I think I'll skip the breakfast and shower and just drive home. Yeah, I can drive. I've driven home when I was in much worse shape than this. The cops know me. They won't stop me."

Bill went home to shower and change clothes. His wife was waiting at the door. "What happened to you last night? That's the first time you've ever stayed out all night without explanation. I've been worried sick about you. I was about to call the police."

"I'm afraid I got a little tipsy at Jason's house, and he was kind enough to let me stay the night. I should have called you. I really wasn't in shape to drive home."

"I really wish you'd do something about that drinking problem of yours," his wife said crossly. "Someday you're going to end up face down in an irrigation ditch."

"Yeah! Yeah! You've told me that before," Bill said as he headed toward the bathroom.

After he had showered and changed, Bill turned on the computer in his home office and checked his personal email. There was another one of those annoying spam messages in his in box, one with from an email address that ended in .ru. The subject read, "You'd better check out this picture, Bill!"

Bill didn't normally open such emails. He had been told that they could contain a virus and might damage his computer. This time, however, he had a sinking feeling that this wasn't a normal spam email. After all, his name was in the subject line. He opened it. A picture of him lying nude on the bed in Jason's guest room next to a nude woman half his age popped up on the screen. The young woman was the same one who had visited Jason's house the night before. He quickly closed the email before his wife could see it. He couldn't stop the tears that welled up in his eyes. If that picture ever became public, he would be a ruined man. If his wife or children ever saw it, his marriage would be over. "Jason's got me by the balls!" he thought to himself.

Bill hadn't been in his office in the State Capitol more than 15 minutes when his phone rang. It was Jason. Jason didn't mention the picture, but he didn't need to. "Bill, I just wanted to give you a heads up. I'm sending over my budget proposal this morning. I would be grateful if you could shepherd it through the legislature and make sure that it gets a fair hearing."

"Sure, Jason. I'll take care of it."

"Oh, and another thing, Bill, I know that you have quite a network of campaign donors. Do you think you could talk to a few of them and ask them to make a nice contribution to my campaign fund?"

"But, Jason, you've just been elected. Why do you need campaign money now?"

"Just do it, Bill. I have plans, and I'm going to need more campaign funds. I can't discuss those plans right now."

"Ok, Jason. I'll talk to my donors and see what I can do."

Jason had no problems getting his bills through the legislature after that conversation. Senate Leader Kandinsky proved very capable when it came to shepherding them through both the house and the senate.

Jason was one of the youngest people to ever sit in the governor's chair in Arizona. He was only 28 years old when he took office, only three years older than the minimum age to qualify for the office. He felt pretty satisfied with his life so far. He had grown up as the son of a laborer and had made himself into a successful leader of the business community and was now governor of one of the 50 states. He had only two problems. He was deeply in debt, and Maricopa County Sheriff Paul Balboni knew too much about the skeletons in his closet. He had to do something to solve both of those problems. He had a feeling that freeing himself from Paul Balboni would be more difficult. Like Jason, Paul had no conscience, and he had a lot more experience both in politics and in life than Jason. Oh, and then there was that actress that Paul had hired to ruin Alice Dickerson's primary campaign. If she talked, she could cause Jason big problems. He had no idea who she was, however. That was another secret that Paul could hold over his head.

Jason soon saw a way to start getting rid of his debts. The few freeways that existed in metropolitan Phoenix were becoming congested and needed widening. Federal funds were available to help with the project, but the Arizona Department of Transportation (ADOT) was heavily involved in the planning and letting of contracts. The project would require enormous amounts of concrete, signs, grading, land acquisition, etc. The bidding process for contracting out various aspect of the project was complicated, and Jason knew that in complexity there was an opportunity to make money. One section of ADOT's rules for letting contracts especially caught Jason's eye. It had to do with the procedure for dealing with errors: "Regardless of the reason [for the error], in order to get the Contractor to equitably adjust unit prices, the Department must show that the error or omission was readily apparent at the time of bidding. If the error or omission becomes apparent during construction, then the Department has no case...."

Jason assigned some of his most trusted administrative assistants to aid ADOT in writing the plans and specifications for the freeway-widening project. These administrative assistants had no knowledge of highway construction, but they were all people whom Jason had personally hired for their knowledge of taking advantage of loopholes. All of them had previously worked for financial organizations and were therefore quite used to putting their own financial advantage ahead of the welfare of their employer. Jason made sure that their interest and his were the same. He promised them fat bonuses in exchange for padding the budget for the construction project.

Under the guidance of Jason's people, the amount of work and materials written into the specifications ballooned far beyond what was required. Because a realistic price for widening the freeways through an urban area could run as high as eight million dollars per mile, there was plenty of room to pad the estimated costs. With more than 60 miles of freeway in the Phoenix metropolitan area to be widened, a realistic price for the whole contract might have been $480. Jason's assistants managed to inflate that to $620 million. Some of the engineers and accountants at ADOT realized that the modifications to the specifications were unrealistically expensive, but every time one of them brought the subject up, he or she received a threatening visit from someone representing the governor. Even decades later, when the fraud came to light, investigators were unable to untangle the complex web of paragraphs, subparagraphs, specifications, cross references, and ungrammatical sentences in the specifications.

Finding a crooked contractor to bid on the contract was not a problem. Arizona had a long history of land and construction swindles every since the first fraudster had managed to sell non-existent lots in a development project to unsuspecting easterners. When the investors came to Arizona carrying their worthless titles with the intention of claiming their lots, they found that the supposed development was located out in the desert far from water and was on federal land to boot.

But back to our story. Jason didn't dare have any direct communication with the firm that was to be awarded the contract in exchange for a substantial kickback. If any of the shenanigans surrounding the project came to light, Jason needed to have deniability. He personally had nothing to do with the contracting process, or at least it had to appear that way.

Once again Sheriff Paul Balboni came in handy. Being a crook himself, the sheriff knew just how to handle the situation, in exchange for a percentage of the kickback, of course. The sheriff had a man with a Russian accent contact Schissen Construction, LLC (Schissco for short) CEO Alexis Medvedev. The company had often been accused of doing substandard work, but so far, it had managed to get off by paying a few fines and was still landing government highway construction projects. Sheriff Baloni's man suggested that Medvedev bid on the entire package of contracts for $610 million and assured him that if he won the contract at that price, he would still be able to make a fat profit. Medvedev was to wire $10 million dollars to a bank account in the Cayman Islands as soon as the contract was awarded. The state would pay Schissco portions of the total contract monthly as work progressed. Schissco was to wire 10% of each payment to the same bank account within five business days of receiving it.

All of the other bids came in a $620 million or higher, and Schissco was awarded the contract. Paul demanded 50 percent of the take for his services. "That's outrageous!" was Jason's reply.

"Take it or leave it," Paul told him. "Without me you wouldn't have been able to set up this caper, and I have expenses. I spent a lot of money getting you elected governor. If you want to back out, we'll just let the whole deal collapse, and you can find your own crooked contractor. However, a novice like you is bound to get caught. You're pretty young to spend a decade or more in prison."

"You used Sheriff's Department funds to back my campaign."

"Oh, yeah? Just try to prove that. I've been playing this game a lot longer than you have."

Jason realized that once more Paul had him by the short hairs. Even after paying off Paul, by the time this construction project was finished, he would be a multimillionaire. In the meantime, he would surely find some additional ways to enrich himself. His car dealership was still making money, even though it was heavily indebted. He wouldn't have to live from his paltry $95,000 a year salary as governor.

One of Jason's problems was now solved. He would be able to pay off his debts, although he would have to do so gradually. Otherwise, he wouldn't be able to explain where he suddenly got the extra income. It was a shame to let so much money sit in an offshore bank while he lived relatively modestly, but someday he would be able to withdraw the money without attracting unwanted attention. He envisaged living anonymously in a villa in the south of France.

He needed some of the money immediately, but the money had to be laundered when he brought it into the country. He found a lawyer who could help him. The lawyer set up and LLC or limited liability company, which was ridiculously easy to do in Arizona. The LLC used money from the offshore account to buy non-existent cars from Wilder Motors, the funds from these imaginary sales were used to meet debt payments to the bank. The whole scheme was very risky, but as stated earlier, Jason thrived on risk.

His problems with Sheriff Paul Balboni were solved in a completely unexpected way. One of the things that made Sheriff Balboni popular among his Republican base was his hard line on immigration. His deputies had made several workplace raids, arresting people who could not prove that they were in the country legally and even some who could. He turned the arrestees over to the Department of Homeland Security for deportation. As his popularity among older white voters soared, he instructed his deputies to be even more proactive in hunting down "illegals." The deputies were to stop Hispanic-appearing drivers on any convenient pretext and ask them and any passengers in the car to prove that they had legal permission to be in the United States. If they couldn't prove it, the deputies were to call the Immigration and Customs Enforcement (ICE) to pick up the driver.

At first, ICE cooperated, but it turned out that many of the people the sheriff's deputies handed over to ICE were legal residents. Some were even US citizens. The resulting bad publicity caused ICE to announce that it would no longer respond to calls from sheriff's deputies. The negative publicity that ICE and Sheriff Balboni received in the national and even in the international press proved a boon to the Sheriff in Arizona. Here was a man who dared to stand up to the federal government.

Sheriff Balboni called a news conference and appeared before the TV cameras in an angry mood. "It's clear that our federal government refuses to protect our borders. We arrest illegals and turn them over to ICE, and what happens? An hour later, these scoundrels are back on the streets. If our government refuses to rid our country of these wets, I will make sure that they are deported from Maricopa County. I hereby declare Maricopa County to be a wetback-free zone."

His stance made him very popular with his political base but caused concern among human rights activists. A spokesperson for the Arizona Latino Rights Organization (ALRO) organized a demonstration against the sheriff in front of his offices on Jackson Street in downtown Phoenix. ALRO spokesperson Leticia Osorio Corona faced the TV cameras and gave interviews in both English and Spanish. "Paul Balboni thinks he is above the law. He cares nothing for the values of this country. He has declared himself to be legislator, judge, jury, and enforcer with no regard for the rights of Latinos. He has made it a crime to be driving while brown."

There was a counter demonstration across the street made up mainly of middle-aged and older white people shouting "Go back to Mexico!" and "Go back to your own country!" Leticia was a third-generation American. Her family had lived in Arizona longer than the families of the people who were trying to shout her down, and these newcomers had the gall to tell her to "go home."

The demonstrations, of course, made Sheriff Balboni even more popular among a certain class of poorly educated and mostly elderly whites who would have preferred to see the backs of everyone with brown skin. His popularity among these people took another jump when he began putting a new deportation plan into action.

Now, instead of turning suspected illegal immigrants over to ICE, sheriff's deputies sent them to the County Jail. Every day, a Sheriff Department bus full of arrestees left the County jailhouse in downtown Phoenix and headed for the Mexican border in Nogales. The bus's occupants were chained to their seats. Once the bus arrived at the border, the detainees were freed one at a time and instructed to walk through the entry gate into Mexico. This informal deportation was in direct violation of federal law, of course, but Sheriff Balboni believed that laws were written for other people to obey, not for him. Again, standing up to the federal government increased his popularity among his supporters in Arizona.

It turned out that not all of the people deported in this manner were in the United States illegally, but once they were deported even United States citizens had trouble getting back into the country, because they had no passports or border-crossing cards with them. How many United States citizens carry proof of citizenship on a daily basis? Spanish-language TV stations in Phoenix reported almost weekly on some American citizen stranded on the Mexican side of the border trying to get back to Arizona.

One case that was highlighted in both the English- and Spanish-language press concerned Susan Bonilla. She had been stopped while driving, allegedly because her car had a broken taillight. It also turned out that her driver's license had expired. She felt sure that she had been stopped solely because she had very dark brown skin. Had she been white, these infractions would have resulted in nothing more than a traffic ticket, but because she was brown, she was taken to jail without being told the reason for her arrest. She was held for three days without being allowed to telephone her family or a lawyer before she was put in a bus, shipped to Nogales, and forced to walk through the border exit gate.

Her husband Emiliano and her two children were crazy with worry, because they didn't know what had happened to her. They reported her missing to the Glendale, Arizona police, but the police officer who came to take their report didn't seem to take the matter seriously. "These Mexicans were always cheating on each other," he told his partner. "She'll be back just as soon as she gets tired of whichever guy she ran off with." However, he did go through the motions of filing a missing-person report.

Emiliano called the Sheriff's Office, because someone who was undocumented and therefore didn't want and direct contact with the police had told him that his wife had been stopped by a sheriff's patrol car, but the deputy who answered the phone denied any knowledge of his wife's whereabouts and insisted that it was a matter for the Glendale Police to handle.

On the Mexican side of the border, Susan was a fish out of water. She was a native-born United States citizen who had never before been in Mexico and who couldn't speak Spanish. She found herself in a foreign country with no money and no identification (her expired driver's license had been confiscated). She didn't even have the Mexican coins needed to use a pay phone.

She went to the border crossing, but officials there refused to believe her claim that she was a United States citizen. Finally, a complete stranger took pity on her and allowed her to use his phone card to call her husband Emiliano in Glendale and ask him to get her birth certificate out of the safe deposit box in the bank and bring it to Nogales. Unfortunately, it was Friday evening when she called, and the bank didn't open until Monday. She spent two nights sleeping in the streets in Nogales, Mexico, and during the second night she was raped.

When Emiliano finally arrived on Monday, the two of them had a difficult time persuading US immigration officials that she was an American citizen who had been unjustly deported by a renegade sheriff. The officials weren't sure that the birth certificate was genuine and belonged to her. However, on Monday evening they finally let her cross the border, and she was soon in her Emiliano's car heading home.

Emiliano called as many news organizations as possible, and at least a dozen reporters showed up to interview her. All of the English-language newspapers buried the story somewhere in the inside pages, and some English-language TV stations didn't cover the story at all. In the Spanish-language media, however, Susan's story was given top billing. The Spanish-language nationwide TV network Spanovisión opened its evening newscast with a live interview of Susan from its affiliate station in Phoenix. Eventually, the story was picked up by the national news media, and it was only then that the English-language press in Phoenix finally gave the story the attention it deserved. It caused a sensation in an already racially divided city.

The Bonilla family filed a lawsuit against Maricopa County for $200 million, which the County settled out of court three years later for half that much. The settlement would come too late to benefit Emiliano, who by that time would be behind bars serving a life sentence, but it would enable Susan and her children to move out of Arizona to Southern California, where they felt more welcome.

Maricopa County frequently paid out large sums of money to settle damage claims caused by Sheriff Balboni's running roughshod over the law, but for some reason, his band of supporters continued to muster enough support to get the sheriff reelected. These damage claims came out of the County's general fund and not out of the Sheriff's Department budget. Because Paul Balboni was an elected official, the County supervisors were powerless to discipline him.

Emiliano was a hothead, and he wasn't about to wait for the slow process of justice to take its course. Even if the family eventually won the suit against the county, Sheriff Balboni wouldn't be affected in the least.

Three weeks after Emiliano brought his wife back from Nogales, as Sheriff Balboni was giving a press conference in front of his office on Jefferson Street to publicize his latest immigration raid, a slim, ordinary-looking brown-skinned man slowly pushed his way through the crowd until he was standing at the sheriff's side. Suddenly he pulled a pistol out of his waistband and fired one shot at close range which struck Sheriff Balboni in the head. Sheriff's deputies wrestled Emiliano to the ground before he could get off a second shot, but the first bullet had done its job. An ambulance arrived within minutes and carried the sheriff away. He never regained consciousness and died the next day in a Phoenix hospital. Emiliano was arrested, held without bail, severely beaten by guards in jail, charged with and tried for murder, and eventually sent to prison. He never regretted what he had done.

Jason's second problem was now solved, and he felt on top of the world. His governorship was proving to be quite lucrative. In addition to his governor's salary, he had considerable income from his auto dealership. Sales had skyrocketed now that he was governor. However, his largest source of income was one that he dare not reveal on his income tax returns, the kickbacks he managed to extort for the awarding of state contracts. He was making progress on paying his debts and had a fortune stashed in his offshore bank account.

Arizona governors are allowed two terms in office, and Jason had decided to run for a second term. He no longer had Paul Balboni to manage his political campaign, but he had built up his own network independent of the Republican Party, and he still had great support among Arizona's large and influential retirement community. He also had Martin Glover's word that the Arizona Republican Party would back him this time and would do its best to stop anyone from opposing him in the primary election. If he could win the nomination, Jason was pretty sure he could triumph in the general election given Arizona's propensity to elect Republicans to statewide office. In Maricopa County it was almost unheard-of for a Republican to lose in a race for a countywide seat, and more than 60 percent of Arizona's population lived in Maricopa County.

Jason had his sights set higher than the governorship of Arizona. In the lofty image he had of his own worth, he could envision himself serving as president of the United States. However, he was still too young to run. Jason's 31st birthday would be on June 13, and presidential candidates had to be at least 35 years old. What a stupid rule! If he wanted to remain influential in politics, his two choices were to run for a second term as governor or to run for the United States Senate. Running for reelection as governor seemed to be the best choice. He didn't want to be some anonymous, first-term senator with no political clout.

Jason had many enemies, and his reelection was far from a sure bet. Civil rights groups including the Association of Latino Voters and the Arizona Latino Rights Organization denounced him. However, voter turnout among Arizona's Hispanic population was low, so Jason gave these groups little notice. The support that still counted most for any Arizona Republican politician was that of older white voters, especially those who lived in the Phoenix-area suburbs and retirement communities and whose only contact with Latinos was with the men who mowed their lawns and the women who cleaned their houses. Despite the fact that those voters were taking advantage of dirt-cheap labor, they believed that Arizona was under assault from hordes of illegal Mexican immigrants, and Jason did all he could to stoke those fears and their mistrust of the distant Federal Government.

"The people in Washington are doing absolutely nothing to secure our border and protect us from these illegals," he started his speech in front of an elderly audience at the Sunrise Retirement Community. "I have done everything possible to get the feds to do their job, and it isn't working. It's time for us to act on our own. When I am reelected, I will double the size of Arizona's National Guard and place 20,000 troops on our border with Mexico. I also have a plan to have armed citizen militias patrol the border to intercept illegal border crossers and greet them with a hail of lead."

His speech was met with applause and cheers from those present but was criticized the next day in editorials in the press and on public television. "I welcome the attacks by the liberal media," was Jason's response. "The more those left-wingers denounce me, the more I know that I'm on the right track. Those snobs who run the liberal media are people who hate America and are trying to turn this great nation into an effeminate country like France. They want to take away our right to bear arms, and they want each of us to live next door to a Mexican. If we don't do something, pretty soon they'll hire Mexicans to go door to door and confiscate our guns."

Jason's opponent in his second campaign for governor was the Democrat Jerry Pierson. Jerry was the son of a former Arizona governor who had served in the times when the proportion of Democrats and Republicans in the state was more equal. He had also served two terms as mayor of Phoenix and was widely regarded by Phoenix residents as having done a good job.

Jason was almost sure that Jerry would carry the vote in the Democratic-leaning cities of Tucson and Phoenix. Jason would have to win the vote of a large majority in the far more conservative suburbs of these cities and in the rural areas and small towns.

Jason had conceded that the liberal-leaning Tucson newspaper *The Daily Star* would back Jerry, but he was taken by surprise when the normally conservative Phoenix paper *The Arizona Republic* also endorsed Jerry and blasted Jason in a front-page editorial as "arguably the worst governor in Arizona history." Worse yet, he was shocked a few days later when one of his aides rushed into his office with a copy of that day's *Republic*. "Boss! you've got to read this!" Below the fold, on the first page, was the headline "Wilder's ex-wife backs Pierson." The story started, "Guadalupe (Lupita) Wilder, the former wife of governor

Jason Wilder, announced at a Pierson rally yesterday evening that she would back Wilder's opponent, Jerry Pierson, for governor of Arizona." Two paragraphs later she was quoted as saying, "I know Jason better than anyone else. I had the misfortune to be married to that jerk, the worst experience of my life. He is not a normal human being with normal feelings and emotions. I entreat all voters in Arizona not to vote for my ex-husband. I will vote for, and I hope you will vote for, Jerry Pierson for governor of Arizona."

Wow! That was a heavy blow!

Then Jason's secretary entered his office. "I've been getting lots of calls from reporters who want to speak with you. I've been putting them off as you usually have me do, but they're getting pretty persistent. Do you want me to keep telling them that you're not available?"

"No, I might as well face the music. Put them through, one at a time."

The first reporter on the phone was from the *Detroit Free Press*. Even the out-of-state news outlets were picking up the story! The reporter wanted to know if Jason had heard his former wife's remarks and what his response was. Jason decided that the best defense was a good offense. It didn't matter whether what he said was true or not. Some of it would stick in voters' minds. Few voters bothered to check facts.

"Yes, I was married to Lupita, and she took me for every penny I had. I was forced to borrow money to pay my legal fees. There is a reason why we divorced. She was more interested in another man than she was in me. Now she's obviously not content with having married and divorced me for my money, she wants to destroy me, as well. She's working with the other Mexicans who want to take over this state and drive us white people out. This is our state, and no Mexican is going to take it over as long as I am governor."

"Are you saying she's lying? Are you accusing her of being part of some sort of conspiracy?"

"Does the bear piss in the woods? Wait! Don't print that! Here's a quote you can use: 'That woman is incapable of telling the truth. She certainly took me for a ride, pretending to love me while she was dilly-dallying with another man.'"

"Are you accusing her of having an affair with Jerry Pierson?"

"No, I'm sure he's not one of her lovers. I don't think Jerry is interested in women. He's not married, and he doesn't even have a girlfriend. There's something funny about him that maybe you should look into. No, Lupita's motive is just pure meanness. She wants to make my life as miserable as possible. She has absolutely no conscience."

Jason himself could see the absurdity of accusing Lupita of very mental problem that he was astute enough to know he himself had. Problem? In his case it wasn't a problem. It gave him an advantage over the weaklings who had stupid ideas such as the difference between right and wrong.

Jason handled the remaining phone calls in a similar fashion, and his lies to the press bore fruit. It didn't matter that Jerry went in front of the microphone to deny Jason's allegations with his girlfriend by his side. Many people thought there was something funny about him. The gossip did not stop.

"Where did Pierson dig up that broad?" was a typical remark heard at one of the Phoenix sports bars. "He must have paid her a lot of money to get her to pretend to be his girlfriend. The latest is that have announced that they're getting engaged. Getting engaged? People don't announce that they're going to get engaged; they just do it. When he was mayor of Phoenix, you never saw him cast a glance at a pretty girl. He was always looking at the little boys."

Jason was elated at having turned a potentially embarrassing situation to his opponent's disadvantage. Almost no one remembered what Lupita had said about him. The debate at the water coolers and in the barrooms became so bizarre that people began to argue about whether or not Jerry was a pedophile, although even Jason had only hinted that he might be and never openly accused him.

Nonetheless, Jason knew that the election was going to be close. Jerry Pierson had been a good mayor of Phoenix, and Jason knew that some voters were smart enough to realize that Jason was a lousy governor, out for his own interests, and not giving a damn about the welfare of the state. What did Lincoln say? You can't fool all of the people all of the time or something like that?

Jason admitted to himself that Jerry Pierson would be a much better governor than he was, but he didn't really care about what was best for the state. The important thing was to be reelected so he could keep lining his own pocket until he found an easier way to keep the money flowing into his offshore bank account.

Jason had learned a lot about campaigning. He knew, for example, that candidates who developed elaborate policies or gave detailed explanations about solving problems were much less frequently elected than were candidates who shot from the hip and made outrageous, disconnected statements. Most voters paid no attention to the fact checkers and considered them to be weirdo lefties who believed in such absurdities as global warming, evolution, and gun control. They were probably all atheists. The important thing was to stress "true conservative values," a phrase that Jason never tired of repeating. Jason wasn't sure what those values were, but he did know how to talk about them in a superficial manner: stress the right of everyone to carry a gun, talk up Protestant Christian values, rail against the oppressive government in Washington, complain that the country was being overrun with illegal immigrants, affirm that the media were controlled by effete liberals, berate the pro-abortion crowd, etc.

It also paid to appeal to people who were likely to vote and ignore everybody else. In the 18-to-35 age group, roughly 20 percent of registered voters went to the polls. In the 60-and-above age group, more than 60 percent of them did. Paradoxically, less-well-educated people were more likely to vote than college students. Only about one third of Arizona's large Hispanic population bothered to vote. Jason's target group was older, lesser-educated white folks. They voted. Let the Democrat appeal to the young and Hispanic, who would sit at home guzzling beer on election day.

Chapter 7 — Presidential Campaign

The year was 2010 Jason was in the second term as Arizona governor when he received a phone call from Luther Hogson, the elder of the two billionaire Hogson brothers who had inherited a fortune from their father and increased it greatly by cornering the silver market a decade earlier. They were known to be generous contributors to ultraconservative political candidates.

"I won't beat around the bush. Willard and I want you to run for president next year. We're willing to finance you to the tune of $300 million dollars. We'll give you 24 hours to think it over."

"President?" Jason was taken completely by surprise. "But, but, don't you think I'm pretty young to be president? I just turned 35 last year. Is this a joke?"

Luther was not so easily deterred. "Believe me, I'm not joking. You're over 35, so you're old enough to be president. It's true that you'll be the youngest president in US history, but there's a first for everything. If Willard and I pick you to be president, you'll be president."

Jason's still couldn't believe that he was talking to one of the richest men in the world. He stalled for time to try to collect his thoughts. "But to run for president, you have to be known nationally. No one outside of Arizona knows who I am."

"Don't worry about getting known. Willard and I will take care of that. If you agree to run as our candidate, on the Republican ticket naturally, we'll make sure that everyone in the world who isn't living in a cave will know who you are. I don't want your answer now. This call has to come as a surprise to you, but I'm not the type of person to be put off. You have 24 hours to make up your mind. I'll call you again tomorrow at about this time."

The phone clicked and the connection was broken. In the old days of metal telephones that sat on desks or tables, you could hear someone slamming down the receiver on the other end. Now, with cordless electronic phones, the person on the other end pushed a button and the connection just went dead. Jason often thought that it made hanging up on someone much less satisfying that it used to be.

Jason was so shaken after the call that he couldn't get up from his seat. The Hogson brothers! Every politician and every political commentator knew who the Hogson Brothers were. They were among the richest billionaires in the world, although no one knew for sure exactly how much money they possessed. *Forbes Magazine* estimated their net worth at $57 billion, but that was probably a low figure. The Hogson Brothers were publicity shy, never gave interviews, and kept their finances as secret as they could. It was rumored that much of their wealth was hidden in a complex network of offshore banks and holding companies that even the Internal Revenue Department couldn't untangle.

In addition to being fantastically rich, they were the most powerful political figures in the United States, perhaps in the world. They pulled strings behind the curtain to get people elected to public office. Many people thought that the Hogson Brothers had the president of the United States in their pockets, and from what Jason had just heard, they apparently did. The president had promised to raise taxes on high income earners during his campaign, but now that he was in office, he seemed to have a cozy relationship with Wall Street. Could that be due to the Hogsons' influence? Some even claimed that the Hogsons were the real power behind Vladimir Putin, although that seemed farfetched.

Jason was in no position to finance even a minimalist campaign for president himself. True, he now had over $100 million stashed away in the Cayman Islands bank account, but he couldn't use that dirty money to finance a campaign. Every dollar that his campaign committee spent would be open to public scrutiny, and he would risk going to jail if it came to light that he had taken bribes and avoided paying income tax on them.

On the other hand, the Hogson Brothers wouldn't finance his run for president unless there was something in it for them. Would there be anything left over for Jason? Jason was used to being in charge, and it would go against his nature to take orders from the Hogsons, even if it meant getting even richer.

There was no one with whom he could talk over the situation. He hadn't spoken to Lupita since shortly after their separation. Oh, Lupita! That reminded him that no one in modern history had been elected president who hadn't had an apparently loving wife by his side. Had there been any bachelor presidents at all? Jason did an online search. Oh, yes, there had been. James Buchanan was a lifelong bachelor, but he was elected in 1857. Times had changed since then. Grover Cleveland was also single when he was inaugurated in 1885. Could Jason be the third bachelor to become president? Actually, bachelor wasn't the correct term. He was divorced, a word that had once had a nasty connotation, but now divorced people were grouped together with the never married under the rubric "single." Ronald Reagan had been divorced when he ran for president, but he had remarried. Being divorced was not the stigma that it used to be.

Jason couldn't sleep well that night. To say that he was an unemotional person was an understatement, but that night he did feel excitement. Even if he were not elected, even if he were not even nominated, the mere fact of running for president would be of immeasurable financial value. After he retired as president, he could picture himself being paid hundreds of thousands of dollars to fill a seat on the board of directors of several large companies, sinecures with juicy salaries that required no work. Even during his term as president, there must be some way of earning some money on the side. After all, Lyndon Johnson started his political carrier as a Texas schoolteacher and ended it as a multimillionaire. Did the Hogson Brothers really have the power to get a 36-year-old divorced man elected president? If they did, would they own him? Was he about to make the Faustian error of selling his soul to the devil? If Hell really existed, which Jason doubted, he had long ago consigned his soul to its eternal fires. In for a penny, in for a pound.

The next day it was Willard who called. "You talked to my brother Luther yesterday, and he made you a proposition. Are you ready to accept?"

"I assume you want something in return." Jason said, still not sure that he was willing to give those brothers so much control over his life.

"If you don't get elected, you'll owe us nothing, but that is not probable. When you do get elected—and with our backing I can guarantee you that you will—we'll want your support on some legislation we'll propose. There'll be people in Congress who will make sure the bills get through both chambers, but we want your word that you won't veto them or oppose them in any way. We also want you to initiate some of them."

Jason was still hesitant to accept and attempted to drag the conversation out. "How are you going to get people in Congress to back your bills?"

"That's our business! Look, I'm not going to spend all day on the phone beating around the bush with you. Either you're with us or you're not. I want to know right now. Are you with us? There are plenty of other people willing to work with us."

"OK," Jason replied, "I'm with you."

"I know you're officially not in good financial shape."—At least the Hogsons didn't know about his offshore bank account.—"Your car lots are a financial mess. We know about your secret offshore bank account, but we also realize that you can't touch that money without getting into trouble with the law."—Damn! These Hogsons seemed to know everything.—"You can save that money for your retirement. You won't have to touch it as long as you're working for us. We'll take care of you.

"You'll soon receive a visit from someone who will give you the number of a secret account in Switzerland into which $100,000 has already been deposited. He'll also give you an ATM card that you can use to withdraw up to $500 a day. You will nominally be in charge of your campaign, but we'll make all the decisions. We'll tell you who to pick as your campaign manager, we'll make sure that you get campaign donations, and we'll establish several independent educational organizations that will run ads against your opponents and praise your ideas, which will be our ideas, of course. All you will do is travel, deliver speeches, hold rallies, and give interviews. We'll write your speeches for you, and we'll supply you with talking points to answer questions from the press. Understood?"

"Yes, I get it."

The phone line suddenly went dead. These Hogsons certainly wasted no time with pleasantries. That was the last that Jason was to hear directly from either of the Hogson brothers until his presidency was over.

Five minutes later Jason's phone rang again. It was his secretary. "There's a gentleman here to see you. He says his name is Gerald Wilkinson. He says you're expecting him." Jason suspected that this visit had something to do with the phone call he had just finished.

"Show him in."

As soon as the door closed behind the visitor, he opened his briefcase and put a wad of $50 bills on Jason's desk. "This should hold you over until you need more. Here's your ATM card for the Swiss account. It looks like a membership card in the American Youth Hostels, but its magnetic strip is programmed as an ATM card. Just insert it in any ATM and you can withdraw money. Your PIN number is the four digit year when your ex-wife was born."

Without giving Jason time to respond, the visitor turned on his heel, opened the office door and walked out, quietly closing the door behind him, and leaving his empty briefcase standing open on the floor next to Jason's desk.

Jason was flabbergasted. It was like something from the mafia days of the 1920s, but even then, politicians had had some independence from the mob. It was hard for him to believe that he had just sold himself to a pair of modern day mobsters passing for legitimate businessmen. However, the pay was good. Jason was used to turning every relationship to his own advantage, but this time he didn't think he could gain control of the situation. The forces that had just taken control of him were much too powerful. He had just sold his soul to the Hogson Brothers, just as Johannes Faust had sold his soul to Mephistopheles in the famous German legend.

About two hours later, his phone rang again, and his secretary told him there was a man named Shawn Killingworth on the phone. "He said to tell you that he represents 'the brothers' and you would want to talk to him."

"Put him through."—Then after a pause, "Mr. Killingworth?"

"Yes, but you should call me Shawn. I'll be your campaign manager in your run for president."

"That was fast! I just talked to Mr. Hogson a bit earlier today."

"Yeah, those Hogsons don't let any grass grow under their feet. At any rate, as I said, I'm your new campaign manager. We need to get started. You have a difficult year and a half ahead of you. Are you up to it?"

Jason was not used to things happening so quickly. "How much do you get paid, and how do I pay you?"

"You needn't concern yourself with those matters. I work for the Hogson Corporation. They pay me. I'm a salaried employee.

However, we have a grueling series of primary elections to get through. If you think running for governor was tough, you ain't seen nuthin' yet. You can plan on spending the next eighteen months living on the point of exhaustion."

"Have you managed presidential campaigns before?" Jason asked.

"Yeah, I guess you have a right to know a little about me. Let me give you a quick summary. I was a young, star-eyed volunteer in Ronald Reagan's campaign in 1980 and again in 1984. By time George Bush senior ran, I had worked my way up to a paid position, and I travelled from state to state as part of a team setting up his campaign appearances in advance. I worked for Bob Dole in 1996, and we got him nominated. We could have had him elected president if he had followed our advice, but after he won the nomination he started to think he didn't need us. He convinced himself that he had won the nomination on his own merits, so we dumped him and left him to his fate. Let that be a lesson to you.

"After the Dole campaign, I was hired by the Hogson Brothers to manage their political interests. It was my organization that got George Bush junior elected. In fact, I was the guy who came up with the phrase 'compassionate conservative.' By the end of his first term, the public realized that he was a lousy president and that our two guys, Cheney and Rumsfeld, were really running the country, but we managed to get him re-elected anyway. Without our help, he would have been a one-term president. Unfortunately, he got uppity and stopped listening to us in the middle of his second term and started doing things his own way. He fired Rumsfeld and stopped listening to Cheney. He refused to take orders from us. Getting Bush reelected was a big mistake. We would have been better off letting John Kerry run the country. Kerry is an honest man, and we would have had no influence with him, but it would have been better for us to have him in the White House than that intellectually challenged bastard who suddenly decided in his sixth year in office that he was going to act like a real president. We learned from that. We won't make that mistake again. In the future, anyone who doesn't toe the line is going to pay a big price and not simply end up as a pariah as Bush has.

"I next managed John McCain's campaign, and I would have gotten him elected, but he insisted on proving that he was a maverick and wouldn't take my orders. He picked that idiot Sarah Palin as his running mate, even though I pleaded with him not to. That was another mistake we made. As we did with Dole, we dumped McCain after we got him nominated. When you make a mistake that big, the best thing to do is discard the candidate and cut your losses."

Jason interrupted. "But Sarah Palin was the sweetheart of the conservatives. Wasn't she a plus on the Republican ticket?"

"She may have been the sweetheart of some of the stupider conservatives, but everybody else could see that she has very little between the ears. Can you imagine what a disaster it would have been if something had happened to McCain in office and Palin had become president? She's too much of an airhead to even understand our orders let alone carry them out."

"I see your point," Jason replied.

"There's a reason I'm telling you all this. If you want to get elected, you'll do things our way. Rebel and we'll drop you like a hot potato, and even worse might happen to you. We know about the skeletons you have in the closet.

"Obama is up for re-election. He's a popular president, and he'll be hard to defeat. He's not a bad president from our point of view. He plays along with us halfway. For example, he made sure that the bankers who made themselves rich and crashed the economy during the Bush administration got off scot-free. The Hogsons made billions from that crash, and Obama made sure that no one's the wiser. The poor bastards whose retirement funds owned the banks' stock and the mortgage-backed securities got stuck with the bill."

Jason was impressed. "There's no way I could run for president at this time of my life if it weren't for you and the Hogson brothers. Don't worry. I'm completely in your hands, but speaking of getting rich, is there any possibility that I might end up well-off?"

"Behave yourself, and do as we tell you, and we'll make sure you get a cut of the action."

"Are you sure you can get me elected?"

"No question. The Supreme Court did us a big favor recently, for which I will modestly claim some of the credit. Starting this year, supposedly independent political action committees will be able to spend unlimited money on the primaries. The Hogson brothers are willing to spend whatever it takes to get their man into the White

House. We'll be running all sorts of 'independent' ads slinging mud at your opponents and praising you, and thanks to our buddies on the Supreme Court, no one will be able to trace where the money came from."

There's not enough space in this book to go through the primary process in detail, so I'll just give you an overview. If I were to print here all of the things that Jason told me in our interviews before his death, you would be astounded. You may be under the impression that the president of the United States is selected by a democratic process. Nothing could be farther from the truth. A small number of very rich, mostly white, and mostly male oligarchs pick the president all the while putting on a show to make it look as if the president were selected by the will of the people.

Campaigning had to begin in 2011. The primaries, which normally begin in February, started right after New Year due to a revolt of the state Republican parties against headquarters in Washington. Traditionally, the primary season begins with the Iowa caucuses in the first week of February followed a week later by the New Hampshire primary. Then come the Nevada caucuses and the South Carolina primary. In 2012, a number of states moved their primaries ahead of Iowa to January in the hopes of getting more national attention by displacing Iowa's reputation as "first in the nation." Not wanting to give up their importance in the nomination race, Iowa and New Hampshire pushed their caucus and primary election respectively to just after New Year. The Iowa caucus was held on January 3, a day when many voters had still not shaken off the effects of their New Year's hangovers. By the time an attenuated Super Tuesday rolled around on March 6, 13 states had already held their presidential primaries.

Jason followed an exhausting schedule flying from state to state to campaign, but he consoled himself with the thought that the other candidates were working even harder, because they did not have the support organization behind them that he had. The other candidates had to spend part of their time begging for donations, for example. Jason didn't have that responsibility. Jason also didn't have to worry about spending time with a team of speechwriters. A week before each campaign appearance, a courier arrived with the speeches he was to give the following week. Luckily, there was enough repetition that he was almost able to memorize the speeches and could deliver them with only an occasional glance at his notes:

"The Constitution guarantees every American citizen the right to bear arms, and I'll make sure that the Constitution is obeyed. When I'm president, every illegal immigrant will be shipped back to Mexico. I promise to scrap the Federal Reserve, which is printing money so fast that it's ruining our country by promoting run-away inflation. I will also do away with the hated Internal Revenue Service that is bleeding Americans dry and taking away money the rightfully belongs to them. If you earned the money, it belongs to you and not to the government. Thanks to the conspiracy between the dysfunctional Obama administration, the big banks, and the Federal Reserve, inflation is eating up the paychecks of the average worker. We can stop inflation dead in its tracks by returning to the gold standard."

Jason now understood why the Hogson brothers had picked him as their candidate. Except for the promise to abolish the Federal Reserve and Internal Revenue Service and go back to the gold standard, most of the points in the speeches could have been lifted from his speeches when he ran for governor. Even Jason realized that these ideas were nuts. Returning to the gold standard was an especially dim-witted idea that appealed to people who didn't know enough about economics to balance their own checkbooks and if implemented would take the United State economy back the Stone Age era of bartering. He couldn't believe that the Hogson brothers wanted any of these things to happen, but he understood their appeal to the dumbbells who voted for rightwing candidates. He was enough of a politician by now to know the wisdom of promising the voters whatever they wanted to hear, even if those promises were beyond ridiculous and you had no intention of keeping them.

However, there were differences in the speeches written for different states. The nominating process began with the caucuses in Iowa. Shawn told him that he would "be spending most of his time in the northwest part of the state. "That's where our people are. It's very important that you come across as a conservative Protestant fundamentalist."

Jason didn't understand. "Why is Iowa so important?. Iowa sends less than one percent of the delegates to the Republican Convention."

"Yeah, but it's 'First in the Nation,' and gets more press coverage than any other state during the primary season. The press writes that whoever wins the Iowa caucuses has 'momentum.' If you can get voters to believe that, you start a bandwagon effect. People want to be able to brag that they voted for the winner."

Jason had another objection, "I'm not religious—in fact I'm an atheist—but I was baptized Catholic. How am I going to come across as a Bible-thumping rightwing Protestant?"

Shawn had an easy answer for that one. "You're a good actor, Jason. Watch the religious TV stations, and you'll soon get a feel for how to scam those people. The preachers on religious TV have the act down to a science. Some of them are boozers and maintain harems of mistresses, but when they're in front of the TV cameras, they slip into a very self-righteous role. Think of Jim and Tammy Baker. If they can fake it, you can fake it. If people think that you have the same religious values that they have, they're not going to question which church you go to."

"Or don't go to," Jason added.

The speeches Jason was to deliver in Iowa all stressed the need for much larger federal government subsidies for ethanol. "Why do we want to push more federal subsidies?" Jason was puzzled. "I thought I was supposed to be against big government."

"You are against big government and for bigger ethanol subsidies at the same time. You don't understand the conservative mind. They're all against big government when they see the other guy's snout in the trough. When it comes to their own interests, they all want to milk the government for every cent they can. Iowa grows lots of corn, which is used to make ethanol. Giving food to the poor is anathema to conservative values. Using taxpayer money to give government subsidies to rich farmers fits right in with conservative ideology."

Jason had known next to nothing about Iowa before the campaign started. He quickly learned that so-called "Christian values," were of utmost important to Iowa Republicans, especially in in the northwest corner of the state where he held up to three rallies a day. He also learned that Christian values had their limit. Fundamentalist Christian values were very much aimed at giving more benefits to the already well off. They did not include sympathy for the poor, the immigrants, or people with a darker skin color. Jason could see the influence of people like the Hogsons in shaping these peoples' opinions. There was no other explanation for the fact that so many people were ready to act against their own interests by demanding that the government give their money to people who were already fabulously wealthy.

Iowa has a largely rural population with scattered small towns and no real cities. Only three percent of the population is black and only a bit over five percent is Latino. Almost 90 percent of the population identifies as white, non-Hispanic compared to 62 percent of the nation as a whole. Most Iowan Republicans had no idea about the problems of non-whites, and most of them didn't want to know. "Send those people back where they came from!" was a popular refrain.

"Ethanol is essential in reducing air pollution in our country," Jason declaimed before one rural gathering after another. "When I am president, I will mandate that gasoline sold in the United States contain at least 30 percent ethanol. That is essential so that our children and grandchildren have clean air to breath." Christian values could include a bit of environmentalism, as long as the environmentalism lined the pockets of the believer.

"I also promise to increase all federal farm subsidies. Our farm families are the backbone of American society, and I promise that I will protect them. My grandparents were small farmers in Europe who came to this country, because in Europe farmers were starving to death. Here they were welcomed. I learned about farming at my grandparents' knees. Farming is in my roots. Our government needs to do more to support farmers and preserve our cherished American values."

His grandparents probably didn't even know which end of a hoe to pick up, and as far as that was concerned, neither did Jason, but this was politics, and "stretching the truth," as Shawn called it, was par for the course.

And on religion: "When I was a young man, I led a life of sin and depravity. I drank alcohol, and I fornicated. Then the Lord appeared to me in a dream and told me that I was saved. He lifted me from my sinful life and set me on a straight path. Glory be to God! I accepted Jesus Christ our Lord as my savior. Hallelujah! And it was God who appeared to me and told me to run for president to save this sinful nation. We are living in the last days. The Lord is about to appear on Earth again, and when he does, those of us who have been saved will go with him to live in Heaven. Those who have not accepted Jesus Christ will descend into the fires of Hell and spend eternity in unspeakable anguish. I am so grateful to the Lord for havin' chosen me to save this great nation and return it to its former splendor. Glory to God!"

To which many in the audience replied in chorus, "Amen."

The whole time Jason was eyeing a particularly buxom woman in the front row and thinking to himself, "Boy! Would I like to screw her!"

"When I am elected president," Jason continued, "I will make sure that this country is run accordin' to strict Christian values."—Jason was trying to remember to drop his g's as he spoke.—I will do everything in my power to overturn Roe v Wade and make sure that the lives of unborn children are held sacred."

Again, there were cries of "Amen!" from the audience, louder this time.

Of course, none of this was true. Jason was not only a baptized Catholic, he hadn't been inside a church since he was a teenager on the rare occasions when his parents had managed to rope him into attending mass. As to abortion, he didn't care one way or another. He was lucky enough to be a man and was never going to get knocked up, so why should he care? Pregnancy and abortions were women's problems.

In New Hampshire, the message was different. In Iowa, only 25 percent of the population had graduated from a university, and most of the college educated were Democrats. In New Hampshire, 33 percent of the population had at least a bachelor's degree, and some college graduates were Republicans, even though the Republican Party had been losing influence among the better educated since the 1990s when the far right began to take over the party. However, Jason's job was to appeal to the conservative Republicans who now formed the core of the New Hampshire Republican Party and not to the people who used to be Republicans. That meant dumbing down his message not quite as much as he had done in Iowa but more than he would have done if he were campaigning in the general election. He would worry about the Democrats and independent voters when the general election rolled around and hope that they had forgotten his primary speeches by then.

"One of the first things I'm gonna' do when I'm elected is overturn Obamacare. People should have the right to choose which healthcare insurance they want to buy or whether they buy health insurance at all. It's un-American to tax people and force them to give money to the big insurance companies against their will. That's not what this great country stands for."

Jason spent most of his time flying back and forth between Iowa and New Hampshire with occasional forays into other early primary states such as South Carolina. He had a bus permanently stationed in Iowa with "Jason for President" painted on both sides in bright red letters. No matter where he was in Iowa, he railed against taxes.

"My plan is to introduce a flat tax. Everyone in America will pay the same tax rate, and it will be fair to all. I will also eliminate corporate income taxes. We need to attract industry back from places like China and Mexico and provide jobs for Americans, not for the Chinese. Zero income tax on corporations will encourage companies like Apple to bring their profits back to America and stop hiding them in overseas accounts. When that money is in America, it will make our economy stronger and make us all more prosperous. It's time to make America great again! This country was chosen by God to lead the world. Under the Democrats, our administration has shown itself to be weak with a pathetic foreign policy. In a Wilder administration, America will again take the place that God intended it to take as the undisputed world superpower. "

After the rally, a New York reporter cornered Jason and asked in a cheeky tone of voice, "Say, Jason, aren't you divorced? How does that play with your claim to be a servant of God?"

"Yes, I am divorced. When I found the Lord, my wife wasn't prepared to walk with me on the path to salvation. She continued her sinful ways under Satan's influence, and we parted."

Lupita was furious when she read Jason's words, or rather a French translation of them. She was flying business class on Air France back to the United States from a sales meeting in Paris, and had tucked a copy of the newspaper *Le Figaro* under her arm to read on the plane. The French press, along with most of the rest of the world, was following the American presidential campaign with great interest. On the front page was a headline that translates into English as "Jason Wilder

Appeals to the Iowa Extreme Right." Under it was what the French press calls a *chapeau* or summary of the article. It read in translation, "Mr. Wilder Says Ex-Wife under Satan's Influence."

Lupita had to restrain herself from screaming out loud in the crowded airplane. Her anger must have shown on her face, because a passing flight attendant stopped and asked her, "*Y-at-il quelque chose qui vous dérange, madame ?* Is something wrong, ma'am?"

"*Non, rien merci.* No, nothing."

Lupita had to change from Air France flight to a United Airlines flight in Newark, and by the time she landed in Phoenix, she was exhausted from lack of sleep. When she arrived home, without bothering to change into something more comfortable, she picked up the phone and dialed her lawyer.

"Lincoln, did you read in the papers what that asshole who's my ex-husband said about me?"

"Yes, I did. You're well rid of that guy."

"That's not the point! I want to know if there's anything I can do to get even. Can I sue the bastard for libel?"

"Claiming that Jason's statement is libelous would be impossible to prove in court, because there's no legal way to prove that Satan even exists. Therefore, it's not possible to say over whom he does or does not exert influence. Am I making sense?"

"No you're not. What you just said sounds like lawyer speak, but I do understand that you think I can't sue him and win. I'm not at all happy with that answer," said Lupita just before she slammed down the phone. "I want to get even with that son-of-a-bitch!" she yelled to herself. Then she took a few breaths. It wasn't fair to take it out on Lincoln. This was a matter between her and Jason. She would find a way to put that bastard in his place. She also vowed to stop swearing. She'd never used that sort of language before she met Jason.

Jason was smart enough to understand why the Hogson brothers were pushing the low tax agenda. The elimination of corporate income tax would benefit them enormously as would a flat tax with its resultant shifting of even more of the tax burden from the rich to the middle class. The country as a whole would suffer. The lowest-income groups would bear the burden of financing the government, and high-income people including the Hogson Brothers would make out like bandits.

Reduced taxes would mean very little money for maintaining the country's roads and bridges, but that wouldn't affect the Hogsons in the least. They didn't drive; they flew in private jets and helicopters. It didn't matter to them if the roads and bridges went to pot and educational standards slipped even farther. As to the rhetoric about eliminating the IRS and putting the country on the gold standard, Jason knew that the Hogsons weren't serious. That was pabulum to feed the unwashed masses.

Jason didn't care about ordinary people, either. He was already seeing himself as a member of the elite. The whole country could go to hell in a hand basket, as far as he was concerned. He was smarter than other people were. He had great confidence in himself and believed that he would come out on top no matter what happened to the rest of the country. He suspected that the Hogsons would do even better.

Just as the primary campaign was, the general election campaign was made very easy for Jason. His job was to travel, hold rallies, and make speeches. He didn't have to worry about financing, planning, or even writing his own speeches. The funds somehow magically appeared from multiple donors. Jason had no idea who the donors were, and given the newer opaque campaign-finance laws made possible by the Hogson-controlled Supreme Court, no one else could trace the money back to its source either. In panel discussion shows on TV news programs, analysts and reporters asked where all of the money was coming from that was financing the attack ads against Barack Obama but no one had the answer.

All the paperwork such as finance reports were taken care of behind the scenes without Jason's intervention. Most of the campaign funding was spent off the books at any rate, making the campaign finance reports pure works of fiction. Jason didn't know how those accounting tricks were pulled, but he was relieved to not have to worry about such details. Jason almost felt as if running for president were an automated process. All he had to do was to show up where he was told to, when he was told to, and say what he was told to say. "This is so simple and automated, I wonder if there's an app for it?" he asked himself whimsically.

Having it easy did not make Jason happy. He was used to being in control, but now unseen persons were manipulating him from behind the scenes. The thought kept coming back to him that he had sold his soul in exchange for a chance at power and riches. Like Faust, he was gaining the power and riches that he had sold his soul to obtain, but in the end, hoped it would be possible to back out of the agreement and keep his soul as Faust had done. At some point, somehow, he would have to get out from under the Hogsons' thumb. Nevertheless, for the moment it was best to play along. The important thing at present was to become president of the United States. He could deal with the Hogsons later from a position of power.

On the other hand, was he really going to win? His poll numbers were depressing. They had him in third place in the Republican primary race nationally. In Iowa he was second, and in New Hampshire he was fourth. The polls also indicated that if he were the Republican nominee, he would lose to Barack Obama in the general election by a wide margin. Fifty-seven percent of the electorate viewed him unfavorably against 31 percent who viewed him favorably. He had good reason to feel depressed. This was not what the Hogsons had promised. Perhaps they were not nearly as powerful as they had led him to believe.

"Don't worry," Shawn assured him, "I promise you everything is in good hands. The poll numbers mean nothing. Trust me on this. This will end just as we want it to."

Jason didn't trust him, and as the race went on, Jason came in second or third in primary after primary, in caucus after caucus. He didn't win a single one of them. Jefferson Cunningham led in the number of delegates, and Andrew Parsons was running a close second. The two were running too close to each other in the delegate race to predict which of them would come out on top. Jason trailed them both. Again, Shawn Killingworth attempted to reassure him. "The voters are under the impression that they decide who is going to be president. They don't. I'm telling you not to worry. You will be nominated. We have this under control."

When the primaries were over, Jason was still third, but he had enough delegates to act as a spoiler. Neither of the other two candidates had enough delegates to claim the nomination outright. Of the 2,286 delegates up for grabs, Jason had only 532 committed to vote for him. Andrew Parsons had 864 delegates and Jefferson Cunningham had 792. Ninety-eight delegates were uncommitted, but few of them appeared to be leaning toward Jason. To win the nomination, a candidate was required to have the support of 50 percent plus one of the delegate votes. Even if all of the uncommitted delegates were to vote for Jefferson Cunningham, he would not have enough to win the nomination. Whoever won would need some of Jason's delegates.

"I thought you were going to make sure that I won this race," Jason complained to Shawn. "Instead, it looks as if I will get to decide which of these other two imbeciles gets the nomination."

"Relax! I keep telling you to leave this to me," was Shawn's answer. "I know what I'm doing. Just hold your pants on; it ain't over 'till the fat lady sings, and she ain't even on stage yet."

"It's hard to have confidence in you and the Hogson brothers when I don't even have a shot of being nominated."

"Take solace from history," Shawn" countered. "James Garfield was also in third place when the Republican Convention began in 1880, but on the 36th ballot he won the nomination and went on to become president."

"That's a bad example. Garfield was shot by a nut job soon after taking office and then died a lingering and painful death at the hands of an incompetent doctor. That's not the way I want to end up."

The Republicans had not had a brokered convention since 1948, so no one could predict the outcome. On the opening ballot, most delegates were required to vote for the candidate they were elected to represent, but if no candidate received a majority of the votes, which seemed assured to happen, delegates would be free on later ballots to switch to another candidate. Ballots would continue to be taken until one candidate prevailed. There would be intense behind-the-scenes negotiations in an attempt to switch delegate votes from one candidate to another.

The Republican Convention was held in Tampa, Florida. The Convention was opened at 2 pm on August 27 and recessed 10 minutes later due to Tropical Storm Isaac's expected arrival. However, the storm veered west and struck the coast of Louisiana. Before balloting could begin, the Party had to settle a kerfuffle among the Maine delegates. Opposing groups of the Maine Republican Party had each sent a slate of delegates to the convention, one slate in favor of Andrew Parsons and the other in favor of Jefferson Cunningham. The dispute ended in a compromise. The official Maine delegation would be made up of half of the proposed delegates from each group. The decision split Maine's delegation down the middle and made it irrelevant in early balloting.

Once all of the boring opening speeches were over, the convention settled down to the business of picking a Republican nominee. However, that proved to be difficult. The convention held ballot after ballot, but neither of the two leading candidates could obtain the 1,144 delegates necessary to win the nomination. For decades, the primary elections had decided who the presidential candidate of both parties would be long before the conventions were held, and the party conventions were viewed as rubber-stamp events whose main purpose was to give the delegates an opportunity to have a good time and feel that they were important. The convention delegates were incapable of doing the job for which they were ostensibly there: To pick a nominee. In the old days when the candidate was selected in "smoke-filled rooms" off the convention floor, things went more smoothly. Party bosses had control over the delegates and decided how they should vote. Now, the skills developed in those days to handle a deadlocked convention had been lost. The delegates were much more ideological and not inclined to be bossed around by self-appointed bigwigs.

Representatives of the three candidates met behind closed doors in an attempt to resolve the impasse. The meetings dragged on without resolution. The leaders of the Parsons and Cunningham campaigns both appealed to Jason's representatives to release Jason's delegates to their candidate, but acting under Shawn's instruction, Jason refused, and his delegates loyally and stubbornly continued to vote for him. Floor vote succeeded floor vote with neither of the leading candidates winning a majority and Jason's coming in third. The press reported a rumor that representatives of the Cunningham campaign had offered some of Jason's male delegates "a good time" in exchange for changing their votes, but when word leaked out, Jason's delegates expressed an even stronger loyalty to him. If they changed their votes now, it would appear that they had been bought.

Cunningham finally conceded that he could not win, but he refused to endorse Parsons, for whom he had developed a deep hatred. The time for gaveling the convention to a close approached, and still no candidate had been nominated. The convention could not end that way.

A candidate had to be nominated, so the convention was extended for an extra day at great expense to its sponsors.

As it became increasingly obvious that neither the Parsons nor Jefferson could win, wiser heads began to exert their influence. They persuaded each of the two leading candidates to release his delegates with the stipulation the other would not be nominated. The only person left in the running was Jason, who began to fill quite complacent. However, his optimism was premature. The Republican establishment at first refused to accept him as a compromise candidate. He stood for the ideas of the "crazy" right wing of the party and not for the establishment's more traditional Republican values.

The party leaders discussed drafting Arizona senator John McCain. However, after some discussion, that idea was discarded as impractical. McCain's expressed political views were all over the map depending on which group he was trying to please. Rather than gaining him popularity, McCain's machinations had angered people in all wings of the Republican Party. The diminishing coterie of moderates considered him far too conservative, and the growing number of Republican right-wingers found him to be too moderate. They called him a RINO, Republican in Name Only.

McCain's ignorance of economic matters was painfully obvious to all. The Republican bigwigs feared that Obama would run circles around John McCain as soon as the subject turned to the nation's economic problems. McCain's only smart economic move had been to marry a rich heiress after his marital infidelity had brought his first marriage to an end. McCain was a war hawk in an era when Americans were tiring of the conflicts in Iraq and Afghanistan. His solution to all foreign problems was to bomb anyone he didn't like out of existence and then send in American troops.

The Republican establishment finally threw in the towel. If neither of the leading two candidates could win the nomination, they would have to accept Jason as the Republican compromise candidate, no matter how distasteful they found the idea. They recognized that his powerful backing by the Hogson brothers gave him an excellent chance of winning the election. In the end, winning was all that mattered, and no one wanted to be on the wrong side of the Hogsons. Parsons and Jefferson, each mollified by the fact that the other would not win the nomination, both put the word out that they were releasing their delegates to vote for Jason Wilder. Perhaps a little behind-the-scenes prodding from the Hogsons helped them reach that decision.

On the next roll-call vote, state after state announced that its delegation was voting for Jason Wilder. Finally, there was a motion from the floor to nominate him by acclamation. The roughest part of the campaigning was over. Only three months remained until November's general election, and this time there was only one opponent, the sitting president, Barack Obama.

The Convention had one more task to complete, the nomination of Jason's vice-presidential running mate. By tradition, the presidential nominee picked the vice-presidential candidate and the Convention delegates rubber stamped the decision. What the delegates didn't know was that Jason would in turn rubber-stamp the candidate that the Hogson brothers had probably already chosen for him. Jason was curious to know who his running mate would be. He hoped the Hogson brothers wouldn't extend an olive branch to either Cunningham or Parsons by offering the vice-presidential slot to one of those idiots. He hated them both.

Jason's suspense didn't last long. The phone rang. It was Shawn. "Your running mate is Chamita Monroe."

"Who?" Jason asked, with his ignorance obvious in his voice.

"Senator Chamita Monroe from Texas."

"Never heard of her," Jason responded, still sounding dubious.

"Well, you'd better start brushing up on her, because you're going to meet her before you make your acceptance speech. Google her and make yourself familiar with her history. For now, I'll give you a quick fill-in. She's the second African-American woman to ever be elected to the United States Senate. The first was Carol Moseley Braun from Illinois, of course. Oh, and while you're Googleing her, I'll have an information packet about her sent over. It will not only tell you who she is, it will tell you why you picked her, well, the reason you're supposed to tell the press. Then this evening the three of us will have a late diner together in my hotel room at 9 pm. I expect you to have done some homework that time. By tomorrow you've got to be able to handle questions from the press about your running mate."

"Why did I pick her?"

"Officially, because she balances the ticket. She's from the South, and you're from the North. She's black, and you're white. She's a woman, and you're a man. The fact that she's African-American will help deflect the accusations that you're a racist. The two of you will be running against the first black president in American history, so it will be very helpful to have a person of color on the ticket. She's also the first African-American of any gender to be elected to the Senate from the South since Hiram Revels and Blanche Bruce represented Mississippi during reconstruction. That was before the Klu Klux Klan took over the state and suppressed the black vote. She's also a great speech-maker."

"OK, those are the official reasons for public consumption. What's the real reason?"

"She's one of ours, of course. She's been doing an outstanding job of looking out for the Hogsons' interests in the Senate since she was first elected. As vice president, she'll preside over the Senate and be able to help us even more."

The late diner did not go well. It was apparent to Jason as soon as he walked into the room that Senator Chamita Monroe had a chip on her shoulder. Instead of addressing Jason by his first name, she insisted on calling him Governor Wilder. "I've read your speeches. It seems that you have a low opinion of black people, Governor Wilder."

Jason suppressed an urge to repeat the cliché "Some of my best friends are black." In truth, he had no black friends and had never had much interaction with anyone didn't have lily-white skin except Lupita since he had moved out of the dorm room he shared with Jimmy Jefferson at Arizona State University decades ago. He came up with a typical politician's evasive response, "I'm sorry you have that impression. I hope that as you get to know me, you'll find out that that isn't true and that we can be friends."

Chamita wasn't buying it, "As I said, I've read your speeches. You not only don't like blacks, you don't like Mexicans. You refer to the United States as a white Christian nation. That sounds pretty racist to me. My opinion of you is that you're a white supremacist."

Jason didn't have an opinion one way or the other about blacks or Mexicans. He didn't give them much thought, just as he didn't give much thought to anyone unless it was to figure out how he could take advantage of the person. However, he wasn't going to admit that. Aloud he said, "From what Shawn has told me, I think you're in a position to know that I didn't write my own speeches. You should know better than to take the content of my speeches as my true beliefs. In my speeches I said what I was told to say. If you've looked into me at all, you should know that my former wife is a Mexican."

"Former wife? Obviously that didn't work out. You chucked her as soon as you entered politics. You couldn't get rid of her fast enough. Were you ashamed to have a brown-skinned wife by your side? However, I admit that I've also had to say things in speeches that I don't believe. That doesn't mean that I'm convinced that you're not a racist. I'll be keeping an eye on you, and we'll see if your actions change my opinion."

"Let's not fight over this," Shawn interrupted. "We had Jason use the tactics that were required to win the Republican nomination. Now that we're switching to the general election, it's time to change tactics. We'll be appealing to the broader electorate from now on, and that means no more references to white America. We need to get some black and Hispanic votes to win this election."

"Is that why I'm on the ticket? Chamita asked. "Am I the token house nigger broad?"

Shawn was a bit taken aback at the vulgarity of Chamita's question, but he didn't completely lose his composure. "The fact that you're black and the fact that you're a woman are both important. Until Obama was elected, no person of color had ever been elected either president or vice president of the United States. I won't deny that your skin color is an advantage in this election. As the first woman and the first black person to be vice president, you will be a role model for others. However, that's not the reason we picked you. We think you're the best person for the job. And, don't forget that vice presidents often go on to become president. You'd make an excellent president if you'd learn to control your tongue."

Jason asked, "Is that a subtle threat aimed at me? Are you implying that if I'm elected president, something could happen to me in office and Senator Monroe would take over?"

"Take it for what you want to. Now stop referring to each other as Governor Wilder and Ms. Monroe. From now on it's first names: Jason and Chamita. Got it?"

"That's not going to be easy," Chamita responded.

Jason and Chamita didn't become friends during the meal, but Jason noted that she was very intelligent with a quick grasp of the facts. She also had a PhD in philosophy and was well versed in international politics. In short, she was much better educated that Jason was, and although he didn't say it aloud, he recognized that she was much better qualified to be president than he was. He was certain that if she were white and male, their roles would be reversed. That made him hate her all the more.

After the convention was over, Jason had a brief respite from politicking. He and Chamita would hit the campaign trail soon—they would start with a joint appearance in Chicago—but in the meantime, there was little chance of getting news coverage. The Democratic Convention, which would be held in Charlotte, North Carolina, was about to start and wouldn't end until September 6. Until then, the Democrats would suck up all of the news coverage, even though it was a foregone conclusion that they would nominate Barack Obama to run for a second presidential term.

Shawn decided that it would be a good time for Jason to visit his parents in Chicago, whom he hadn't seen since the Christmas vacation he spent with them during his freshman year at Arizona State. Maybe they could use the visit to drum up some press coverage. Shawn said that showing himself as a loving son from working-class Chicago would help him with the Illinois vote. Obama was also from Chicago, so the Chicago papers billed the presidential election as a battle between two hometown boys, Obama, the elite and wealthy black constitutional lawyer from the Southside and Jason, the working-class white boy from the Northside. Obama would have more support in the city itself, which leaned heavily Democratic, but Jason could count on support from the suburbs, which were largely white and Republican. Obama would probably carry Illinois, but Shawn wanted Jason to at least put up the appearance of trying to win votes in the city where he was born. It would be a big upset if Obama were to lose the election in his home state.

Jason didn't call his parents to arrange the visit. In fact, he wasn't keen on the idea of visiting them at all. He left it up to Shawn and his people to arrange the visit and to book Jason's airplane ticket. The Secret Service would book the tickets for Jason's security detail. The airplane that he would use during the campaign was still being repainted with the Wilder & Monroe logo in large letters on both sides, so he flew first class on a commercial flight.

The first communication Craig and Irene had with Jason was when the latter stepped off the plane at O'Hare Airport. Shawn's people had arranged for his parents to be chauffeured to the airport in a luxurious limousine with a Secret Service and police escort and also made sure that the Chicago press was there to record the family reunion when Shawn emerged from airport security and gave a big hug, first to his Mom, Irene, and then to his dad, Craig.

How his parents had aged! Craig was now 88 years old and had to use a walker to get around. He had been diagnosed with lung cancer had a persistent cough. At 74, Irene was getting up in age, too. Jason wondered if his father would survive long enough to see him inaugurated as president of the United States in January. Well, if he didn't, too bad for him. Absence had not made Jason's heart grow fonder of his parents.

It was no longer simple for Jason to travel even a short distance. He and his parents were driven to the house on Fletcher Street in a caravan of black SUVs and limousines that also carried members of the press and Jason's Secret Service bodyguards. His parents were now also assigned their own Secret Service detail. The entire caravan that left the airport must have consisted of 30 automobiles, all with tinted windows. A Secret Service agent who rode in the limousine with the family explained that many of the other automobiles were decoys so that any possible terrorists wouldn't know which car to attack.

Jason didn't know what to say to his parents in the car, but Craig started the conversation, "You come a long way, Jason, and you done it on your own. I still regret that your Mom and me weren't able to help you more when you were a student."

Jason remained quiet. This was not a comfortable situation.

After a while, Craig continued, "Your Mom and me never thought you'd break off all contact with us. So now you come back, now that you're a big shot."

"Look, Dad! I'm no happier with this situation than you are. Let's just try to get along for the few days I'm here. I promise you and Mom will be well compensated."

Irene, who had been silent since they entered the car, finally spoke up, "We don't want your money Jason. What we wanted was a son, but we didn't get one. No amount of money can make up for that."

"Suit yourself, Mom. The money's available. It really doesn't matter to me if you take it or not."

It made quite an impression when the whole entourage entered the Fletcher Street in a long caravan. Jason would never travel alone again. For the rest of his short life, he would constantly be surrounded by Secret Service agents and often by the press as well. Members of both groups would accompany him in a caravan of black cars with darkly tinted windows whenever he traveled by land and would surround him in the plane wherever he flew.

The neighbors' initial enthusiasm wore thin when police blockaded Fletcher Street and much of the surrounding neighborhood. TV trucks with high microwave towers set up operations in front of Craig and Irene's house, and Secret Service agents began going from door to door asking residents about their overseas connections and if they owned guns. Few of them did. Entering and leaving the street became difficult, and even sleep was disturbed by the noisy reporters who filled the street 24 hours a day. Neighbor women, who were used to dropping by to have a cup of tea and a half hour of gossip in Irene's kitchen, were blocked from approaching the Wilder house by men wearing dark suits and dark glasses with an earphone in one ear.

Reporters vied with each other to interview the Wilders' neighbors since the Secret Service kept them away from the Wilders themselves. "What was Jason like as a kid? Is there anything special about him that sticks in your memory? How did he get along with the other kids? What was he like as a teenager? Did you know when he was growing up that he would someday run for the presidency of the United States?"

Jason had been a rotten kid, of course, but now that he was famous, the neighbors all remembered him as a marvelous child. They all knew even when he was small that he was destined for great things. Many of them claimed to be Greg and Irene's best friends. Not one of them remembered that Jason sometimes smoked pot in the alley, was mean to animals, and made the lives of the younger neighborhood kids miserable. The neighbors grumbled among themselves about the fact that the neighborhood had been taken over by a gang of men in dark suits wearing dark sunglasses, but secretly each of them was proud of the attention. When speaking to the press, they all claimed to be delighted that one of theirs had become so famous.

"I remember when he first learned to ride a bicycle," one of the neighbors said. "He kept falling down, so I held onto the bike and ran alongside him until he got the hang of it. To think that I taught the future president of the United States how to ride a bike."

Another woman claimed that she had always baked cookies "especially for Jason. He would come over to my house and sit in the kitchen, because he always knew that I had milk and cookies for him."

Inside the Wilder house, things were not going well. Jason didn't want to be there, and he didn't hide that fact from his parents. He wasn't even allowed to walk out the front door without making arrangements with his Secret Service detail in advance so that a small army of men could walk with him, keeping him surrounded at all times. He wondered if someone was spying on him when he went to the bathroom to take a piss. "If I asked one of those guys to come in here and wipe my ass for me, he'd probably do it," Jason thought.

There was no sense going outside or anywhere else if it was so complicated. He felt penned up in the house. He went to his old bedroom and closed the door. It was the only place where he could be alone. He called Shawn on his cell phone."

"Shawn, you gotta' get me outa' here. I can't take this. No way am I gonna' stay cooped up in this house. I can't stand my parents, and they can't stand me. There is no way we can continue bottled up together like this. This visit wasn't a good idea."

"You're going to have to show some patience, Jason. We need to create the impression that you come from a loving family."

"Loving family? Christ! You should be here! I'm telling you I can't take this for a week. A few more hours of this, and I'm gonna' explode."

"OK. A couple of us will put our heads together and see what we can come up with. In the meantime, you've got to act the part of a loving son."

"Sweet Jesus! That's not gonna' be easy. Make it quick, please," and he hung up.

Irene had cooked supper for the three of them. That's not quite true. Shawn had arranged for a caterer to deliver a meal in advance, and Irene had heated it in the microwave. Jason's cell phone rang. It was

Shawn. "Jason, I've arranged for ABC News to get an exclusive of the happy family sitting around the diner table. Let them in to shoot some video. They need to film you eating and talking to each other. It's a way to squeeze in a few words about our side amid the blanket TV coverage of the Democratic Convention."

Jason's parents were more than happy to have a normal conversation with him while the TV crew filmed. The family tried to act as if the TV crew and the off-camera Secret Service agents were not present. The crew shot an hour of video, which was going to be edited down to a one-minute blurb on the national news. The family made a show of eating and talking while the crew filmed. Occasionally the director would give them orders such as, "Jason, hold your fork in your right hand, look toward your father, and talk to him. It doesn't matter what you say. The audio, is off. We'll do a voice-over when we show the video clip on the news."

"You know, Pop, one thing I miss about being in Chicago is going to see the Cubs. I hope when this campaign is over that I have time to relax and watch a baseball game."

Craig nodded attentively as the cameras recorded the scene. Inwardly he thought, "What the hell? The kid never went with me to see the Cubs when he was living at home."

The TV crew also wanted some shots of other rooms in the house: the living room, the kitchen with Irene standing at the stove and stirring a pot of stew, which in reality was a pan of cold water placed there as a prop. The director also wanted to film Jason's bedroom. "Don't you have a Teddy Bear or something that you used to sleep with when you were a kid?"

"A teddy bear? What kind of a weirdo kid do you think I was? No, I used to read in bed. I never cared for stuffed animals."

"Well, what did you read? We'll get a shot of you reading one of your old books."

Jason looked at the bookshelf in his room. The books were just as he had left them when he moved to Arizona years ago. He grabbed the copy of Gabriel García Márquez's *One Hundred Years of Solitude* that he had borrowed from the public library as a teen and never returned. He didn't have many pleasant memories of his life in Chicago as a teen, but now he remembered how he had enjoyed reading this book. He wondered how many hundred dollars in overdue-book fines he now owed.

"It would look better if you picked a book by an American author," the director told him. "It would look more patriotic."

Jason sighed, put down the book and said, "I guess you're right." He picked up a slim volume of John Steinbeck's *Of Mice and Men* that he had been required to read in a junior high school English course. What a dumb story that was about a couple of losers. However, he asked the reporter, "Will this do? Who could be more American than John Steinbeck?"

No sooner had the TV crew left than the front doorbell rang. It was Shawn. "Jason, I hate to drag you away from your family, but we have a minor emergency. Your house has been broken into back home in Phoenix. You need to fly back and tell the police what was stolen. I've got a car to take you to the airport."

Jason made the necessary excuses to his parents. "I'm sorry to have to go. I was really looking forward to spending some time with you."

"We understand," Irene answered. "You've got to go. We understand."

"We'll miss you son," Craig lied.

"I'll miss both of you, too," Jason replied with equal insincerity as he gave them a big hug.

Jason's parents were just as glad to see his back as he was to be getting out of the house.

Sitting in the back of the chauffeured limousine with Shawn, as the caravan of black SUVs motored down the freeway Jason said, "This isn't the way to O'Hare Airport!"

"We're not going to O'Hare. There's a private jet waiting at Midway to fly us to Phoenix."

"A private jet? But I thought my campaign plane wasn't ready yet."

"It's not your campaign plane. We've made other arrangements."

Jason was astounded to see that the private jet wasn't a small business aircraft but a full-sized Boeing 737. He didn't have to ask who the plane belonged to. The plane was crewed by a pilot, a copilot, and a steward who served them champagne as they settled into the large, comfortable bucket seats in the front compartment of the plane, which was equipped as a spacious office. Before them was a large mahogany desk with a telephone, and on the wall was a giant plasma TV screen. "Please buckle yourselves in until we take off," the steward said as he took their now-empty champagne glasses. Once we're in the air, you can move around the plane, and I'll be serving some light snacks."

The "light snacks" turned out to be Russian caviar with crackers and another bottle of champagne. "Man! I could get used to traveling this way!" Jason sighed.

"You'll travel better than this beginning in January," Shawn told him. "Don't forget that with the presidency come two official Boeing 747s, and whichever one you're riding in will be called Air Force One."

"By the way, was my house really broken into?"

"No, I had someone throw a rock through one of your windows, which set off the burglar alarm. I made sure he wore a black hood so he couldn't be identified on closed-circuit TV and wore surgical gloves so as not to leave fingerprints. The supposed burglar's getaway car was picked up on closed-circuit TV cameras, but it was stolen. Sooner or later the police will find it abandoned in the desert north of Scottsdale with no fingerprints. We had the car sanitized before it was abandoned. Don't worry, the guy barely entered your house, and nothing was taken, but no one will doubt that it was a real burglary attempt. We have people working for us who know how to do this sort of thing."

When they arrived at Jason's home, there were two Paradise Valley police cars plus three Arizona Department of Public Safety squad cars parked in front, and the street was blocked with yellow police tape. One of the Secret Service officers identified them to a police officer who lifted the police tape and allowed the limousine to pass. The rest of the motorcade parked in the streets around the house.

Jason unlocked the front door and entered with two of the police officers and three Secret Service agents. He made a show of inspecting every room. "I don't think anything was taken," he said finally. "I owe that to the prompt police response. You officers did a great job."

"Thanks, Governor," one of them replied. Jason was no longer governor, but everyone in Paradise Valley remembered that he had been.

Jason and Chamita kicked off their campaign with a joint appearance in Chicago, even though they had no hope of carrying the city and only a small hope of carrying the State of Illinois. In addition to picking up the conservative vote in the Chicago suburbs, they hoped to pick up the vote of a few liberals, who were disillusioned with Barack Obama's performance in office. It wasn't their decision to begin the campaign in Chicago. Shawn had said it would seem like an insult not to start it in the city where Jason was born. He tried to get Jason's parents to attend the rally and appear onstage with their son, but they refused. Jason and Chamita assumed that Shawn knew what he was doing, and they did as they were told.

Chamita turned out to be a better speaker than Jason was. There was a certain rhythm in her voice as she read off the speeches that Shawn and his assistants supplied her as she railed against Obama's and Clinton's trade agreements, which she claimed were costing American jobs. "When we are in the White House, we will put a high tariff on Chinese imports and bring those high-paying manufacturing jobs back to America. Our country is being flooded with cheap, low-quality imports from Chinese factories. The Chinese are using those products to spy on us. Every time you make a call using a Chinese-built cell phone, or every time your call or Internet connection goes through a piece of Chinese-built telecommunications equipment, someone in China is listening in. Obama refuses to do anything about Chinese spying and economic cheating. When Jason and I are in office, we will put China in its place.

"NAFTA is a bad deal pushed onto the American people by the Clinton administration. Ross Perot was right when he said that NAFTA would cause 'a giant sucking sound' as American jobs disappeared south of the border. That is exactly what has happened. Clinton promised us that NAFTA would make Mexico more prosperous and reduce illegal immigration, and what happened? NAFTA made Mexicans poorer, so millions of them poured across our border, willing to work for a few dollars a day and taking jobs away from hard-working American families. When Jason and I are elected, one of the first things we will do is to demand that Congress renounce NAFTA. NAFTA is bad for the United States. NAFTA is bad for Mexico.

"Climate change is a liberal fraud perpetrated on us by the Chinese government and the Obama administration who want to undermine the good-paying jobs that used to exist in American factories. Does anyone here doubt that Obama has been a nightmare for the American worker?"

"NO!" the crowd shouted in chorus.

"Hell no!" Chamita added.

"HELL NO!" the crowd responded.

"American companies spend billions of dollars trying to comply with government red tape that the Obama administration put into place in the name of preventing climate change to the point where our companies are no longer competitive. Do Chinese companies cut their emissions?"

This time the crowd shouted, " HELL NO!"

"Chinese government officials laugh all the way to the bank at the fraud they have managed to foist off on the American liberal left, a fraud that is strangling our economy. And, what happens when Obama's climate-change rules get too expensive for American companies? They pull up stakes and move to China, taking good-paying manufacturing jobs with them.

"Those of us who are black were excited when Obama was elected president, but he has let us down. Has he helped you?"

"HELL NO!" came the response.

"A black male born today has a 30-percent chance of winding up in prison. Police officers, who are supposed to protect us, are gunning down our people in the streets all across the nation. Far too many of our people continue to live in poverty in crime-infested neighborhoods where drugs are sold openly while Obama's buddies on Wall Street get richer and richer. Obama has betrayed black Americans. Obama has betrayed white Americans. Obama has betrayed Latino-Americans. Obama has betrayed Asian-Americans. Obama has betrayed us all. Are we going to put up with this?"

"HELL NO!"

Shawn was on the phone with Luther Hogson. "Luther, I think and Willard have really made a mistake this time. I've been spending a lot of time with Jason ever since we started his primary campaign last year, and I've come to believe that we shouldn't trust him as far as I could throw him. He's a real slimy character."

"What makes you think that Willard and I trust him?"

"But, you're about to have him elected president, and I'm almost sure that once he's in office, he'll turn on you."

"Of course he will," Luther agreed.

"Luther, wouldn't it have been much better to have picked Chamita to run? She's been working for us for a long time, and I'm pretty sure she's the person we want sitting in the Oval Office. She's certainly a better campaigner than Jason is."

"It would have been much harder to get Chamita elected. She's a smart cookie, but some of her votes in the Senate have been questionable. They were votes made in our interest, of course, but they've aroused a bit of public suspicion. No, Jason was the right choice. We've got Chamita in the right place to take over when Jason gets, err, I mean to say if Jason gets out of line. It's a dangerous world out there, and accidents happen to people all the time."

Shawn got an uneasy feeling. "I hope you don't mean that Jason is going to meet an untimely death."

"No!' Luther replied sharply, "don't even think that when you're talking on a telephone line where who knows what government agency is listening in! Murdering a president would be a terrible crime if someone were so inclined. Let me make it clear to you and to anyone who might be listening in that such a thing is out of the question. Besides, law enforcement techniques have advanced by leaps and bounds since the time Kennedy was assassinated. Anyone behind such an assassination would be caught. If we need to get rid of Jason, we can do so without laying a finger on him."

"The Kennedy assassination was a real professional job," Shawn said admiringly. "They never did find out who put Oswald up to it."

"Yeah, but we can't get away with that sort of thing these days."

"We? Were you and Willard behind the Kennedy assassination?"

"I said no such thing!" Luther retorted. "I want it clearly understood that I know nothing about Kennedy's death except what was written in the press. At any rate, if Jason doesn't play ball with us, anything that happens to him will be legal and aboveboard. He will be the cause of his own downfall. That's all I'm going to say on the matter."

Unseating a sitting president is not an easy matter, and Barack Obama still had a residue of goodwill among the voters, despite his failure to deliver on his agenda during his first term. Jason and Chamita campaigned hard to nourish the seeds of doubt that had already taken place in voters' minds about Obama's performance in office.

"Obama took office with the promise of putting American back to work," Jason hammered away on his stump speeches. "However, millions of Americans are still unable to find jobs, and those that can are flipping burgers and making the minimum wage. You can't support a family on that sort of income.

"And why hasn't he put more effort into creating decent jobs for decent people? Because he's too busy pushing the liberal agenda. Thanks to Obama, men can marry men, and women can marry women. If he has his way, people will soon be able to marry animals. The mere thought of men having sex with men and women having sex with women and both of them having sex with animals is disgusting. It's time that we stopped tolerating this sodomy in our midst and returned to the Christian values upon which this nation was founded."

Actually, although Jason had never tried it, he couldn't help but wonder what it would be like to have sex with another man. If he weren't running for president, he might risk it just to satisfy his curiosity.

The history of the Obama-Wilder campaign has been well documented, so I will not go into great detail about it here. Chamita attacked Barack Obama from the left to win the black vote, and Jason attacked him from the right to win the white vote. Suffice it to say that the night of the election was a real nail biter, as you probably remember. NBC first declared Barack Obama the winner and then recanted as more Pennsylvania precincts reported, and it appeared that Jason Wilder might carry the state. Then enough votes were counted in Ohio that the TV networks felt confident in declaring Obama the winner there. Pennsylvania turned out to be a cliffhanger, however. Obama only needed two more electoral votes to be declared the winner, and Pennsylvania had 20 them up for grabs. By three am, all Pennsylvania precincts had reported except those in Somerset County in a state where Obama had only a slight edge of 322 votes in the precincts reported so far. No one could figure out why some precincts in Somerset County had not reported their vote totals, but for some reason hour after hour passed, and the final tallies did not come in.

Finally, the networks signed off their election coverage for the night and went back to running old movies, and people went to bed still not knowing who had won the election.

When the nation awoke the next morning, the election was still undecided. It turned out that Pennsylvania was still using an ancient punch-card system, the same system that had enabled the Supreme Court to snatch victory away from Al Gore in the State of Florida 12 years earlier. This time the problems revolved around a single precinct in Windber, a city of only about four thousand inhabitants. Several hundred ballots that had apparently been cast for Obama had been torn, and local officials had declared them invalid. If the decision were allowed to stand and the ballots were not counted, Wilder would carry the precinct and therefore claim Pennsylvania's twenty electoral votes by the slimmest of margins. That would make him the president elect.

No one could explain how the ballots had become torn, although conspiracy theories abounded. The Obama campaign protested, of course, and the matter was sent to the courts to settle. Given the urgency of reaching a decision, the Supreme Court decided to hear the case directly and to give it priority. It took only two days for the Court to reach a decision. The Supreme Court was dominated by Republican appointees, just as it was in the days when it awarded the presidency to George W. Bush despite Al Gore's overwhelming lead in the popular vote. It was not hard to predict that history would repeat itself and the court would again rule in favor of the Republican candidate, Jason Wilder, just as it had ruled in favor of George W. Bush in the Florida ballot dispute 12 years earlier. That is exactly what happened.

Jason was jubilant. To think that a humble person like him, born the son of a working-class construction worker in Chicago, could become president of the greatest country on Earth. He was busy on the phone answering calls from people who were anxious to congratulate him. Now that he was going to be president, everyone wanted to be his friend. It didn't occur to him until later that his parents hadn't called. Oh, well, no big loss.

Another person who didn't call him and whom he didn't call either was Chamita. She still couldn't stand Jason. That also didn't bother Jason. Many past vice presidents had spent their years in irrelevancy. She would be living in a house on the grounds of the Naval

Observatory with the address One Observatory Circle, and although her offices would be on the White House grounds, there was no reason why Jason had to see her. She could appear at his side when he gave important speeches and even sit in an elevated position behind him when he addressed Congress, but that didn't mean that they had to speak to each other in private.

Jason felt time heavy on his hands while he waited to be sworn in as president in late January. He had expected to be overwhelmed with duties during the transition, but Shawn and his team were taking care of everything. Anytime Jason tried to get involved, Jason told him that he needed trouble himself. His people had everything in hand. Rather than being pleased at being released from responsibility, Jason was annoyed. It irked him to take orders instead of being in charge. "Just wait until I'm sworn in," Jason thought to himself. "I'll show Shawn and these Hog-nosed brothers who's boss. I may have to take their crap now, but soon the shoe will be on the other foot."

Chapter 8 — Jason's Comeuppance

Finally, the big day came. Although not required by law, by tradition the Chief Justice of the Supreme Court swore in the new president in a public ceremony. The soon-to-be president raised his right hand and placed his left hand on a Bible. Shawn's people had obtained a Roman Catholic Bible for the occasion, as Shawn had been baptized into that religion, although Jason himself had no preference and could have been sworn in on a Superman comic book as far as he was concerned. He had long ago given up any loyalty to any religion, although he made a public pretense of being a devote Catholic for political purposes. He thought God was a superstitious creation designed to pacify the masses. Karl Marx had been right about that at least, even if the rest of his ideas were idiotic.

The press referred to Jason as the second Catholic president; John Kennedy had been the first, of course. As far as Jason knew, he was actually the first atheist president. He didn't want to meet the fate that befell the true Catholic president.

After the swearing-in ceremony, President Wilder gave his inauguration address, which had been written for him by Shawn Killingworth's speechwriters. Advance copies were distributed to the press shortly before Jason began speaking.

"Vice President Monroe, Mr. Chief Justice, members of the United States Congress, distinguished guests, and fellow citizens: Once again our democratic system has triumphed, and the reins of our great country have been handed over to a new president."

At this point he was supposed to launch into his proposals for his first administration, reducing the federal budget, boosting the economy by cutting federal taxes "on those men and women who create jobs by running the companies that keep our nation strong," limiting the "bloated bureaucracy" of the Securities and Exchange Commission, "sealing our borders to keep our country from being overrun by illegal immigrants and inundated in drugs," etc. Instead of reading the speech, Jason let it fall to the floor. It was finally time to show those Hogsons who was really in charge.

Ignoring the words on the teleprompter, Jason continued, "Unfortunately, our democratic system has once again triumphed in placing our destiny, our very lives, into the hands of a small group of people, mostly white men, who control our political process, run our industries, set our wage scale, and play off our country against low-wage countries in the Third World. Our whole tax system is designed to transfer wealth from working- and middle-class men and women into the bank accounts of the very richest among us." Jason was hitting his stride now. He paused for applause, but the crowd was strangely silent, astonished at hearing the unfamiliar words from Jason's mouth. "For far too long, those of us who form the backbone of this country have been treated as virtual serfs by the undeserving superrich." He stopped again, waiting for the applause that he was sure would come. Instead he heard a lone male voice shout, "Boo! Traitor!"

The members of the press were befuddled. They frantically searched through the advance copies of the speech that they had been given, but the words Jason was speaking had no connection with the words printed on the pages before them. Nothing like this had ever occurred before in the history of the presidency.

The crowd finally broke out of its stupor and began taking up the cry, "Traitor! Leftwing radical!" Soon half the crowd was shouting in unison, "TRAI! TOR! — TRAI! TOR!" with a pause between each syllable. The Jason they had supported in the campaign was not the Jason who was speaking into the microphone. Attacking the rich was un-American. The rich were the ones who created jobs.

Jason leaned over the microphone and tried to regain control, "Please! Listen to me! This is important!" His words had no effect. Finally, he leaned over the microphone again and shouted, "Screw all of you! I'm president now. I don't need to pretend to be nice to anyone anymore!" Some in the crowd attempted to break through the security cordon in front of the stage to get at Jason.

A pair of rough hands grabbed each of his arms, and he found himself being hurried away from the podium and out a side door. "That was a close call, Sir," a voice behind one of the pairs of hands told him. "We couldn't have held back that crowd."

The two pairs of hands belonged to Secret Service agents, who continued to rush him down a hall and into a side room, where they released their grasp. "Please wait here, sir, until we find a safe way to get you out of this building and back to the White House."

Jason could not believe what had just happened. All of his life he had lied to people, and they had swallowed every word he said.

Finally, he told the truth, and a hall full of people turned against him. Dishonesty was obviously the best policy when it came to politics. Why had he told the truth in his first speech? It was certainly not out of a sense of altruism. He cared not a fig for the people or the nation. If they wanted to let rich people lead them around by the nose, it didn't bother Jason in the least. No, it had to do with the Hogsons. He had to show the Hogsons that no matter how important they thought they were, they could not control Jason Wilder. Jason Wilder kowtowed to no one.

As the Secret Service worked out the logistics of getting Jason safely away from the angry crowd, Shawn Killingworth was on the phone with Luther Hogson. "You see what happened, Luther? Don't say I didn't warn you."

"Yeah, you were right, Shawn. I knew we'd have trouble with him, but I didn't expect it to happen during his inaugural address."

"So what are you going to do about it, Luther?"

"Shawn, your place is to carry out orders, not to plan. We have experience dealing with problems like this. You're too young to remember, but Kennedy also rebelled against us."

"You're not saying that you're going to have Jason shot, are you?"

"No! No! No! I told you once that you can't get away with that sort of thing nowadays. Those days were different. Law enforcement didn't have the technology it has today, and we had the Warren Commission packed with our people."

"Are you saying that you're the people who had Kennedy shot?

"No! No! No!" Luther countered. "I'm saying no such thing. Willard and I were much too young then. Our father still ran the business, and he never talked to us about what he did. The Warren Commission came to the conclusion that Lee Harvey Oswald acted alone. I'm prepared to believe that. Let sleeping dogs lie. As to you, I told you before that you should be more careful about what you say over the telephone. I hope I don't have to tell you a third time. Every word we're saying is being recorded in some National Security Agency database, and you never know when someone might start digging through the data and find this conversation."

"OK, just tell me what you want me to do about Jason."

"We don't need you for this. Just sit back and watch events unfold. Take a vacation. You've been working too hard, and it's time for you to take a rest. We'll handle everything from here."

Shawn resigned himself to the fact that any role he had to play where this particular candidate was concerned was over. He said his good-byes and hung up the phone. Still, he couldn't help but wondering how much information about the Kennedy assassination had been covered up. He also realized that his own life might be in danger. He knew far too much about the Hogsons' political machinations. Why did he ever allow himself to get into this mess? The best thing for him to do was to keep his mouth shut, do as he was told, lie low for a time, and hope that he came out of this situation OK.

Jason had no real objection to the Hogsons' political goals. What he wanted was for the Hogsons to come groveling to him willing to accept any terms that he might dictate. They would have to recognize that he was in the driver's seat now and that they were beholden to him. He would play ball with them but under terms that he would dictate.

It turned out that not everyone objected to the speech that Jason had tried to give. There were many people who felt that the rich were running the country and that ordinary people had no say in matters. It seemed to them that working stiffs were getting poorer and poorer while a small group of rich people, "the one percent" they called them, were getting wealthier and wealthier. But, I'm getting away from the story.

It was Tuesday February 5, just over two weeks after Jason's inauguration, that Jason's telephone rang. His secretary said, "Mr. President, your mother is on the line. It's important. I think you should take the call." Jason had instructed his staff not to put through any calls from family members.

"Jason," his mother began, "I have terrible news. Your father passed away this morning."

Jason tried to put a touch of grief into his voice. "How did it happen, Mom? He seemed OK when I visited you."

"He didn't want you to know, son, but his lung cancer was terminal. He knew he was going to die even when you visited us.

However, it was his heart that finally gave way. He died in the hospital this morning after suffering a massive heart attack last night."

"I'll be out there as soon as I can, Mom. When's the funeral?"

"It's on Friday, 2 pm at Henderson's Funeral Home."

"I'll be there, Mom."

This was a nuisance. He was just beginning to get the hang of being president, and now this interruption. He would have to go, of course.

The president would normally be ferried to Andrews Air Force Base in a Marine Corps helicopter where he would board the VC-25A aircraft, a modified Boeing 747, that would receive the designation Air Force One as soon as he was on board. However, the entire East Coast was being assaulted by a nor'easter with high winds and an almost unprecedented snowfall, and the Marine Corps decided it wasn't safe to fly the helicopter. President Wilder was shuttled through the storm in a motorcade. The White House press corps was also included in the motorcade and would have seats on Air Force One.

"Is it really safe to fly this plane?" Jason asked when the convoy arrived at Andrews. He hoped the answer would be no so that he would not have to undergo the trip.

"That's still being worked out," a member of his staff informed him. "There will be a delay until the weather people decide if there will be a break in the storm. It's snowing in Chicago, too, so the problem isn't just the weather here. Before we take off, we have to make sure that we can safely land in Chicago when we get there."

It didn't look promising. Air Force One could take off, but it would be a rough ascent. However, no one wanted to be responsible for putting the president's safety in jeopardy. It was finally decided not to risk the flight, and the president's motorcade returned him to the White House.

At least he had made the attempt. At a hastily called press conference in the White House Jason expressed his grief at his father's death and lamented the fact that the weather had prevented him from attending his father's funeral. He wiped his eyes with his handkerchief, and the press later reported that Jason was so moved that he broke into tears.

Lupita Wilder no longer thought often of Jason. She was now making good money as the international sales manager of Olivari Technology and had been made a vice president. Some thought she was being groomed to be the next CEO. She insisted on keeping her office in Mesa, Arizona, rather than move to the firm's headquarters in Milan, Italy. If she became CEO, she would relocate the company's headquarters to Phoenix. With video conferencing and the Internet, communication among senior officers located in different parts of the world was no longer difficult. It was also a great advantage that almost all international technology companies operated in English these days, no matter where their company headquarters were located. As an additional advantage, Mesa was just a short two-hour plane ride from Silicon Valley, where Olivari had a semiconductor plant and its research laboratories.

It was a warm and sunny morning in March 2013 when Lupita arrived at her office, turned on her computer, and walked down the hall to have her morning cup of coffee with Jacques, her new boyfriend, as had become part of her morning ritual. Perhaps having a boyfriend who worked at the same company was not a good idea, especially as Jacques was her junior, but Lupita hadn't planned to fall in love with him. She had knocked over a bowl of soup one day in the cafeteria and couldn't suppress an explicative that she had unfortunately picked up in Paris, "*Merde !*" Jacques, who was sitting at the next table replied, "*Ne dites pas ça, ma chère !*, Don't say that, my dear!"

When they discovered that they both spoke French, they agreed to meet again in the cafeteria to practice, but the language experiment didn't work out well. It turned out that Jacques, or Jacques du Bois to give him his full name, was a Cajun from Louisiana and had grown up speaking Cajun French at home and English at school. His coworkers called him Jack, not realizing that Jacques is actually French for James. Jacques could understand Lupita's Parisian French perfectly well, but she couldn't understand his Cajun, which is an old French dialect that has disappeared in France but has been kept alive in parts of Louisiana, Texas, northern Maine, and in some isolated towns in the Maritime Provinces of Canada. So, they gave up the idea of practicing French and spoke to each other in English, but they nevertheless developed a friendship and the habit of spending fifteen minutes together in the morning over coffee before beginning work and sometimes they went out for dinner together in the evening.

"I've got a pile of work on my desk," Jacques said. "I can't linger too long over coffee."

"Yeah," Lupita responded, "I always have an inbox full of emails to take care of first thing in the morning. Sometimes I wonder if I wouldn't get more work done if the Internet hadn't been invented."

When Lupita returned to her desk and opened up her email program, she found the usual 40 or 50 emails in her inbox. There was an eight-hour time difference between Milan and Mesa in winter and a nine-hour difference the rest of the year when Europe went on summer time. Arizona, almost alone among the states in the US, had the good sense to not observe daylight saving time. The time difference meant, however, that most people at headquarters in Milan had already gone home when Lupita arrived at the office. Unlike Americans, Italians were not known for working long days. Being called a workaholic was viewed by many as a complement in the United States, but in Italy it was more of an insult.

Lupita frequently came to work as early as 3 am to communicate with her colleagues in Milan. There were the usual emails about pending and possible sales that required the boss's attention. Her input was needed on a pending deal with NXP, which most people still referred to under its former name of Philips Semiconductors, to set up a joint manufacturing plant to produce gallium arsenide integrated circuits in Poland. Lupita would have to soon take a trip to Eindhoven, the Netherlands to meet with her counterparts at NXP and seal the deal.

Then, about halfway down the list, the subject of an email jumped out at her, "Jason's offshore bank account." She hesitated. She didn't know whether to open the email or to assign it to her spam folder. She opened it.

"¡Híjole!" she involuntarily exclaimed in her native Mexican Spanish. This was serious! "Dear Ms. Wilder, It has come to our attention that your ex-husband, President Wilders, has hundreds of millions of dollars stashed in a secret bank account in the Cayman Islands. I wish to see this information made public. If it is not made public by the end of the month, there will be serious consequences."

Following the message was the name of a bank in the Cayman Islands renowned for not asking very many questions of its depositors and a bank account number, which I have been asked not to publish in this book, because it is the subject of an active and ongoing criminal investigation.

Lupita didn't know what to do. Should she report it to her boss in Milan? No, because of the time difference he wouldn't get the information until the next morning. Also, this was not a company matter. It was a threat against her that had nothing to do with her job. She needed some advice. She picked up the phone and dialed Jacques' extension. *"Jacques ! Puis-tu venir à mon bureau tout de suite ?"* She thought that asking him in French would give him a sense of the urgency of the message and keep anyone who might overhear the conversation from understanding it.

She had barely hung up the phone when Jacques entered the office. "Close the door," she told him, "and then come and take a look at this email message on my computer screen."

"Wow!" was his response after reading the message. *"C'est grave !* This is serious!"

"Yes, but what should I do about it. Should I report it to our Internet Technology Department?"

"No, you should call the police, Lupita. This is a criminal matter. It's for law enforcement to sort out, not our people in the IT Department."

"OK, but stay with me, please. I really don't know how to handle this." She picked up the phone and dialed 911.

While they were waiting for the police to arrive, Jacques examined the message's header. It had been sent from a computer with a .ru suffix, Russia. It was almost certainly a spoofed address. The sender could be anywhere in the world. "It's highly unlikely that the Russians will help track down where this message originated. That's why so many people use Russian drone computers for their illegal activity. The Russians have little interest in investigating threats against Westerners."

Lupita's phone rang. It was reception. "There are two uniformed Mesa police officers here. They say you called them."

"Yes, please have someone show them up."

It caused quite a stir when the two police officers came marching down the hall toward Lupita's office wearing visitor's badges, that the receptionist had insisted that they put on. Their guide showed them into Lupita's office and then closed the door. The police presence meant that something illegal was going on. Had Lupita broken some law? Were they going to arrest her? Was Jacques involved?

The two police officers read the email, and then one of them turned to Lupita. "This is a serious matter, but we're out of our depth here. We take this type of threat very seriously, but we're not technologists. Aren't you the former wife of the President of the United States?"

"Yes, I'm not proud of it, but I am."

"That makes this a federal matter. Is there somewhere private where I can make a phone call?"

"Sure, there's a vacant office next to mine that you can use."

The officer called his sergeant, who in turn talked to the lieutenant, who in turn brought the matter up with the Mesa chief of police. He in turn called the FBI, where someone in turn called the Secret Service. Within an hour, the building was crawling with officers from five or six different local, state, and federal agencies. Some were in uniform, wearing bulletproof vests labeled "Federal Officer," or "Arizona Department of Public Safety, and others were wearing black suits. The whole building was in turmoil. What was going on in Lupita's office?

The matter couldn't be kept secret. Everyone knew that Lupita was President Wilder's ex-wife, and the sudden appearance of so many law enforcement officers implied that whatever was going on must have something to do with the president. Remarks between police officers in the hall that were overheard by employees confirmed that fact. No one could be sure who the source was, but the rumor began circulating that the threat was made in an email and had something to do with illegal money that her former husband had stashed away.

It didn't take long for the press to get wind of the affair. The police set up a cordon around the building and refused to let reporters enter, but one of them had a wife who worked in the building, and he called her. She told him about the rumors but begged him to keep her out of the affair.

News helicopters began circulating overhead, and local TV stations began interrupting their regular programming with live bulletins from reporters in Olivari's parking lot. There were few facts to report, but that didn't stop the reporters from filling in the gaps with rumors and speculation.

The next time someone who appeared to be a government official came out of the building, the reporter yelled several questions at him, "Is it true that there is a threat against Ms. Wilder? What do you know about the rumors that the president has money in an offshore bank account?"

The man, who was a Secret Service agent, emitted a brusque "No comment!" and kept walking to his car.

The other managers in the building begged the FBI and the Secret Service to let them work normally. They could not be cooped up in this building. The Secret Service decided that Lupita needed a 24-hour guard detail. That would make her work difficult. They decided to move her to a safe house in Phoenix until the big cheeses in Washington decided that it was safe for her to return to work. In the meantime, she could work by telephone and over the Internet. Her apartment would be too difficult to secure, hence the decision to house her in an undisclosed house that the government owned for just such contingencies.

However, the government agencies couldn't stop the press from speculating and from piecing together bits of information that it had obtained or surmised. Again, it was Channel Six Speedy News that first broke the story. "Federal authorities today placed President Wilder's former wife in protective custody, allegedly because of a threat against her. Channel Six Speedy News has learned that the threat came in the form of an anonymous email, whose source federal investigators are trying to determine. According to rumors, which Channel Six Speedy News has been unable to confirm, the email concerns an offshore bank account, whose owner the email alleges is President Jason Wilder."

It also didn't take long for someone to figure out that Lupita wasn't the only person in Olivari Technology's Mesa office who must have seen the email. One reporter learned from talking to an employee that Jacque du Bois had been in Lupita's office when the police first arrived. He must know as much as Lupita did.

Jacques had refused to speak with the press under police orders, but an enterprising cub reporter for the Spanish-language TV station Hispanovisión was determined to find out what he knew. A more experienced reporter might not have bothered interviewing Jacques du Bois just to hear him repeat the phrase "No comment!" but Claudia was not an experienced reporter. She had recently graduated from the Cronkite School of Journalism and Mass Communications at Arizona State University, and, thanks to the fact that she was fluent in both Spanish and English, she had landed a job as a cub reporter for the number two Spanish-language TV station in Phoenix.

It proved to be very simple to find out where Jacques lived; he was listed in the phone book. She drove to his house in the suburban Gilbert. She expected the house to be surrounded by a herd of reporters and police officers, but she was pleasantly surprised when she arrived to see that the street where Jacques lived was empty. She parked in front of the house, walked up to the front door, and rang the bell. Jacques answered.

"Mr. du Bois, my name is Claudia O'Reilly, and I'm a reporter for Hispanovisión. May I talk to you? It's about your co-worker Ms. Wilder."

"No comment! I'm under police orders not to talk to anyone."

"Do you know where your co-worker Ms. Wilder is at this moment?"

"No, I don't. I'm sorry, but I'm not allowed to talk to you."

"Aren't your worried about her? I have reason to suspect that she has knowledge that could put her in danger, and I think you may know the same things. Do you believe that Ms. Wilder is in safe hands?"

"I don't know. Honestly, I don't know what those guys from the government have up their sleeves. I'm sorry, but I am not allowed to discuss this."

"Mr. du Bois, I think you may be in danger, too. If your are also arrested, then the only two people who know what is in that email will be in the custody of the Justice Department, whose boss is Ms. Wilder's ex-husband, Jason Wilder. How long to you think it will be before someone realizes that it was a mistake to let you go? I think that you should let me in the house and we should talk about this. I don't think you understand how much danger both you and Ms. Wilder may be in. May I come in, please?"

Jacques hesitated a moment and then stood aside to let her pass and followed her into the house where he showed her into the living room. "Can I get you a cup of coffee? I'm afraid I don't have anything stronger in the house."

"A cup of coffee would be fine."

Claudia took a seat on the couch and sized up the living room while Jacques was in the kitchen making coffee. Her training as a reporter had taught her to be observant. It was obvious that Jacques lived alone. A mountain bike was parked in one corner of the room. That explained Jacques' athletic figure. In another corner there was a desk with a computer and printer on top of it. There was no television set. There was a large bookcase, however. Claudia got out of her chair and walked over to examine the books. Most were classic fiction, the majority of them in English, but some were in French.

Jacques was soon back with a tray containing two cups of coffee, a small pitcher of cream, a sugar bowl, and some biscuits. He placed the tray on the coffee table in front of Claudia, took one of the cups of coffee for himself, and invited Claudia to help herself to the biscuits.

"I see you're quite the fan of good literature," Claudia began. "Where did you get all of these books?"

"I'm an addict. I can't enter a bookstore without buying an armload of books. I wish I had time to read all of them."

"And I wish I had your love of literature."

Jacques changed the subject. "You said your last name is O'Reilly. That's an unusual last name for someone working for a Spanish-language news organization."

"My husband is Irish," Claudia explained. "We've only been married a few months, and it's still difficult for me to get used to being called O'Reilly. My maiden name is Osorio. Marrying an Irishman was a good idea. The Irish and the Mexicans have very similar temperaments."

It was time to get to the point. "Exactly what is it that you want to talk about?" Jacques asked.

"The rumor going around is that Ms. Wilder received an email that caused all of the police activity at your office. Because she is the former wife of President Wilder, I assume that the email had something to do with him. I'm not a conspiracy theorist, but I do find it strange that she was taken into protective custody in some undisclosed location.

Other than Mrs. Wilder, the police and the feds, I suspect that you are the only person who knows what was in that email. If the email had something to do with the president and he wants to cover it up, I can see your being taken into 'protective custody' next."

"The email was a threat against her. That's why the Secret Service is protecting her."

Claudia wasn't one to give up that easily. She suspected that there was much more to that email than Jacques was letting on.

"Mr. du Bois, is there anything else about that email that you would like to tell me? Is there something about that email that would be covered up if you were to disappear?"

"I'm not supposed to talk about the email. I think I've already said too much."

"Again, I'm not a believer in conspiracy theories, but if I'm wrong and there is something else in that email that the government doesn't want to be made public, that secret may be something that you take to the grave. Your only protection is to have that information made public so that there would be no purpose in silencing you."

"Yeah, you may be right, but I'll be in big trouble if word gets out that I revealed a government secret."

"Aren't there a lot of people who have seen the email?"

"Other than Lupita and I, the Mesa Police, the FBI, and the Secret Service."

"Then you don't need to worry, Mr. du Bois. Just tell me what was in that email, and I will report that the information came from a talkative anonymous source in law enforcement. If so many cops know about the email, there's bound to be a leak sooner or later in any case."

"OK, Ms. O'Reilly. There was something else in the email. It said that President Wilder has a secret bank account. Lupita is supposed to make the account information public, or something bad will happen to her. At any rate, that's what the email claimed. The whole matter is in law enforcement hands now."

"Do you know anything more about this supposed bank account?"

"Yeah, the email said it is in Cayman Islands. It's a numbered bank account. I wrote down the number on a slip of paper and stuck it into my pocket before the police arrived. Here, I'll write it down for you. No. On second thought, it would be better if you copied it down. That way no one will be able to tie the leak to me by analyzing my handwriting."

"Thank you, Mr. du Bois. I assure you that you did the right thing for yourself, for Ms. Wilder, and for the good of the country."

As Lupita drove away, she noticed two black SUVs driving in the opposite direction. Apparently, she had reached Jacques just in time.

When she got back to the Hispanovisión studio, Claudia told news director Javier Sepúlveda that she had a hot story about a secret bank account that President Wilder allegedly had in the Cayman Islands. "Javier, there is no way I can reveal my source, even to you. If we go with this story, we'll have to independently verify the accuracy of the information."

Javier was skeptical. "I don't mean to be disrespectful, Claudia, but you are not an experienced reporter. How could it be that you managed to ferret out a story that so many reporters from the national press appear to be unaware of?"

"I can't tell you that without revealing my source."

"Well, you're going to have to tell me who your source is if we're to pursue this story. You know we have a code of conduct around here. I promise I won't make your source public."

"I absolutely will not do that. There is one thing we could do tonight to get the ball rolling until we develop an independent source. We can put a story on the air stating that we believe that the president's former wife and one of her co-workers are being held and that there are allegations that they have knowledge that could prove embarrassing to the president. We could ask the FBI about the president's alleged secret bank account, and if they refuse to confirm or deny its existence, that would in itself be news."

"Which coworker is being held?"

"I have reason to believe that a man named Jacques du Bois is now in federal custody, although I haven't verified it."

"I think you've brought in enough information for us to get started, Claudia. I'll get a team working on the story right away so we can break it on the 10 pm news."

"Javier, I'm the one who brought you this story, and I want to be the one who goes on camera to break it. Oh, and I almost forgot. I have the number of the president's alleged secret account."

"WHAT?! Excellent! let me have it! I have a contact in the CIA who can check it out. He won't be deterred by political considerations. If it turns out to be true that the account belongs to Jason Wilder, we'll go public with that and attribute the information to an anonymous source in the CIA. Then you won't be the only person under pressure to reveal a source. I'll have to resist pressure from the feds to reveal mine. I'd go to jail before I'd do that.

OK, I agree with you. You keep your source secret, and I'll keep mine secret from you and from everybody else. That way, when the pressure is on, neither of us will have the whole story in case one of us breaks under government pressure."

Javier didn't wait for the information about the secret account to be confirmed. His CIA contact promised to look into it and to give him a short period of exclusivity before turning the information over to his boss if it turned out to be correct. Javier decided to go on the air with what he knew for sure and to report the rumor for what it was, an unconfirmed rumor. He also agreed to give Claudia the lead on the story.

The news was broadcast in Spanish, of course, and because the reader may not understand that language, I'll skip the details and merely state that the reader already knows its contents from subsequent news reports. Because the story was not broadcast in English, it went unnoticed by the mainstream news media at first. It was not until the following afternoon that the English-language media picked it up. By evening, the story led on all of the local newscasts and had even been picked up by the national and foreign news outlets. Samuel B. Goodrich, the special agent in charge of the Phoenix FBI office consented to a short interview on Channel Six Speedy News with anchor Alison Copper. "Is it true that President Jason Wilder's former spouse, Guadalupe Wilder, and her co-worker, Jacques du Bois, are in FBI custody?"

"No! That's not true!" Agent Goodrich responded. "They are not in custody at all. Because of threats against their lives by persons unknown they are in a safe location under the protection of the Secret Service. They are free to leave anytime they want to."

"Why is the Secret Service protecting them? Isn't that the job of the local police?" Alison responded.

"Normally, it would be, but as you know, the Secret Service is in charge of protecting the president and his family."

"Guadalupe Wilder is no longer married to the president and is therefore not a member of his family. Jacques du Bois has no relationship with the president whatsoever. Why would the Secret Service be in charge of protecting them?"

"While it's true that Ms. Wilder is no longer married to the president, she once was, and the Secret Service feels that is reason enough to protect her. As to Mr. du Bois, he is under threat by the same person or persons as Ms. Wilder, so it makes sense to offer them both the same protection."

Alison wasn't one to take official statements at face value. "Can we speak with Ms. Wilder and Mr. du Bois to get their viewpoints?"

"No, I'm afraid that's impossible. The Secret Service doesn't want to take the slightest risk of having their location discovered. They have both agreed to remain incommunicado for their own safety."

The next day Javier Sepúlveda called Claudia into his office. "Close the door. This is for your ears only. I've heard back from my contact inside the CIA. The account exists, and it apparently does in fact belong to the president. My contact has asked me to sit on the information for the present. The CIA is trying to trace the movement of money into and out of the account."

"Boss, we can't just sit on a story like this. This is too important."

"It's only for a few days, Claudia. And my contact promised me that if we cooperate, we will have the story in advance of other news organizations. Imagine our local Spanish-language TV station breaking a story that even the *New York Times* has no inkling of! I think we're headed for the big time."

"Well, you're the boss, Javy," she said using the familiar nickname that she knew he hated. "Just keep me in mind when it comes time to break the story."

"I will, Clau. That's why you're the only one I'm telling this to. But if you call me Javi one more time, the deal's off."

As it turned out, Noticiero Hispanovisión didn't get the chance to break the news. Someone inside the CIA leaked the story to a Republican senator. The reader may be excused for thinking that the Democrats in

Washington would be the first to jump on the rumor of Jason's offshore bank account and demand an explanation, but traditional Republicans felt a deep hatred toward Jason whereas most Democrats merely regarded him as an annoyance. Senator Wentworth Ellington, Republican of Oklahoma, called a news conference for 9 am on Monday, April 1 to announce "something of international importance." Some reporters thought it might be some sort of April Fool's joke, but Senator Ellington was deadly serious.

"Good morning, ladies and gentlemen, and welcome to this press conference. I have the sad duty to report that the FBI and other federal law enforcement agencies are investigating an offshore bank account that appears to belong to our president, Jason Wilder. The account contains over one billion US dollars and was opened when Jason Wilder was governor of Arizona. The earliest transfers into the account, to the tune of several hundred million dollars, have been traced to Beschissen Construction, LLC, a company that did highway work for the State of Arizona. Money has continued to flow into the account even after Jason Wilder's inauguration as president, although the later deposits were laundered through multiple bank accounts, and investigators have not yet been able to trace them to their source.

"I have shared this information with House Speaker Joshua Clapton who has agreed that the House of Representatives should set up a committee to investigate this allegation, and if it proves to be true, draw up articles of impeachment. I will now take a few brief questions."

"Senator Ellington, where did you get the information about the president's bank account."

"That I am not at liberty to divulge. Let's just say that it is from a responsible investigative arm of government."

"Senator, how long have you had this information?"

"I can't reveal that either."

"Do you know where the money came from?"

"As I said in my introductory remarks, part of it to the tune of several hundred million dollars, has been traced to Beschissen Construction, LLC. We have not been able to track down the source of the more recent deposits."

"Which were larger, the deposits when Jason Wilder was governor or the more recent deposits?"

"The more recent deposits are much larger. Ladies and gentlemen, those are all of the questions that I'll take at this time. I'm sure that other officials will keep the press informed as information is developed. I apologize for not being more forthcoming, but this is an active investigation."

Senator Ellington turned, walked across the platform, and disappeared behind a curtain. Reporters continued to shout questions to him, but he paid them no heed.

At the White House, the telephones in offices of the president's press secretary were ringing faster than her office staff could answer them. "I'm sorry, but Press Secretary Sanders has no information to impart at this time," was the standard answer given to all callers. Then the answer changed. "Secretary Sanders will make a brief announcement in the press room at 3 pm. Only credentialed White House reporters may attend." That word was also sent down to the reporters gathered in the White House pressroom.

Press Secretary Shelia Sanders' announcement was televised live by all of the major networks in the United States, Europe, and Asia, but it was a disappointment. "I have only a brief announcement to make, and afterwards there will be no questions. President Wilder has asked me to tell you that the accusations made by Senator Ellington are completely unfounded. He is looking forward to clearing his name and to continue to serve the people of the United States. He asked me to tell you that he is not a crook. Thank you, ladies and gentlemen."

With that, Shelia Sanders picked up her coffee and left the podium, ignoring the shouted questions of members of the press corps. "I'm sorry, but I said I will not be able to take questions."

One of the old-timers turned to the reporter to her left and said, "I've been covering the White House for a long time, and I heard that statement once before. It was Richard Nixon who said 'I'm not a crook' not long before he resigned his office to avoid impeachment."

By this time, members of the House of Representatives of both parties were angered by what they regarded as Jason's arrogant conduct. The very next day the House Judiciary Committee met to take up the matter of drawing up articles of impeachment. Jason thought it was time to have a conversation with Chamita, who would succeed him as president if he were impeached and convicted. He summoned her to the Oval Office.

"Vice President Monroe," he began, "we've never gotten along. May I call you Chamita?"

"You're the president. You can do pretty much whatever your want."

"I was hoping we could have a civilized conversation for once." Jason could be very charming when he put his mind to it. "My presidency is going to end sooner or later, and you'll become President of the United States. I'd like the transition to go as smoothly as possible. If I'm impeached by the House and tried in the Senate, this whole matter could drag out for a long time, perhaps for a year. During that time, the government will come to a standstill, and you will continue to be a nonentity in the background. It takes a two-thirds majority to convict in the Senate, and that may not be easy to obtain."

"I think you're wrong there, Mr. President. I don't think there are many senators from either party who aren't anxious to get rid of you."

"Call me Jason, please. At any rate, there are two ways this can proceed. It can end quickly, and you can be president as soon as a few days from now, or it can drag on for months with an uncertain outcome while you sit on your hands. Even in the case of Richard Nixon, things dragged on for a long time before he resigned, and if he hadn't resigned and had let the impeachment proceedings continue, he would have stayed in office much longer leaving the country leaderless."

"Are you saying that you're prepared to resign, Mr. President?" Chamita could not bring herself to address Jason by his first name.

"Well, that's a complicated matter. Once I leave office, be it by resignation or by impeachment, I will be subject to criminal prosecution for avoiding income taxes if for nothing else. I'm completely innocent, of course, but proving my innocence would cost me a fortune in lawyers' fees. I'd be dead broke by the time it was over, and I'd probably lose a year of my life fighting court battles."

"Yes, you're right. Your life isn't going to be pleasant, but you deserve everything you get, Mr. President."

Being called Mr. President when he was trying to set a more casual tone was beginning to grate on Jason's nerves, but he suppressed his irritation and managed to force himself to maintain a friendly demeanor. "You may remember that Richard Nixon and Gerald Ford came to an understanding. Nixon resigned, and Ford pardoned him so that he wouldn't face criminal charges."

"Ah! Now I see where this is leading! You're going to tell me that you're willing to resign as long as you can be sure that I'll grant you a pardon once I'm president. You want to make the same deal with me that Richard Nixon made with Gerald Ford, don't you?"

"Ah,... Something like that, sure."

"Now, suppose I agree to this deal. How can you be sure that I will adhere to it once you're out of office and I'm president?"

"I've thought that through, Chamita. I know you're a tool of the Hogsons, just as I was before I rebelled. I know enough to bring the Hogsons down and you with them. If I'm ever brought to trial, everything I know will come out, and I don't think either you or the Hogsons want that to happen."

Chamita hesitated and looked thoughtful. Finally she said, "I can't give you an answer now. I need to think this over."

"I thought you might need to make a phone call. I suggest doing it over a secure phone. Let me know what the Hogsons decide."

Two days later, Jason called a press conference. "Ladies and gentlemen of the press, as you know serious accusations have been made against me. I assure you that they are completely baseless. However, it would be selfish of me to put the country though months or perhaps as long as a year of turmoil until this case plays out, although I assure you I would be found innocent in the end. Therefore, in the interest of maintaining a functional executive branch, I submitted my letter of resignation to the Secretary of State fifteen minutes ago. I will not take any questions, and I will now step aside so that you can witness the swearing in of the new president. My resignation takes effect immediately."

With that, Jason walked off stage, and the Chief Justice of the Supreme Court and Vice President Chamita Monroe took his place. The Chief Justice was carrying a Bible, which he opened to the Book of James, which Chamita had previously selected. "Raise you right hand," the Chief Justice commanded. Chamita raised her right hand and placed her left hand on the open Bible. She then recited the short oath of office from memory. She had rehearsed it many times over the past year. "I do solemnly swear that I will faithfully execute of Office of President of

United States, and will to the best of my ability, preserve, protect and defend the Constitution of the United States." Then she added a familiar phrase that is not in the formal oath, "So help me God."

Jason, meanwhile, had been escorted to the White House South Lawn where the presidential helicopter, Marine One, was waiting to fly him to Andrews Air Force Base. As usual, the helicopter flew in a group with four other identical helicopters in a shifting formation designed to conceal in which aircraft the president, or in this case, the former president, was riding.

At Andrews Air Force Base, Jason boarded one of the two Boeing 747's that were assigned to the president. Chamita, as a last gesture, had arranged for the plane to fly him back to Phoenix. She would have preferred to send him back in a Greyhound bus, but Luther Hogson had suggested that giving him a last flight on the presidential airplane was a good publicity move. It made her look magnanimous. The plane did not use the call Air Force One, because the dignitary it was transporting was no longer the president.

While he was on the plane, the steward come to him and said, "Mr. President, there's a phone call for you. You can pick it up using the phone over at the desk."

"Who is it?"

"I don't know, but the call came in over a secure connection. The caller refused to identify himself. It's a man's voice."

Jason picked up the phone. "Hello."

"Jason, this is Willard Hogson. I warned you not to cross us. I'm just calling to let you know that we're not finished with you yet. Watch your back."

And, the phone went dead.

Chapter 9 — Revenge

Back in his Paradise Valley home near Phoenix, Jason was bored. Because he was a former president, he was still guarded by a Secret Service detail, which would have accompanied him if he had left the house. However, he had no desire to go outside. He still feared the Hogson brothers. At least here he was protected unless they had someone fire a rocket at the house.

He spent most of his time seated in an overstuffed chair in his living room in semidarkness with the blinds pulled. He was depressed, angry, and fearful at the same. He was angry at the Hogsons for having betrayed him, but at the same time he feared for his life. He knew too much. Would the Secret Service really defend him if the Hogsons ordered his assassination? For all he knew, one of more members of his Secret Service detail might be on the Hogsons' payroll. If the Hogsons were going to have him killed, he was going to do everything he could to make sure that they were taken down with him.

He was also disappointed with his record as president. Richard Nixon had at least served one full term and had left his mark on the nation in the form of increased welfare benefits and the opening of diplomatic relations with China. Jason had accomplished nothing. He had no time to take advantage of the ample opportunities for graft that the presidency would have provided him, and his overseas bank account had been seized. The Hogsons had also cut all ties with him and stopped their under-the-counter payments to him. Chamita had not yet kept her promise to pardon him. Would she? Jason began to doubt it. Well, he'd get even with her, too, if she didn't. If he was going to be indicted and go to jail, he was going to make sure that he took a few people to the slammer with him including Chamita. The people he most wanted to bring down, however, were the Hogsons.

His desire for revenge drove him so hard that Jason had no energy for other projects. Nixon had at least authored several books after he resigned the presidency. The mere thought of writing a book left Jason cold. Only idiots wrote books.

But, wait a minute! Maybe writing a book was a good idea. It might fit into his plans to get revenge. He didn't have to write it himself. He was sure that he would have no trouble finding a ghostwriter. He didn't have to worry about incriminating himself; he was already incriminated. The evidence against him was overwhelming. He could still bring down all of the people who had betrayed him, the Hogsons especially, but also Chamita, his ex-wife Lupita, Martin Glover, Bill Kandinsky, Shawn Killingworth, and perhaps a few more. Well, maybe he couldn't bring down Lupita. She was too honest. There were no skeletons in her closet. He wished that he could do something to make her suffer, too, but he probably couldn't. However, he could get the rest of those bastards.

Jason had a lot of information that it was better not to share with anyone until it was time to spring his trap. It would be best to not share some of the most sensitive knowledge even with the ghostwriter until the book was almost completed. What Jason had to reveal had to come as a complete surprise and catch his enemies off guard. The government had provided him with a secretary and a small staff on government salary, but he didn't trust any of them. They were probably spying for Chamita, Shawn, and the Hogsons. He certainly wasn't going to entrust any of the sensitive information to them.

Jason began to make discreet inquiries about a ghostwriter. He needed someone who wrote well but was not well known to the public. He wanted someone who was hungry enough to take on this job. He began searching online blogs, and that's how he discovered me. He found that I had several blogs and an author's page on Amazon, all well written but very dull, which meant that I had few followers and was therefore almost completely unknown. He looked me up in the Library of Congress and found that I had written a number of books about the semiconductor and wireless communications market plus two out-of-print textbooks. He decided that I was just the person he needed to ghostwrite his book. With a bit more investigating, he discovered that I was a retiree living on a modest Social Security check. That was the deciding factor. I was hungry. I needed the money.

When my phone rang, an unknown number popped up on the caller ID. I had a recluse's tendency of seldom answering calls from numbers I didn't recognize. It was probably one more telemarketer with spoofed caller-ID information. I was going to let the call go to voice mail, but then out of boredom I decided to answer it. At least I could entertain myself by wasting a few minutes of some telemarketer's time. My time wasn't valuable; I had nothing better to do.

"Mr. Quinn?"

"Yes, who's calling, please?"

"My name is Jason Wilder. You may recognize the name."

"The only Jason Wilder whose name I know is the one who used to be President of the United States."

"Yep, that's right. That's me."

"This must be some sort of a joke or scam. It's the first time someone has called me pretending to be the President of the United States. I suppose you need my credit card or checking account number, because you need some place to stash a few hundred million dollars."

"I assure you that the call is legit, Mr. Quinn. I understand you're a writer, and I need someone to ghostwrite a book for me. I promise you I will pay well."

Suddenly, I was interested. "What kind of book?"

"It will be an autobiography. I've never written a book myself, but I know that you've written several. Look! I'd like you to come by my house, say tomorrow afternoon at 3 pm. Are you free then?"

"Yes, I am." This smelled of money, and money was one commodity that I lacked.

He then gave me his address and phone number. I already had his phone number on my caller ID, and the one he gave me was identical. After we hung up, I checked the address on Google Maps. It checked out. Then I looked up the property on the State of Arizona website. Sure enough, the title to the property was registered to Jason Wilder. Lastly, I did a name search for him on the Maricopa County Registrar's website. A number of documents popped up in his name including a quitclaim signed by Guadalupe Wilder giving Jason full title to the house. It really did seem as if I was about to negotiate a ghostwriting contract with the former president.

I have the bad habit of always arriving early for appointments. The following afternoon I arrived at Jason Wilder's house 15 minutes before the appointed time and parked in the street in front of his house. I did not get to walk up to the front door and ring the bell as I had expected. On the front sidewalk, I was stopped by a dark-suited man who seemed to appear out of nowhere. He asked me who I was and what I was doing there. When I told him I was Jack Quinn and that I was there to see President Jason Wilder, he nodded but demanded that I show him identification. When he was satisfied that my face matched the picture on my driver's license, he leaned over, squeezed a fold on the front of his shirt, and whispered something into his chest that my budget hearing aids were unable to capture. That's when I noticed that he also had an earphone in his right ear. He seemed to listen for a few moments, and then he led me to the front door. He opened it and motioned me to enter.

Another dark-suited man was waiting for me inside the door. "Mr. Quinn, empty your pockets, please, and place everything in them on this table." He passed a wand over my body much like the wand that the security personnel at the airport use to screen passengers. He examined the items I had placed on the table before saying, "You may put these items back into your pockets except for your Swiss Army knife, and then follow me. I'll give you the knife back when you leave. Come along, and I'll show you to the president now."

I entered the dimly lit living room, and it took my eyes a few moments to adjust to the gloom. Then I recognized Jason sitting in his chair from the many times I had seen him on TV. However, he had aged considerably. He now had thinning gray hair, was slightly stoop-shouldered, and lost a considerable amount of weight. He seemed comfortable in his overstuffed chair and did not bother to rise or to offer me his hand when I entered the room. He motioned me into a chair across from him. Seated to his right was an attractive middle-aged woman. Judging from her athletic figure, she must spend a lot of time in the gym.

"Mr. Quinn," Jason began, "this is Elisa McIntosh. She's one of my attorneys. She'll help us work out this book contract."

Elisa nodded, but she also did not offer me her hand.

"Here's what I'm thinking," Jason continued. "I want to write a book about my life, but I am not a writer. Even if I could write, I absolutely do not have the patience to write anything as long as a book. So, my idea is to have you interview me and tape our conversations. Elisa will supply you with documents that will fill in some of the blanks. I also want you to interview other people in my life, my Mom, my ex-wife, other people with whom I am associated. You will write the book as if I were telling the story. Your name will not appear anywhere in connection with the book. My name will be on the cover as the book's author. For all of this, you will be well compensated. I think that's how things work when someone is having a book ghostwritten. Am I right?"

"I've never been asked to ghostwrite a book before, but that sounds acceptable so far, depending on the compensation," I replied. "I think I need to get a lawyer, too, and have him work things out with Ms. McIntosh. There is a lot to think about. What if something happens to you before the book is finished? Do I still get paid? How do I get paid in that case? Does the book still get published?"

"If you'll just listen to me, I think I have the answers to those questions. I've given all of those questions some thought, and Elisa is going to include answers to them in the proposed contract. I have some very powerful enemies, and you're right to worry about something happening to me. If I die of natural causes or am assassinated before the book is finished, I'll be beyond caring what happens to the book. I don't believe in life after death, so I won't know or care what happens if my life should end suddenly, as is likely. I plan to be around to see this book cause a sensation, but if I'm not, I'll die more content if I can be sure that this book will see the light of day.

"Here's what I'm thinking. I'll pay you $50,000 total to write the book. You'll get $1,000 a month while you're working on it and the balance in a lump sum when the book is ready for publishing. I'll pay an editor and a proofreader. I'm sure this book will be popular, but I'm not concerned with the profits. I want this book to have a major negative impact on certain people."

I was dying to get the book contract, and $50,000 would be a windfall for someone of my modest means, but I tried to appear lackadaisical and in need of convincing. "How can you be sure that the book will sell?"

"All books by former presidents sell. Look at that book that Clinton wrote; what was it called?"

"*My Life*," I answered.

"Yeah, *My Life*. It is very poorly written, and probably no one who buys it reads it all the way to the end, but it's still selling thousands of copies this many years after his presidency is over. Nixon's books are still selling, too. I hope you write better than whoever the hack is who wrote Clinton's book for him."

I let that pass. I wasn't going to venture an opinion about my own writing skill. It was time to bargain. "$50,000 isn't much money for so much work. It'll probably take me a year of hard work to write the book, and after that I'll still have to work with the editor and proofreader on changes and corrections." I was stretching the truth a bit, I was sure I could crank the book out in less than six months. I was wrong as it turned out. I had no idea how complicated this project would be.

"Mr. Quinn, I did some investigating and made sure that I learned a lot about you before I decided to offer you the chance to write my book. I know that you're living on Social Security, and you can't be making much money from that book you're selling on Amazon about that pilgrimage you made. What's it called, Elisa?"

"*A Senior Citizen Walks the Camino de Santiago.*"

"Ah, yes, that's it. You can't be making much from that crappy book about doing a dumb pilgrimage. There must be a million books about the Camino de Santiago. Even if yours is written better than most, nothing makes it stand out, and I'll bet you're lucky to sell a dozen copies a day. $50,000 is more than you'll make from that dumb book even if it sells for the next 20 years, which it won't."

"That's not quite true," I responded, even though it was perfectly true. "I think $100,000 would be fairer."

However, Jason was smarter than I gave him credit for. He knew I couldn't refuse. "If you don't accept my terms, I can easily find someone who will. There's a lot of starving writers out there who would jump at the chance to earn $50,000."

I had to admit that he was right. $50,000 was a lot of money to someone in my financial position, but I had one more objection. "If something happens to you before I finish the book, how do I know that I'll get the balance of the $50,000?"

"Good point!" Jason admitted. "I may not be around much longer, and if I'm not, my estate could be tied up for years. I'll tell you what. We'll write into the contract that if I die, disappear, or become mentally incapacitated before the book is finished, you become the sole owner of the rights to the book. You get the copyright, and you can do with the book whatever you want, even publish it under your own name. I'll be beyond caring. You needn't be concerned about the rest of the advance in that case. A book about me and my downfall should make you a fortune."

I noticed that during this conversation Elisa was taking copious notes.

"If you'll tentatively agree, Mr. Quinn, I think we're finished for today. Please give Elisa your attorney's contact information, and she'll send over a tentative contract."

I stood up to leave and expected Jason to also stand to shake hands. He looked away from me and made a motion with the back of his hand that I understood to mean that I was dismissed.

The contract that Elisa sent to my attorney turned out to be perfectly acceptable. I had no changes to suggest. I wish that I could have weaseled more money out of Jason for the deal, but beggars can't be choosers.

I was about to call Jason to set up an appointment for our first interview when I received a call from someone on his staff. "The President will see you tomorrow from 2 to 4 pm and thereafter every Tuesday and Thursday at the same time until you have as much information from him as you need to write the book. Bring your own recording device, and make sure that you come on time and alone."

When I arrived for the appointment, 15 minutes early as usual, I had to go through the same security procedure as on my last visit. This time I was smart enough to leave my pocket knife at home. Then I was shown into the dimly lit living room where Jason was seated in the same chair as if he hadn't moved since I last saw him. This time he and I were alone. He didn't want anyone but me to hear his story.

I sat the recorder on the table between us, and he began talking about his early life in Chicago. I interrupted him from time to time to ask questions to clarify certain details, and each time I did so, Jason shot me an irritated look. However, I wanted to get the story straight, and I persisted in my interruptions despite his displeasure. When we finished the first session, Jason handed me a slip of paper and a sealed, padded envelope.

"The number on the slip of paper is my Mom's telephone number in Chicago. I already spoke with her, and she promised to help in any way she can. She's expecting you to call her. The envelope is to be opened only in case of my death. If I should disappear or if I should die, I want you to incorporate the contents of this envelope into the book. I'm trusting you not to open it before that, and I'm trusting you to do the right thing with the contents if anything does happen to me."

I did call Irene, Jason's mother. I still have the recordings of our several telephone conversations. We spoke several times. I got the impression that she was lonely and was glad to have the distraction of our conversations. I pieced together what she told me with the information I got from Jason, and I wrote the rough draft of the first chapter of this book.

My Tuesday and Thursday meetings with Jason became a ritual. I spent much of the time I was not talking with Jason or his mother at my computer transcribing the recordings and then editing the transcriptions into the first draft of the narrative that you have been reading. I didn't know at the time that I would have to go back and revise everything once I opened the envelope that Jason had given me.

My twice-weekly meetings with Jason went on for just over two months. After the last interview, we never met again, although I did speak to him several times on the telephone to clear up certain points in the narrative or to ask for more detail. There was, of course, the final fateful phone call, but again, I am getting ahead of the story.

I had been sure that I would be able to finish the book in less than six months, but six months after our first meeting, I still hadn't finished. I had typed all of the information I had into my computer, but it still wasn't properly organized in a form suitable for publication. I had grossly underestimated the amount of editing and rewriting I would have to do before I could organize Jason's meandering monologues into a manuscript that would be ready to submit to a proofreader let alone to a publisher.

Jason hired an editor to keep tabs on me—I don't think Jason completely trusted me—and I emailed the editor weekly updates. I think Jason would have done better not to trust the editor who never gave me any detailed suggestions. I would receive emails from him with remarks such as "It looks good" or "it needs more polishing" or "you need to flush out the communication with the Hogsons a bit more." Given Jason's preoccupation with secrecy, I was surprised that he would allow an editor to read the manuscript, but I assumed the person he hired must have been someone in whom he had confidence. For my part, I wondered if the so-called editor even bothered to do more than take Jason's money and skim the material I sent him.

Finally, I reached the point where I could see the end of my work in sight. It was well organized, although some sections still needed some minor polishing. Jason had told me from the beginning that he wanted this to be a revenge autobiography, a tool for getting even with all the people he believed had wronged him, especially the Hogsons. I didn't see how that could work. Jason made plenty of accusations during our conversation, and I incorporated those accusations into the book, but none of them were backed by evidence. To me it seemed a case of "he said, she said." I didn't realize at the time that Jason had already given me all of the necessary evidence to back up his accusations.

I had been steadily writing for over a month with no word from Jason when one day unexpectedly he telephoned me. "How's the book coming along?" he asked with no preliminaries.

"I think I have everything written, but it's still not quite polished. I need another month to clean it up and make the text flow more smoothly."

"I'm glad to hear that you've made so much progress. Do you remember that padded envelope I gave you?"

"Yes, certainly, I do."

"Please do as I say and don't ask any questions. When we finish this call, open the envelope and make a copy of everything in it. Don't take the time to read anything. You need to do this as quickly as you can. Do you have any spare flash drives?"

"Yes, I always keep a few blank ones handy."

"You're going to need at least one. Do you have a copy machine, I mean for copying documents?

"No, but I have a scanner and a printer. I can scan documents into the computer and then print them."

"That's not the best idea, because it will leave copies on your hard drive, and even if you delete them, they can still be recovered. Go to a copy shop and make photocopies there of the documents in the envelope."

"This is sounding pretty mysterious. Is there something going on that I should know about?"

"I said don't ask questions! Now, you'll also have to copy the text file of my book onto a flash drive plus a copy any supporting information you have on the computer, your notes, audio files, etcetera. Is there safe place you can leave the copies where no one would think of looking for them?"

"Yes, I can leave them with...."

"Don't tell me where! Someone is almost certainly recording this call. Just do as I asked and have it done before 5 pm. Then put all of the originals back into the envelope and leave it in your house. Later, you'll understand the reason for all of this.

"I am very depressed. The book's rights belong to you, by the way. Oh, speaking of the book, you need to make a backup of it and any other files on your computer that you need to keep and put them on the flash drive, too. All of the copies you make need to be stored in a place that no one will think of."

"You're repeating yourself," I said. "You told me that already."

"Sorry, I am very agitated, and I'm not thinking straight. I'm afraid I have some bad news for you. Once you go over the contents of the envelope, you'll have a lot of rewriting to do before the book is ready to be punished. It's not nearly as complete as you thought.

"The good news is that once the book starts to sell, you'll be paid handsomely for the extra work. All of the royalties will go to you. I'm sorry about the remaining money I owe you, but your book royalties should more than make up for it. Do the things I told you quickly. There may not be much time. As I said, I imagine this call is being monitored."

The phone went dead. I was quite alarmed. Jason didn't sound quite sane, and what he said about the book's rights belonging to me alarmed me especially. He had said that the book would belong to me in the event of his death. I dialed Jason's number, but he wasn't the person who answered. "Yes?" asked a gruff male voice.

"This is Jack Quinn. I'd like to speak with President Wilder."

"The president left instructions that he does not want any more phone calls this evening."

"But, this may be important."

The phone clicked, and the connection was broken. The person on the other end of the call didn't even have the courtesy to say good-bye.

I sat stunned for a few moment before I sprang into action. Jason had sounded very insistent when he told me to make copies and get them to a secure location as quickly as possible. He must have had a good reason.

I opened the envelope. There was a flash drive inside and several sheets of paper. The paper had a list of names, dates, and mp3 computer file names. I guessed that they pertained to the files on the flash drive. Without investigating farther, I scanned and printed the few sheets of paper, and I used my computer to copy the files from the flash drive to a blank one. I also copied the book manuscript from my computer's hard drive onto the flash drive. Then I placed the original flash drive and the original sheets of paper back into the original envelope and placed the copies into a second envelope, which I sealed and addressed to a friend, adding the words on the outside of the envelope "Please hold unopened for Jack Quinn." I knew that my friend would do as I asked. I dared not call him. I remembered Jason's warning about the possibility of the call's being recorded.

I had a program that was advertised as being able to permanently erase all traces of any files that had been deleted from a computer's disk. I started the program running and used the computer's mouse to check the onscreen box that would cause the program to shut itself off and shut down the computer when the program had finished running. I hoped it would erase any traces of the documents that I had copied using the computer in defiance of Jason's instructions.

I was in the habit of going for a walk every evening soon after sundown to relieve the stress of sitting in front of the computer all day. I suffer from insomnia, and the walk helps to calm me down and makes it easier for me to sleep. There was a blue mailbox just a few blocks from my house, and my normal evening walk took me past it. I took the envelope with the copies along as I set out on my walk. I left the envelope that Jason had given me on the desk beside my computer. When I reached the mailbox, I dropped the envelope with the copies into it. Then I continued my walk, which lasted about another half hour, enjoying the pleasant Phoenix evening weather.

When I got back to my house, there were several black SUVs parked in front of it, and several of my neighbors were standing at a respectful distance looking on with evident curiosity. One of the black-suited men whom I had seen at Jason's house asked me gruffly, "Where were you, Mr. Quinn?"

"I just went out for a walk. I go for a walk every evening. What's going on, anyway? Why are you all here?" However, after Jason's call, I had already divined what had happened.

"Where did you walk to?"

"I didn't walk to any special destination. I have a circuit that I walk almost every evening. It's just a random path through the neighborhood; I'm not very imaginative. I walk the same circuit every evening. It's the only exercise I get. Are you going to tell me what's going on?"

"We'll discuss that in presently. In the meantime, I want you to go inside."

I didn't have to unlock the door to let us in. The latch had been smashed, and the door was standing wide open. Several other black-suited men were already in the house ransacking it. The man who had intercepted me before my house barked an order at two of the others, "Get some yellow tape placed around this place out front, and tell those neighbors to get the hell off the street and stay in their goddamned houses."

One of the men was sitting on my couch with my laptop on the coffee table in front of him. "What's the password to this computer?" he asked me in a harsh tone.

"Unless you have a search warrant, that computer's private, and I'm not going to tell you how to get into it. There's nothing in the computer that could interest you anyway."

"Never mind! We'll just take the computer. We can read the disk without your help. We'll decide what interests us."

"I want to see a warrant," I insisted. "Unless you have a warrant from a court, you have no right to break into my house and destroy everything. And, get your goddamned hands off my computer." I seldom use strong language. That fact that I had used a swearword now showed the extent of my anger.

The man hit me across the face with the back of his hand. "Shut up!" he barked. I'll ask the questions, and you'll keep your mouth shut except to answer them."

Another black-suited man was busily dismantling my desktop computer. He removed the hard drive and put it in a black bag. Another held up the padded envelope that Jason had given me. "Did you take anything out of this envelope?"

"No, Jason called me this afternoon and told me to open it. I did, but the things inside made no sense to me. I was going to put the flash drive into my computer and examine it when I got back from my walk." Strictly speaking, I wasn't lying. They didn't ask me if I had made copies.

"Are you sure that everything that was in the envelope when you opened it is still there?"

"Yes, I looked at everything and put it back into the envelope."

"And, what did you find on the flash drive?"

"I didn't find anything on the flash drive. As I told you, I was going to check it out when I got back from my walk. I have no idea what's on it." That was not completely true. If there were mp3 files on the drive, they weren't likely to be Jason's classical music collection. I was pretty sure that they were recorded conversations of some sort.

I was getting increasingly angry, especially as I saw my desk drawers being opened and their contents dumped onto the floor. One of the agents even began slashing open my couch and easy chair cushions and dumping the stuffing onto the rug. These guys were making a mess of the place. No, they were destroying it. It would cost me a fortune to get everything fixed.

"Would someone please tell me what's going on here? What right do you guys have to break into my house and ransack it?"

"This is a crime investigation," one of the black-suited men growled. "That's all you need to know. Do you have a cell phone?"

"Yes, it's in my pocket."

"Give it here. Is it password protected? What's the password?"

"You have no right to take my cell phone, and I'm not going to give you my password."

He didn't answer me. He stuffed the cell phone into the same bag where he had already placed my laptop, the envelope, and the hard drive from my computer. I heard a motor in front of my house and got up to look out the window. A flatbed truck was out front, and two men were loading my car onto it. In Phoenix, it's hard to go anywhere without a car. Everything is too far away to walk to, and public transportation is primitive.

It was three am when the guys finally left. "Don't go anywhere!" one of them commanded. We may be back, and if we are, you'd better be here."

I had nowhere to go and no way to go there if I did. All I wanted to do was sleep. I couldn't use my bed, because the mystery men, obviously from the Secret Service, had slashed open the mattress. I found a blanket rolled up in a corner, spread it out on the floor, fell on top of it fully dressed, and fell asleep. I still had no idea why my house had been ransacked.

I awoke at about 9 am and surveyed the mess. Almost everything I owned had been tossed onto the floor. I went into the living room to switch on the TV and watch the morning news, but the TV was gone. I searched among the rubble in the bathroom for the portable radio that I sometimes used to listen to the news while showering and shaving, but it was gone, too. The kitchen was a mess, so I couldn't even fix breakfast without cleaning it up. I decided to lower my dietary standards and walk the six blocks to the nearest McDonald's for breakfast. One of the advantages of living in Phoenix instead of in a ritzy suburb like Paradise Valley is that there is a McDonald's to walk to. Half of the snooty residents of Paradise Valley would probably put their homes up for sale if a McDonald's would open in their town.

There was a newspaper vending machine next to the McDonald's main entrance. I found four quarters in my pocket and bought a copy of the *Arizona Republic*. I didn't see the headline on the front page at first. There was a time when the *Republic* made sure that the top half of the front page of the paper and the main headline were visible in the vending machine window, but standards had fallen, and the front page was now covered by an advertising circular. I ordered a big breakfast and a senior coffee at the counter and stood around until my order was ready. I carried my tray and the newspaper to a table in the back of the restaurant, took a sip of coffee, and ripped off the advertising that was covering the front page of the newspaper. The headline popped into view, written in enormous letters:

FORMER PRESIDENT WILDER FOUND DEAD IN HIS PARADISE VALLEY HOME

You might think that I would be stunned to read the headline, but I wasn't. I suspected from all that had happened the night before that something serious had happened to Jason. I took another sip of coffee and let my breakfast stand and get cold while I tried to muster up the effort to read the article. I felt the same way as I felt when I was about to take my blood pressure or step on the scale: I didn't really want to know. However, I had no choice.

"Jason Wilder, the former president of the United States, was found dead in his Paradise Valley Home yesterday. According to an FBI spokesperson and Paradise Valley Police, who were called to the scene by his Secret Service detail, his death appears to be a suicide. The Secret Service agent who was sitting with him in his living room, said he got up from his chair around 8 pm and went to the bathroom. When he did not return 15 minutes later, the agent became concerned and knocked on the door. Receiving no response, the agent broke through the door and found President Wilder hanging by his belt fastened to an overhead ventilator.

"'Although this appears to be a suicide, we are not ruling anything out,' according to an FBI spokesperson who asked to remain anonymous. 'Anytime someone under Secret Service protection dies under suspicious circumstances, we conduct a thorough investigation.'

"The spokesperson further said that President Wilder's body would be autopsied and the official cause of death would be determined once the results of the autopsy and of the laboratory analysis of bodily tissue and fluid samples were available. The spokesperson added that everyone who had been in touch with President Wilder during the past week was being interrogated, and that a number of documents, computers, and hard drives were being analyzed."

I could read no further. Even though I had interviewed Jason several times a week while I was conducting the research needed to write his biography, no friendship had developed between us. Jason was not the type of person who made friends. Nevertheless, I was shaken at the news of his having taken his own life. I can't explain why, but I felt a sense of loss.

When I returned home, two FBI agents were waiting inside my house. The door had not yet been repaired, so anyone could walk in. "We need to talk to you," one of them said. "I thought we told you not to leave the house."

"I just walked out for breakfast. Your boys last night made sure that any food left in the house would not be fit to eat."

"Never mind that! As I said, we need to talk to you."

"Fine, let's see if we can find three chairs that you didn't smash last night and sit down and talk," was my sarcastic reply.

"No, we need to do this downtown. Come! We'll drive you there."

I was interrogated all day long and into the evening. I was never able to obtain a transcript of the interrogation, but different interrogators asked me the same questions over and over until I had unconsciously memorized the answers and began reciting them from memory. Even if I had a transcript, I would not bore you by including the repetitious questions and answers here. The interrogators wanted to know my relationship with Jason, and I told them truthfully that he had hired me to ghostwrite a book. I added that they should know that already, because they had confiscated my laptop and the hard drive and had almost certainly listened to my phone calls.

I answered every question truthfully. They didn't seem to believe that I had anything to do with Jason's death. They were more concerned with the contents of the envelope that Jason had given me. When I was asked if I had made backup copies of my hard drive and the contents of the envelope, I hesitated, but then decided that lying to the FBI during the course of an investigation was not a good idea. They were sure to have known that I had made copies and were testing me. Jason had said during his last call that our conversation was probably being recorded.

"Yes, I made copies of everything. No, I am not going to tell you where I hid those copies. I'm engaged in a journalistic exercise, and as a journalist, I have the right to keep that information private. If you're charging me with a crime, I want all questioning to stop now until I can call a lawyer."

"We have to detain you until you tell us where to find the copies of what President Wilder gave you."

I decided it was time to tell a white lie after all. "The person who has the copies will make them public if I am detained for more than 24 hours."

I realize now that I should have demanded the presence of a lawyer right from the beginning of the interrogation and refused to answer any questions until the lawyer was seated by my side, but I wasn't thinking straight from lack of sleep. Maybe it would have made no difference. These guys didn't seem bound by the niceties of legal procedure.

I had only gotten a few hours sleep the night before. I was in a daze when I was finally allowed to leave at around 9 pm. No one offered me a ride home just as no one had allowed me to call a lawyer. I telephoned a friend (not the same person to whom I had mailed the copies, of course) and asked her for a ride to my house. "On second thought," I added, "could you put me up for a night? My house is a disaster. I'll tell you the story in the car."

After that, I basically put the book on hold for several months. It now legally belonged to me, of course, and I had every right to publish it and reveal myself as its true author. However, I thought it best to postpone any work on the book until things calmed down. I had become quite paranoid and thought I might be followed, but after a few days, I realized there was no reason to think that. Then I received a call from an FBI agent who asked that I not reveal her name. "Mr. Quinn, I'm sorry what we put you through. As to the copies you made of the documents that Jason gave you, our only concern is that premature publication could interfere with a criminal investigation. Also, if certain parties think that you have the only copies of that information, your life could be in danger. Not from us, from the people we're investigating. Although you're under no legal obligation to do so, we're asking you not to mention to anyone that you have the recordings of certain telephone conversations. We're mainly asking for the sake of our own investigation, but it's for your own safety."

"Telephone conversations? I didn't even know there were recorded telephone conversations. Are they on the flash drive?"

"There no sense in playing coy with me, Mr. Quinn. I'm sure that you know what I'm talking about. You need to understand that there are people who want to suppress the information you have and that merely by possessing that information, you are in danger. It might take several months for our investigation to conclude. Then we'll make everything public, and once certain parties realize that law enforcement already has the documents, they will no longer be interested in you."

I had no idea what she was talking about. At that time I hadn't had the courage to retrieve the copies out of fear that I was being observed. Therefore I hadn't read any of the documents or listened to any of the mp3 files and didn't know what a bombshell they were. However, given what I was just told on the phone, I decided it would be a good idea to take the information and disappear with it for a time. I booked a flight to Puerto Vallarta, Mexico, coincidentally that same city where Lupita had been born.

Before leaving, I visited my friend with whom I had left the copies of the flash drive and the documents. I made two more copies of everything. I left the original copies with my friend, placed a second set in a safe deposit box in Phoenix, and took the third set with me on the plane along with the new laptop computer that I had purchased to replace the one that the FBI had confiscated and still not returned. I instructed my friend, who asked not to be identified, not to open the envelope unless something happened to me. If something did happen to me, I asked him to turn the information over to the press. As I wrote a few paragraphs ago, I had become very paranoid. Just because an FBI agent had told me that the government wasn't trying to take the information away from me didn't mean that it was true.

The plane ride to Puerto Vallarta was bumpy. It was the summer monsoon season, the period when thunderstorms form over Mexico and move northward through Arizona bringing summer rains. For some reason the pilot flew southward through the storm track. I am not a good flier and felt quite uneasy as the plane bounced violently around the sky, or at least the turbulence seemed violent to me. I couldn't understand why the pilot did not take a flight path a bit farther west over the Sea of Cortez, where the air would have been calmer.

Despite my fears, the plane landed safely at the Puerto Vallarta airport, a few miles to the north of the city. I am a cheapskate, and I had been to Vallarta before. I knew how to save a few bucks on transportation from the airport into the city and to my hotel. I am also a light traveler, and I had packed everything I needed into a small backpack, which I had carried onto the plane. I ignored the taxi drivers who tried in a mixture of English and Spanish to convince me to hire them and walked out to the highway, where I flagged down a city bus. The bus dropped me off right in front of my budget hotel on the city's north side.

I spent a full month at the hotel, walking on the beach in the early morning, working on this book in the afternoon, and stopping at the same restaurant every evening for supper followed by a few beers. I and got to know the hotel personnel and a number of people who worked in businesses in the hotel zone quite well. They seemed mystified by this gringo who appeared to have moved into town to stay. Most tourists stay only a week or so, but week after week passed, and I was still there. I had the same routine every day. Perhaps I should have visited Lupita's parents to get their take on things, but I was afraid that if they knew I was in Puerto Vallarta, the word might get back to Phoenix.

My Spanish is not good, but I can read a newspaper article with occasional help from a Spanish-English dictionary. I would buy a newspaper on my morning walk to read over breakfast and then take the newspaper back to the hotel and read as much of it as I could during the short breaks I took from my writing.

My evening walk took me all the way downtown, where day-old American newspapers were for sale. I would read the newspaper over supper and the beers I drank for desert and then hop a city bus back to the hotel in time to do some more writing on this book before I went to bed.

I had a considerable amount of new material to incorporate into the book. I discovered from the mp3 files on the flash drive that Jason had recorded all of his phone calls starting with his conversations with Sheriff Balboni when he first decided to run for governor. He even recorded some of Lupita's conversations. I was especially interested in his phone conversations with the Hogsons and with his campaign manager, Shawn Killingworth. For a biographer, all of this information was a gold mine.

Jason had also kept a meticulous diary on his computer, and I found that diary among the files on the flash drive. Some of the entries in the diary made even me blush, but I have left the most scandalous entries out of this book. Jason's reputation is bad enough, and I have no desire to make it worse. Let him take a few of his worst secrets to the grave.

I now understood why the material I had could have put me in danger. The recordings and diary entries not only incriminated President Chamita Monroe, they incriminated the Hogson brothers, as well. Everyone knew that they were involved in political machinations, but up until that time, no one had been able to pin any criminal activities on them.

As fascinating as all of this information was, I had mixed feelings about its existence. It meant that I had to rewrite the entire book to incorporate it or at least to incorporate that part of the information that I felt was relevant to Jason's story. I wished that I had the time to sit on the beach and sip drinks that came with a paper umbrella like the other tourists, but I spent most of my time locked up in my hotel room writing and revising on my laptop.

It was during my fourth week in Puerto Vallarta that I read in the American paper the headline, "**Hogson Brothers Indicted**" The article continued, "The Justice Department announced this morning that it was filing criminal charges against the Hogson brothers, Luther and Willard, for bribery, illicit enrichment, and income tax evasion. Simultaneously, the FBI released scores of computer files including recordings of telephone conversations between the Hogson brothers and the late president Jason Wilder. The telephone conversations also implicate President Monroe in bribery and tax evasion charges.

"The Hogson brothers were arrested late yesterday afternoon, the Justice Department revealed. They are being held pending a bail hearing. The Justice Department maintains that given their great wealth, the Hogson brothers are flight risk and should not be granted bail. Their defense lawyers point out that their passports have been confiscated and maintain that the Hogsons have shown a respect for the American justice system.

"Jason Wilder's former campaign manager, Shawn Killingworth, was also arrested and charged with income tax evasion and with paying and receiving illicit bribes. The FBI is currently examining his cell phone and computer records. The Justice Department reports directly to President Monroe. However, the head of the Justice Department Magdalena Flores, was appointed by her predecessor, the late President Jason Wilder and claims that her department is capable of conducting an impartial investigation. Nevertheless, Congress has demanded that the matter be turned over to an independent investigator appointed by someone outside the administration."

I had read enough. It appeared that Jason was getting his revenge from beyond the grave. It was time for me to fly back to Phoenix. I took the bus out to the airport and booked a flight back to Phoenix for the following week. I still needed some time to polish this book.

There is nothing interesting to relate about my last week in Puerto Vallarta. I spend most of it working. Finally, the day of my flight came, and I took a city bus to the airport as usual. In truth, the bus dropped me off some distance from the airport, and I had to walk the last stretch, but even at my old age, I am used to walking.

When I went through security at the airport, the young man who was operating the X-ray machine was reading a comic book and didn't bother to look at the computer screen as my carry-on bag was scanned. If I had been a terrorist, I could have smuggled a bomb on board.

Inside the secure zone, things were no better. I knew that no food would be served on the plane, so I ordered a chicken sandwich at one of the restaurants. At a US airport, the sandwich would have been made up days in advance, and it would have been tasteless, but here, sandwiches were made to order. The young lady behind the counter opened a drawer and pulled out a fresh bread roll, which she then cut open with an enormous sharp knife. Again I was surprised at the lack of security. I imagine that if I had offered her twenty dollars for the knife, she would have sold it to me, and I could have carried the knife onto the plane. So much for post 911 security.

My journey back to Phoenix was uneventful. This time we flew through no monsoon storms, so the flight was calm. I landed at Sky Harbor Airport anxious to get my book finished and published.

Epilog

The events that followed are mostly well known, so I will summarize them here rather than discuss them in detail.

Jason had requested in a suicide note that his body be cremated and there be no memorial services. I have been unable to determine what became of his ashes. What is left of his fortune is still tied up in lawsuits and claims by creditors. If the plaintiffs and the lawyers don't get it all, I don't know what will become of the balance. He has no immediate family left. Some have suggested that Lupita is his heir, but she is adamant in declaring that she wants "nothing to do with his filthy money." Perhaps his cousin Lucy, whose Barbie doll he destroyed as a child, will get the money. She is currently in a drug rehab program in Chicago and could probably use a hand up.

I drove by one of Jason's car lots last week, and it was vacant. All of the cars had been removed from the lot, but the large sign with the words "Wilder Motors" was still standing. It appears that the creditors are liquidating his assets.

As this book goes to press, the Hogson brothers are both in jail awaiting trial on bribery charges and for participating in organized criminal activity. They were denied bail, because the judge felt that their enormous financial resources made them a flight risk. Both continue to maintain their innocence, although no believes them.

Documents seized from the Hogson Brothers' offices revealed that one of the people that they bribed was President Chamita Monroe. Impeachment proceedings against her have been initiated in the House of Representatives. I predict that she will be impeached and then criminally charged. She will likely spend several years in prison. As I write this, she is still tenaciously clinging to office and refuses to resign. I suspect she's holding out for some sort of plea bargain and would resign if she could obtain a promise of a reduced prison sentence. Because she has not named a Vice President, Speaker of the House Blaydon Gutenberg is in line to be the next president of the United States.

I am sad to report that Irene Wilder, Jason's mother, passed away three weeks ago. I flew to Chicago to attend her memorial service, which had to be held in a spacious hall due to the large attendance. Not only were her neighbors there, many political figures attended as well.

Lupita and Jacques were there, of course. May Irene Wilder rest in peace.

Lupita Wilder is now Lupita du Bois. She and Jacques married in a private ceremony that seems to have been planned on the spur of the moment. I was the best man. They are expecting a child. *Malas lenguas* or gossipers claim that the pregnancy motivated the hasty marriage, but I am not one to count off the months on my fingers, so I have no opinion on the matter. After the child is born, Jacques plans to take a year's leave from work to care for her (it's going to be a girl). Lupita makes more money that he does, so that seems to be a sensible decision. They have asked me to be the child's godfather.

Here in Phoenix, things have gone from bad under Jason Wilder's governorship to worse under the present governor, who has been working with the legislator to cut taxes and state spending "to make Arizona more business friendly." It has become friendly only to industries such as warehouses and call centers that are looking for a place where they can pay low wages. Amazon has a warehouse here. Most high technology companies avoid the state due to its bottom-of-the-barrel educational system. The governor and legislature have cut funds for the State's three public universities and many community colleges. Funding for public schools is dismal.

Arizona public schools can hardly get much worse than they are now, but the state administration is doing its best to make them that way. Arizona ranks 47th or 48th in the nation in public school education, depending on which study you believe. At least our schools are still better than those in West Virginia and North Carolina. We have something to brag about. We're not in last place! Arizona does rank dead last in public school spending per student, however. Things are unquestionably worse in Arizona now than they were when Jason Wilder was governor.

There is also no funding for infrastructure. Phoenix's streets, which used to be smooth as glass, are now pothole ridden and full of large cracks. Driving on them beats a car to death.

Why do Arizona's politicians want to make Arizona the worst educated state in the Union? Jason Wilder could answer that question. Uneducated people vote for politicians like him.

The present sheriff in Maricopa County, where Phoenix is located, is no improvement over Paul Balboni either. Perhaps you have read that he was convicted on civil contempt of court charges and is still being tried on criminal charges. His department has done such a poor job that the courts have appointed a monitor who is to attempt to make sure that the Maricopa County Sheriff's Department obeys the law. Stacks of un-served arrest warrants have piled up in his office allowing criminals to remain free while he devotes the Sheriff's Department resources to insuring his reelection. He appears on television and brags that he is the West's toughest sheriff. Yes, he is tough on innocent people. Criminals have little to fear from him.

This is a great state for retirees. If you are retired, you may want to move here. If you are still working, I suggest you don't unless you want a low-paying job with no benefits. Good jobs are rare.

As to me, I am glad that this period of excitement in my life is over. Once this book is published, I plan to fly to Europe and spend several months in France, Spain, and Portugal. Perhaps I will do the pilgrimage on foot from France to Santiago de Compostela in Spain yet again. It's a good way to escape the stress of modern life. For week after week, one gets up every morning with no more responsibility than to carry one's backpack to the village where one is going to spend the next night. If I do, I will post my progress on quinnblog.com so that anyone who is interested can follow me.

If you have enjoyed reading this book, I will be eternally if you will leave an honest review on Amazon.com Thanks in advance.

You may be interested in my Kindle book about my 2015 pilgrimage, *A Senior Citizen Walks the Camino de Santiago*, which is for sale exclusively on Amazon. As mentioned previously, I also write a blog and make entries almost daily. If you're interested, the URL is quinblog.com.